PUBLIC RELATIONS

NICOLE S. GOODIN

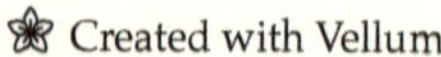 Created with Vellum

Public Relations

INTERNATIONAL BESTSELLING AUTHOR

NICOLE S. GOODIN

DISCLAIMER

This book is a work of fiction. All names, characters, places and incidents either are products of the author's imagination or are used fictitiously. Any resemblance to events, places, or persons, living or dead, is purely coincidental, if not a little inspired.

The author acknowledges all song titles, song lyrics, film titles, film characters, trademarked statuses and brands mentioned in this book are the property of, and belong to, their respective owners.

Nicole Goodin is in no way affiliated with any of the brands, songs, musicians or artists mentioned in this book.

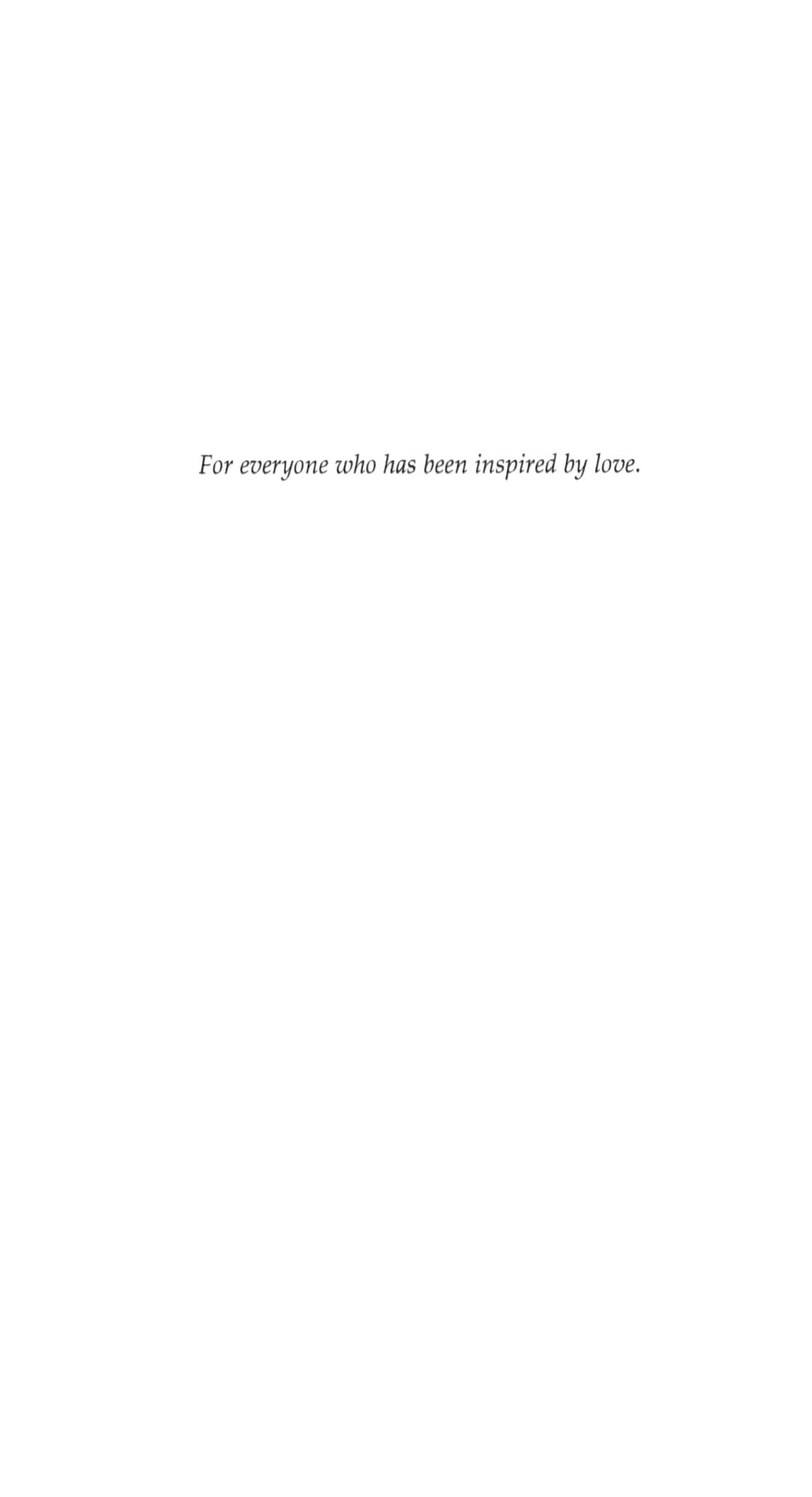

For everyone who has been inspired by love.

AUTHOR'S NOTE

This book has been written using UK English and may contain euphemisms and slang words that form part of the New Zealand spoken word.
Please remember that the words are not misspelled. They are slang terms and form part of everyday, New Zealand vernacular.
I.e: I'm from New Zealand and sometimes we say weird things down here... please try and be cool about it.

PROLOGUE

ELLY

I'd love to organise a public execution for the moron who thought it was smart to stage the PR stunt to end all other PR stunts.

The most famous pop singer in the world and the golden boy of the NBA.

Two of the biggest names on the planet coming together, two totally different worlds colliding with a bang that is being heard in nearly every corner of the globe.

A love story for the ages, and an absolute circus for a public relations executive.

The brain behind this operation deserves to be strung up by their balls.

Only problem is, *she* doesn't have balls, and if I really were to point the finger, I'd have to do it in the mirror, because the person responsible for making my life one hundred million times harder, is *me*.

This was all *my* idea.

I'm a genius, the best of the best at my job, and I have a feeling I'm going to wind up hating myself for it.

ELLY

"No, Morgan *won't* be taking any interviews on this subject."

I don't even bother with the pleasantries of saying goodbye, I just end the call and wait for the next one to come, because it will. *Oh god it will.* The phone hasn't stopped ringing for more than about thirty seconds all day.

Everyone is desperate for the exclusive on this story.

International pop singer Morgan Rhodes sits courtside at legend Tom Daniels' game last night.

It's all anyone can talk about.

I swear most people are more invested in this love story than they are in their own relationships.

Her being spotted there alongside the wives and girlfriends of the team in the VIP suite has sent social media into an absolute spiral. Her sitting courtside is another level entirely. TikToks with millions and millions of views, merch and ticket sales through the roof... the chatter is *crazy*. The frenzy is real.

The world loves them, both individually and even more together.

The fans are saying this is *it*, after all the heartbreak, that he's the one for our girl Morgan. No more break-up ballads. They're pretty much planning the wedding already.

I knew this was going to blow up, but even *I* had no idea just how out of hand it would get.

Talk about zero to one hundred. More like one hundred *million*.

We've left the fans following a very subtle trail of crumbs for a few weeks now, and while there was speculation something was coming, even the most onto it fans didn't expect a launch quite this hard.

An in-person, game day, courtside appearance was straight A up the guts, full force, little warning and absolutely no lube, kind of hard launch.

The phone rings again, but I ignore it this time, rubbing my temples instead until the noise stops. I haven't got another 'no comment' in me right now.

I wonder if Walker has his hands as full as I do.

Walker Brooks is Tom's PR manager. He's also his brother. And he's also a gigantic pain in my ass.

It's my bad really. If I'd known that Tom Daniels came hand in hand with what has to be the cockiest human on the face of the planet, I might have thought twice about this plan.

It's too late now though. We're in this together for as long as it takes.

Tom and Morgan are set to play the long game, and while I don't really care too much about *Tom's* reputation and feelings, I do care about Morgan's. She might technically be my client, but she's also one of my closest friends, and I won't see her dragged through the mud again so soon after her last break up.

That's the last thing I want to see happen. It's a big part of why we're here.

This whole thing started when Tom and some of his friends showed up in a VIP tent at one of Morgan's shows on her current tour.

He's a big name in sports, an even bigger man in person, and with all due respect, he's off-the-charts hot.

The *Rhode Runners* noticed.

The *world* noticed.

You can't look like that, dance and sing along like *that*, and not get noticed.

The fact that he had a huge sign asking her out on a date raised above his head for half the show, certainly didn't do anything to die down the hype.

A few phone calls, endless endorsement deals, airtight contracts later, and here we are. As far as the world is concerned, they've just launched their budding relationship to the world.

It doesn't matter that it's all fake.

It doesn't matter that it's all about money and marketing.

It doesn't matter that this was specifically engineered to shift focus from one thing to another.

The fans believe what they want to believe. They believe what *I* want them to believe.

And right now, they're eating out of the palm of my hand.

All those viral videos where the events match up perfectly with themes and lyrics from Morgan's songs… not so coincidental.

I guess I have to give *some* of the credit to Walker, he and his team came up with a lot of it, and it's a lot more romantic than I would have thought they'd be willing to get. For a slick NBA player, Tom pulls off sweet and dreamy much better than I expected.

It's all a stroke of genius. I'd hate to have to admit that to Walker. The last thing he needs is praise. He thinks enough of himself as it is.

The guy is a nightmare. Sexy as hell, and he knows it all too well. Like his brother, he's tall, built, handsome and charismatic. Unlike Tom, Walker is also pushy, arrogant and overly confident.

Six months to a year, I remind myself.

I can put up with *anything* for a year.

Things will die down in a month or two, and I might be able to breathe again. For now, I can remain professional and do my job. It'll make one of us.

My phone rings again, and I resist the urge to throw it over the balcony of my twentieth-floor apartment.

It's lucky I don't, because it's Morgan calling this time.

Finally, someone I can actually have a real conversation with without wanting to rip my hair out of my scalp.

I feel my headache ease as I hit the answer button.

"Well hello, future Mrs. Daniels, how is the happy couple this morning?"

Her soft laugh tinkles down the phone. "Morgan Daniels doesn't have the worst ring to it. I can picture it on the front of the next album."

I lift open my laptop and look at the follower count for Morgan's Instagram. We're up one hundred thousand in just one day. I flick to Tom's. His has grown by over four hundred thousand now.

The power of this fandom is insane. She's got the most dedicated following I think I've ever seen. They've seen she's excited about him and they're excited too.

"So, how was it?" I ask her.

"*Crazy*," she breathes. "I still don't know how word gets out so quickly, but the fans were *everywhere* after the game. We snuck out the back."

I already know all this, of course, but I let her tell me anyway. Sometimes I think she forgets that even when I'm not there, I'm everywhere. I co-ordinated the viral clip of the two of them sneaking out the back of the arena, not that they probably needed instruction.

"I didn't know he could drive a motorcycle. It was pretty cool."

"It suits him," I agree. "That was their idea."

"It was a good one." She sounds impressed.

I am too, if I'm honest. The bike was a nice touch by the boys. Those video clips have fitted perfectly with her song *Escape Route*, where she sings about taking off on the back of some guy's bike. It's like handing the fans content on a silver platter.

The whole thing is a stroke of genius. Perfection. They're trending everywhere.

Ten out of ten, if I do say so myself. The followers are eating it up.

"And the after party?"

"*So* much fun. I thought some of those women would have been bitchy as, since they were friends with his ex and everything, but they were all so nice. I had a few drinks, we danced. He's funny. You did good with him."

If I didn't know better, I'd say she had a little crush.

Maybe if her last boyfriend hadn't ripped her heart clean out of her chest eight months ago, I might believe it.

Poor bitch has only just started to recover from that. It was brutal, the worst one so far, and that's really saying something. It resulted in a great album though.

I never liked that guy, but at least he was good for something.

"Your fans are in love," I tell her.

She giggles again, and I frown. I don't think I've ever heard her giggle like such a girl before. *Interesting.*

"He *did* make a three pointer in the last few seconds to win the game," she brags.

It's really going to help that she's such a basketball fan. This would have been a real tough gig if she had to feign enthusiasm for a bunch of guys throwing a ball around a court. It's so genuine though. It feels authentic because it *is*.

The Bears are two-time NBA champs, and on track

to make it a third. Tom was part of the team that won last season, and he's desperate to make it a back-to-back double.

"I saw. It was a hell of a shot."

I hear chatter in the background around her. I try to listen, but I can't make out whose voice it is.

"Where are you?"

"I'm at Tom's hotel. Zayn and his wife are coming over for breakfast."

Talk about committing to the bit.

I don't quite know what to make of that, but she's a nearly thirty-year-old woman, if she wants to sleep-over at her fake boyfriend's hotel room, then she can have at it. They'll be doing a stellar job of convincing those closest to him that they're the real deal, if nothing else.

I don't think it'll be hard to make anyone believe it.

They're kind of on the same vibe. I could see them being good friends. I hope they can be when this is all said and done.

"You did good. Enjoy your breakfast and give me a call later today when you're home. We'll talk over the scope of the next week. Shall I get tickets for the home game?"

"Ooh yes, can you try and get me like half a dozen? I talked to Cam and Liv, and I think Adam and Jones want to come with as well."

She's bringing out the big guns. Next thing she'll be cuddling up to Tom's ma.

"Sure thing. Should I just get five then?"

"And one for you."

"*Me?*"

"Yes *you*. You're coming too. It's *so* fun. You'll love it. You're taking the day off and we're going to have fun. We'll stay in the suite this time."

"Morgs, I don't know if that's a good idea."

Me and fun don't really belong in the same room anymore.

"Fine then, you're working that day, and I need you to come to the game to make sure I'm not messing things up."

I roll my eyes. She's something else.

"You know, I can feel it, I'm going to say something silly to the wrong person. Maybe I might get really drunk again and dance badly. The media loves that," she carries on.

"Fine. I'll come. You don't need to threaten me."

She laughs. "It'll be fun, I promise."

The last time she promised me a fun night out, we ended up absolutely hammered, doing a runner from her security – that I personally hired – to sneak into a *McDonalds* for a cheeseburger. I don't know where the logic went that night, but it sure as hell wasn't with us.

We got swamped by fans. Never did get that cheeseburger.

"If you say so. I'll send a car for you in about an hour? He can wait until you're ready to head to the airport."

She'll already have three members of her personal security close by – they go wherever she does, and they have their own vehicle, but she doesn't like riding with them. She thinks it makes her feel like someone is going to come at her with a bomb or something.

"Thank you, Elly." She says it like she's thanking her mother.

"Just doing my job."

"You're doing amazing, sweetie."

I laugh at the reference. It's been too long since we had a *Kardashian* binge.

"Talk to you later," I tell her.

"See ya, love you, bye," she replies cheerily.

I end the call and see I missed four calls during that short conversation. Far out. I can't even keep up. I put it on do not disturb, just for a while. It's not life and death. It's just gossip and money. The world will keep spinning if they don't get the tea.

It's only going to get worse once she turns up to the next game. People are still speculating to a certain extent, but a reappearance will confirm it. Some people think she was just there because he openly told her that she'd have to come see him rock a sold-out crowd the same way he watched her, others are convinced they're just toying with the media.

But she'll be back, and they're only going to get more and more comfortable in front of the camera. The league is eating it up.

He's the most eligible bachelor in the NBA and she's possibly the most famous person on the planet right now. Heads are going to *roll*. It's going to blow the roof off the place.

There's already talk of his bitch of an ex doing an exclusive tell-all interview. I don't know what she thinks she's going to tell; the guy seems like an open book, unless he's got some weird kink fetish.

I'd be willing to bet there's not a single thought

that crosses his mind that doesn't immediately come out of his mouth.

What you see is what you get with Tom Daniels, and I think half the women in the world would be more than happy to get what you see when you look at him.

The guy is *gorgeous*.

It amuses me how quickly these things move though. He's a multi-millionaire, he's a legend of the game, easily one of the best shooting guards to ever grace the court. He's a big deal on his own merit, but throw him together with someone like Morgan, and suddenly the money grabbers appear like magic.

His ex is an absolute piece of work, and I doubt she has anything to say that is worth hearing, but it's a situation I need to keep an eye on. We don't need anything coming out that would be best kept hidden.

I make a note to talk to Walker – *shudder* – about it. I don't know how close the brothers are, but as his PR manager, it's his job to know everything about Tom.

I go back to Google and type in their names together.

Tom and Morgan.

There are hundreds of results. Photos, videos, TikToks, reels, memes…

It makes me laugh that so many people are over the moon that she can wear heels and he's still towering over her.

I can't say it's an issue I've ever personally had, but she's a tall girlie, it's nice that she still has to look up at him. Women get all hot and bothered about that. She really should have considered dating a ball player before now, if for nothing other than the height.

They look good together. They really do look like two people who are still a bit nervous in each other's company. Like maybe they've been talking and hanging out but haven't quite become a couple yet. It's very believable.

They know what they're doing.

Tom looks the most nervous. It's actually quite cute. I watch a clip of them leaving out the back and heading towards his motorcycle. He looks like he wants to touch her but isn't sure if he should or not. It's adorable really, his hand is hovering behind her but never making contact.

It's sweet to see such a confident man look like he's freaking out a bit.

He's a big personality with a big reputation, and the idea that he's nervous to be around her is going to get people swooning.

I find another video talking about his ex, and how sources say that she's kicking off behind the scenes.

I'd love to make this girl disappear, but I'm going to have to gather some intel and wait and see what eventuates.

I know who my best source is for that intel, but I'm procrastinating hard, doing anything and everything to fill time before I have to put on my big girl panties and call the dipshit in charge.

He is a *long* day.

I'll likely have to wade through twenty minutes of shit talk before he'll even be willing to get to the point.

Nothing is quick and easy with Walker Brooks.

I type his name into the search bar and scroll through his photos.

I hate how handsome he is. He looks cheeky and fun. He probably *is* cheeky and fun. He might even be charming when your entire career doesn't hinge on him doing his job well.

I must ask Tom how he copes with his brother. I don't know how he's done it his whole life. I've only been putting up with him for a matter of weeks and my patience is almost entirely run out.

I click on a photo of Walker when he was younger. God, I bet that guy sank some skirt in college. He looks like he's sculpted from stone. Floppy blond hair, devious look in his eye and a smirk on those sexy lips.

That's enough of those.

I hit the little 'x' and close out the page.

Looking at him isn't going to help me – nothing is.

I can do it. I *can* be professional. I can be patient. *He will not beat me,* I tell myself over and over.

I take a deep breath and prepare myself for what will no doubt be a conversation that'll make me seriously consider sticking pins in my eyes.

WALKER

"Okay, Elly-May, leave it with me, I'll take care of it."

I grin widely as she reminds me her name *isn't* Elly-May. She hasn't cussed me out about it yet though. I'm pretty keen to find out how hard I have to push to make that happen.

There's something about this girl that brings out my petty inner child. She's professional, calm and collected. I actually admire her; she's very good at what she does, but I also want to see her crack and lose just a little bit of that control. I don't know why that is.

Ma always has accused me of being a shit stirrer, and Ma knows everything, so it must be true.

Elly's saying something about follower counts and revenue streams, but I don't bother myself with listening. I hate numbers, I'm a words man. If you can't talk the talk, you're dead in this game. Numbers aren't open to interpretation, they can't be swayed with a smile and some charm, so I don't have a lot of time for them.

"I'm going to stop you right there, Elly-May, I've got people for that. *You've* got people for that. Have your people send my people a chart or some shit, because you're wasting your breath with me."

I swear I can hear her clenching her teeth, but when she talks, she's as composed as ever.

"Okay then. Some of us prefer to have the *whole* picture so we can make sure we're doing our job," she replies, snarky as hell.

Oooh. A jab. Shots fired by the tiny brunette.

I knew I preferred blondes for a reason. These dark-haired ones take themselves too seriously.

"How about *you* worry about doing *your* job and let *me* worry about doing *mine*?" I reply, biting back the laugh that's so fucking desperate to escape.

"Suits me. Suit me better if my job wasn't directly linked to yours, but thems the breaks," she mutters.

Speaking of jobs... I scrawl down a note about checking out Tom's piece-of-shit ex. I'll have to ask him if she's got any dirty laundry to air, or if it's just her bad attitude in general. I'm not overly worried about her, but I won't underestimate her either.

Elly and I might not have agreed on much so far, but we both have the same view when it comes to my brother's former lover – she's trash and needs to be kept quiet.

I scribble down *stuff for Elly* and a few other notes.

"Is Elly your real name? Like legit, on the birth

certificate? Out of all the names in the world, they picked that?" I ask her, steering the conversation abruptly in a totally different direction.

She actually sighs in defeat this time, and ohhh damn, it's satisfying as hell.

I grin wider.

"What's it to you?"

Clipped tone. Her patience is wearing thin.

I lift my legs up and cross my ankles on top of my desk as I lean back in my chair, enjoying myself.

"*Elly*… I mean, I guess it's sweet and all. Kinda cutesy though, don't you think?"

"Your name is *Walker*," she deadpans. "It's awful rich of you to be throwing stones. At least I'm not named after an exercise that's even less exciting than running."

I chuckle.

"What can I say? My mother hated me from the minute I was born."

She goes quiet for a minute, and that's how I know she's researched me thoroughly. It's not the best kept secret, but it's also not widely available to people with no resources. Only those closest to me know my dad got dumped with me a few hours after I was born because my mother 'didn't feel like looking after a baby'. He met Sandra a few months later and only a few months after that they were married and preg-nant. Tom was born about a year and a half after me. My sister was born two years after Tom. Ma has raised me like her own from the minute she met me.

The only thing my biological mother gave me was my grey eyes and my name.

My name is legally Walker Daniels now, but I prefer Walker Brooks – her last name – for business. Sometimes I want to be known on my own merit, and not because I'm the G.O.A.T's brother.

"Well, can't say I blame her…" Elly finally says. "I'm not too fond of you so far either."

My grin is so wide, my face hurts. I love dark humour.

That was not half bad, and so unexpected – my favourite kind of banter.

"Maybe you should let me take you out sometime, see if we can change that."

"You *can't* be serious," she replies dryly.

"Dead serious. You know you feel this between us."

"The only thing I feel between us is impending doom."

I chuckle. She's lying, I've seen her check me out. "I could argue that's not true."

"Of course you could. You could start an argument in an empty room."

I shouldn't keep laughing, it's only fuelling her rage, but this is just so much fun. For me at least.

"Alright, sugar plum, as much as I'd love to sit here and have insults thrown at me all afternoon, some of us prefer to actually do some work. You know, *so we can make sure we're doing our job*," I mimic her.

I can feel the 'fuck you' vibes coming through the phone at me.

I don't get a response; the line just goes dead.
Sassy.

I've been dismissed again by miss Elly-May Johnson. It's becoming a recurring theme. I don't know why that fucking tickles me the way it does, but I'm enjoying myself.

She's one hell of a woman. I've got a mouth the size of a truck, but she has the unique ability to keep me in check. Like when she took charge of our joint public relations meeting the other day and controlled a group of people with a mere click of her fingers. I couldn't do anything but sit back, shut up and do what I was told.

It was *hot*.

I slide open my messages and text my brother. Elly told me he's hosting his BFF Zayn for breakfast today, and that he and Morgan are doing an all too convincing job of playing the new lovers role. Sounds like she even had a sleepover.

I know my brother though, and I'd be willing to bet he gave her the spare room like the gentleman he is.

Walker: Morning super star. How's the Mrs?

Tom Spanks: Morgan is good, as beautiful as ever.

Walker: Did you get a chance to show her your microphone?

No pun intended, but I'll roll with it.

Walker: Unintentional reference to your penis being tiny there, but I'm happy with it.

Tom Spanks: Nah. Kept the python in its cage.

I'm chuckling as another message comes through.

Tom Spanks: I thought I wasn't allowed to sleep with her?

Walker: You're not. Doesn't mean you won't do it anyway.

Tom Spanks: Roger.

Walker: Killer game last night, bro. I'm proud of you.

Tom Spanks: Had to come through for my girl <3

Walker: Love changes a man.

Tom Spanks: You're still my #1 princess xoxo

He's such a fucking clown. Cheekiest dude around.

I toss the phone onto my desk and sit soaking in the quiet for a minute. I've been going all day.

No comment this, *quit fucking calling me* that.

It hasn't stopped.

I knew this chick was a big deal, it's not like I live under a rock, but *fuck me*, her fans are something else.

I can appreciate she's a talented singer and song writer and whatever, but her stuff has never really been my jam. Not like my brother. He went to her gig, and it wasn't for hype or PR. It was because he's a legit fucking fan boy.

Pretty sure he even went home with a tour t-shirt.

Embarrassing.

Led us here to this, though. Whether or not that's a good thing still remains to be seen.

I'm sceptical.

I think he's going to get his heart all bent out of shape here. He thinks he's in control of this situation, but I have my doubts. I can see it all unfolding and turning to shit.

The boy's got a crush. I've never seen him look as nervous as he did yesterday, and it had nothing to do with the game and everything to do with the leggy raven-haired woman sitting courtside.

He's a big boy though. He agreed to this, and it's not my job as his PR manager to protect his feelings. It's my job to protect his image, and I'll do that if it kills me.

As his brother, my morals lie in a slightly different space, but I can't be everything to everyone, all the time.

He's a grown-ass man – he can make his own decisions.

I swing my legs down and fire off a few emails to the appropriate people, relaying a message from Tom that he wants to up his security for a while. I don't know if that's for Morgan's benefit or his, but I can't argue that it's a good idea. We've never been swamped like that leaving a game before.

Those fangirls work fast and materialise even faster.

I didn't think anything could have excited a group of women more than a team of NBA players, but I was wrong... girl's girls are nuts.

They must have some kind of exclusive network they communicate on, or an alert goes out so they can come together to scream and shit. We really should put them in charge when there's a missing persons case; they know how to get things done fast.

I strum my fingers on my desk. Elly's boring chat about percentage increases didn't interest me in the slightest, but the idea of Tom's socials blowing up gives my ego a bit of a stiffy.

I pull up his gram account, and sure enough, he's

gone from under three and a half million followers to nearly four.

Fuck.

This shit is mental.

She's probably going to have to write a whole album about this 'break-up' once this is all said and done – that might lose Tom a bit of support, but it'd be worth it for the experience.

I hurt my feelings a little by looking at Morgan's page next. She outnumbers him times a hundred, which when you're dealing in the millions, is even more outrageous to think about.

The girl is *big time* famous.

She's also stunning.

She's cool too. I didn't expect her to be so… *fun.* She's real, and I like that. I like that for Tommy. I'm starting to think that maybe we've screwed him here by doing this collaboration, maybe they could have been good for each other in real life, under different circumstances, but realistically, if not for this, he wouldn't have had a shot at getting close to her. That's just straight up fact.

This PR campaign is the only reason he and Morgan have spoken a word to each other.

There's only the four of us who know this is a stunt. Morgan and Tom, and me and Elly. Even the rest of our PR teams don't know – they think we're just doing normal media control like we would for any new relationship, and that's exactly how it's going to stay.

The NBA would probably flip a lid if they knew, but if we do it right, no one will ever find out. Tommy probably has the most to gain, but Morgan has the most to lose. She's got her own agenda with this whole thing, and I know Tom just happened to be the chosen one – but I can't argue that it's doing good things for his personal image. He's the same basketball player he's always been – the best in the game, but now he's being seen by an entirely new demographic.

He's the sweet, smiling, nervous guy who is all jumpy because his new girlfriend came to watch him play ball.

This shit is so wholesome it makes me want to hurl.

"Has anyone ever told you that your relentless persistence is one of the most annoying things about you?"

"It's a transferable skill."

"Is it though? Seems to me that it's just a giant pain in the ass."

"Elaine?" I guess again, ignoring her.

"Look, let's just keep this simple and easy. I need you to focus for about five minutes and find me the contract for the promotion deal with *Miles*, that running shoe brand, do you remember? I need you to find it and email it to me please. Do you think you can do that without driving me mental in the process?"

"Honestly, probably not, no."

I can picture her rubbing her temples.

"Come on, Walker, I've got things to do today. I don't have time for your theatrics. I just need the contract."

"Why was *I* made responsible for the only copy?"

I hear her take a deep breath. "*Because* you insisted on giving them *your* email, just in case they decided to email you and give you free shit, and because you were meant to send me a copy as soon as you got home, and you *didn't*. I trusted you and I shouldn't have."

"That doesn't sound like me."

"Are you sure about that? Even in my limited subject knowledge I think it sounds *exactly* like you."

"Why don't you come over and pick it up in person?"

"Because unlike you, I have a lot to do, and driving across town to look at your smug face isn't one of them."

"Come on. We could make pizzas."

"It's ten AM. I don't want pizza, and honestly, I'm less than keen on you too. I'm not coming over."

"I'm hearing that you want me to deliver it. The contract. And the pizza. Obviously."

She takes a deep breath.

"I swear to God, you turn up to this building and I will have you thrown in a federal prison."

I laugh loudly. "I bet you're fun at parties."

"Walker Brooks, I swear to *God.*"

"Oh, come on, Elly-May, you know you want to see me."

She sighs. "I have a meeting, Walker. I don't have

time for this. I can assure you, if you show up here, you will *not* be met with a warm reception."

I think I've severely overestimated my market value. Elly isn't the least bit impressed by me. She's remained thoroughly averse by my attempts to get closer to her. I've tried charming, pesky, annoying, sweet and polite. It's entertaining though, at least from where I'm sitting.

I know I bother the hell out of her, but she won't do anything about it. She hasn't lost her shit even once, not even when I drive her to the brink of insanity.

She's good. She's *real* good.

"Is it Elizabeth?"

"You don't *ever* stop, do you?"

"Not until I get what I want. You'd be smart to remember that."

"You'd be smart to remember that I don't have to answer your phone calls."

"But you *will*," I reply, my tone a lot smugger than what is probably wise.

"The odds are starting to swing," she warns me.

"Elise?"

"This gives me absolutely no peace."

I chuckle. What more could I ask for.

"*Good.* Disrupting your peace *was* on my bingo card for today."

"I bet it's on tomorrow's too," she replies dryly. "May as well mark that one off already."

I can think of plenty of other things I'd like to check off where she's concerned.

"Look, *Walker*." She's fed up with me, but she's hanging in there – credit to her. "I just need you to send over that contract, *okay*? Do you think you can manage that?"

"If you're asking me to do something for you, shouldn't you be willing to do something for me in return?"

"I'm not asking for a favour, I'm asking you to do your *job*."

"It's not as exciting when you put it like that."

"It's not exciting no matter which way I put it. It's an email of a boring document. One that I needed twenty minutes ago," she snaps.

"All I'm hearing is that you need me."

"Are you seriously okay? Like have you been checked out by a professional, because I'm starting to think that maybe you need medication."

I laugh loudly.

"Do you see a therapist? If you do, stop. And if you don't, start. Do the opposite of whatever you're doing, because right now, whatever you're doing, it isn't working."

Fuck, I almost can't breathe, I'm laughing so hard.

She's fucking hysterical.

"Ohhh god, you kill me, Elly-May."

"You keep this up, and I just might."

I wipe the tears out of the corners of my eyes.

"Death threats even, I've really gotten under your skin, haven't I?"

"My tolerance for man children was never particularly high in the first place, but if it makes you happy, then yes, I do find you considerably more annoying than most."

"Are you flirting with me?"

"*Jesus Christ*," she mutters. "I'm *insulting* you. There is something catastrophically wrong inside that head of yours."

"Sounds like more flirting to me."

"Walker. The contract."

"In a minute. I've got more guesses in me."

"Get. Me. The. Contract," she says, trying to sound tough.

"*Ellen*?"

"Do you *crave* chaos or something?"

"I mean sometimes, yeah. A little chaos can be exciting, right?"

"I wouldn't like to speculate on what excites that tiny brain of yours."

"Elodie?"

"*No*, good lord, give it a rest."

"Elaine?"

"Go and play on the road," she says between gritted teeth.

"That was mean… do it again."

"You're unwell."

"Let's make a deal, I'll send you what you want, but you have to tell me what your real, full name is."

I could get my team to find out for me in about forty-five seconds flat, but that's not as satisfying as this will be when she finally cracks and tells me.

"Send me the contract. *Please*. Do it now, and if you have any questions for me… just… don't." She's starting to sound a touch frantic, still more composed than ninety percent of the population, but by her standards, stressed.

I think I need to chill. I want to get in her head

enough that she'll still be thinking about me later, not ruin her entire day.

"I sent it as soon as you asked; I'm just messing with you now, Elly-May."

"Seriously?"

"*Seriously.*"

The line goes dead, but I swear I hear her mutter 'motherfucker' before it does.

I'm grinning wide.

Am I acting like a mature adult? *No.*

Is it getting me the girl? *No.*

Am I going stop doing it? *Also no.*

"What are you smiling about?"

I just about jump out of my chair. I didn't even hear him come in. Tommy is looking at me like he's considering whether or not I've lost my marbles.

"Nothing that'd interest you."

"Alright, well can you send Elly some contract or something? Morgan called just before and said that you'd know what it was, and that Elly's instructions were for me to dangle you over the balcony by your ankles if you didn't do it immediately."

I chuckle. "I just got off the phone with her. It's done, no murder attempts necessary."

"Now I know why you've got that look on your face then." He looks at me knowingly.

"I don't have any look. This is just my face."

"That's your face when you're acting like a schoolboy in the playground, teasing the girl you're crushing on. I know you, bro."

"I do like games."

"Are you going to pull her pigtails next?"

I get a visual of pulling her hair as she's bent over in front of me, and Jesus, that's not going to be appropriate to be thinking about at work, even for me.

"I tell you what, Tommy, I sure as hell hope so," I say with a smirk.

ELLY

It's dark when I get woken by the shrill sound of my phone ringing.

I don't know what god damn time it is, but it's too early for phone calls, I know that much.

I reach around for it blindly, I don't have my contacts in, and I can't see shit all.

I find it, but it's just a bright light, I can't make out anything on the screen – the time included.

I groan. I don't want to answer it, but it could be important, and this is the job.

Some days I really wish I'd gone into real estate like my parents wanted me to.

"I bet no one tries to buy a house in the middle of the night," I grumble.

I slide my thumb blindly across the screen several times until it unlocks and bring it up to my ear.

"Hello?" I say, my voice scratchy and rough from sleep.

"Elly-May," I hear his voice say, the humour already thick in it, like he knows how pissed I'm going to be and that entertains him.

Asshole.

I absolutely cannot stand the fact that my brain knows his voice.

It's a ridiculous thing to be worried about, we've spent countless hours talking to one another on the phone this past week, while the world goes crazy over all things Tom and Morgan, so it's not unreasonable that I'd recognise his voice, but it still irks me.

He's become no less annoying than he was on the day I met him, in fact, he's got considerably worse.

Calling in the middle of the night is a new low though. This better be an emergency.

I don't even bother wasting our time by pretending to be nice.

"What do you want, Walker?"

"Good morning to you too, honey bunch."

"Is it even morning?" I growl.

There's a pause, I assume for him to check, and then he's back. "Technically, yes."

Great.

"What do you want, Walker?" I repeat.

"I couldn't sleep."

Fucking unbelievable.

"Well, I could."

He chuckles.

"This is the part where you apologise for waking me up."

I hear him crunching on something. Chips by the sound. Delightful. Nothing I love more in the middle of the night than listening to some douche bag chew.

"You want me to say sorry when I'm not?"

I take a deep breath in my nose and out my mouth while I dig deep, looking for my last shred of patience.

"I want you to *be* sorry."

"Right. I see. Yeah… that's unfortunate."

Infuriating. This mother fucker is the definition of infuriating.

"If you don't have anything to tell me about Morgan or Tom, then you need to hang up and go and dial a booty call or something. I've got *nothing* to offer you at this hour of the night."

"What might you have to offer me at say, eight?"

"How about a restraining order?"

He howls with laughter.

"I'm glad you're amused," I snap.

"Oh, I'm more than amused. You're quite the little *pocket rocket*, aren't you? Are you sure the PR in your job description stands for *public relations*?"

"I'm hanging up."

He laughs again. "No, you're not. You don't give warning; you just hang up." You're enjoying the bants, Elly-May, just admit it."

I hate that he knows something about me.

"You know, when I Googled you, it said you were thirty-three, but that can't be true. You act like you're nineteen years old and still waiting for puberty… *and* maturity to arrive."

I realise my mistake as soon as I've made it, but he's ever quicker.

"So, you Googled me, huh?" It's obvious that pleases him.

Maybe if he was more thorough at his job, he'd have Googled me too.

"You're *insufferable*. I seriously hope your brother isn't as punishing as you are, because this thing with Morgan won't last five minutes if he is."

"Don't try and change the subject, honey, tell me what you learned in your little search."

"Don't call me *honey*, and you're not my parent in the car ride home from school, I don't need to tell you what I learned in class today."

"But you want to, though, don't you?" I can picture the obnoxious waggle of his brows as he speaks.

"Not even a little bit. You probably search your own name once a week, I'm sure you know what it says."

"Did you see the shirtless pictures from my game days?"

I certainly did see them, but I'm not going to admit that to him. They were hot. He was hot. He's *still* hot. Damn him.

I don't even know why I'm still on this call. Maybe I'm dreaming. There's no real logical explanation as to why he's calling me in the middle of the night, just to chat, so this very well could be a creation entirely from my imagination.

I don't know which would be worse – this actually happening, or my mind coming up with it when it isn't. Either way, he's in my head, taking up real estate when he shouldn't be.

"Basketball players aren't really my type. I wasn't that impressed."

"Lucky I'm not a basketball player anymore then."

I roll my eyes. He's such a flirt.

Walker was a decent player, or so Google tells me. It sounds like he and Tom both played college ball at the University of California and got drafted into the NBA upon their respectful graduations, but after his first season, Walker got injury after injury, resulting in him retiring entirely from the game in his mid-twenties, while Tom's career went to new heights at a rapid rate.

Walker became Tom's manager shortly after, and the rest is history.

"What *would* be lucky, is if I were still sleeping and you were bothering somebody who isn't me."

"Guess *I'm* the one with the luck then," he retorts.

This man. He's exhausting. Always has to have the last word.

"Only reason I haven't hung up is because I can't see."

I try to reach around for the glasses I keep on my bedside table, but I can't find them.

Fuck it, at this point I'd be willing to sacrifice the phone to get rid of him.

"Huh?"

"I can't find my glasses."

"You wear glasses?"

"Sometimes. Need something if I want to see."

"You've been wearing contacts?"

"I have, but not while I'm sleeping, so you see my predicament."

"Well, that's something new I learned about you, Elly-May."

"Great," I reply sarcastically. 'What an educational day for you."

"You should get laser eye surgery."

"Please, for the love of all things holy, can you tell me what you want, because I'm certain you didn't call me in the middle of the night to talk about laser eye surgery."

He chuckles. "You never know."

I stab at the screen of my phone, hoping to end the call. It makes a few shrill beeps, but no luck.

"Wait, wait, wait," he says quickly. "I wanted to talk to you about the game this weekend."

"What about it?"

"I got you guys tickets in the suite with us."

I pinch the bridge of my nose. "*You're* going to be there too?"

"What's the matter? Google couldn't tell you that?"

Google could not.

"Wonderful."

"Rain, hail or shine, I'll be there."

"*Perfect.*"

"*As if* I was going to miss this game. Especially not when Morgan is bringing Jones Knight with her. That girl is all kinds of hot, and I heard she's about to be single. Do you reckon?"

I've had enough. I simply cannot take any more of this man's shit right now.

I find the power button on the side of my phone and turn it off.

That's one way to end a call.

I lie awake a long time, thinking about how utterly ridiculous the guy I'm forced to work with is. Of all the PR managers, for all the different single men, I had to get into a hypothetical bed with this one.

I finally fall asleep, but when I wake up in the morning and turn on my phone, I see he sent me a message at one thirty AM.

Walker Brooks: Good chat Elly-May x sweet dreams.

I might have to start doing meditation or yoga if I'm going to be expected to deal with this muppet on a daily basis and still maintain my sanity.

I swipe away the message. I'm not going to give him the satisfaction of getting a response.

I will *not* reward bad behaviour.

I don't know what I'm meant to wear to a basketball game. I haven't been to one since I was a kid and we moved to America. Dad took us to one of each of all the big sporting events, but none of them really stuck for me.

I think I remember going to a game with a boyfriend in high school, but that could have been ice hockey now that I think about it – clearly, I didn't pay much attention to the actual game. I always got caught up watching the people in the stands instead.

I'm still the people watcher I always was, and I

doubt today will be any different. I love watching people in crowds, seeing their interactions, guessing who they are outside of that situation.

I could find myself distracted through anything. It's a blessing and a curse.

I push another outfit to the side in my closet.

I don't know why I care. It's not like I haven't been photographed with Morgan a million times before, but I feel like I need to look good today. Really good.

I try to remove the idea from my brain that it's because I know Walker is going to be there, but it refuses to leave.

It's not that I want to *impress* him, but I do want to look good in front of him. I can admit that. I need to be on top of my game, as full of confidence as I can be if I'm going to have a chance at coming out of our interactions even mildly unscathed.

The man is like a tornado, and I'm genuinely worried about getting swept away.

I put on a pair of jeans that make my ass look great, but I can't manage to find a pair of shoes that go with them, so they end up on the discard pile on my bed.

I try three dresses and passionately hate each of them for entirely different reasons.

Pants are next, and the ones that don't make me look even shorter than I am, make my hips look huge.

I'm having one of those days. I'm about thirty seconds away from having a total menty-b and deciding I'm not going.

I grab my phone off my bed to text Morgan and see what she's wearing. This is always much easier if I know what the vibe is.

As much as *I* can vibe with a multi-platinum recording artist who looks like a supermodel.

There's already a message there from her, bless her heart.

Morgan: I'm wearing short shorts, knee high boots and a tank. Jacket for if it's cold.

She knows me well.

Elly: I have a wardrobe situation.

Morgan: Mini skirt and a sweater. You can't go wrong.

She really is a genius. Never mind the singing or the song writing, the directing or the acting or any of that stuff, I'm here purely for the outfit advice today, and I think she's pointed me in the direction of a winner.

I toss my cell back down and head for the wardrobe to find exactly what she suggested when my phone beeps again.

Maybe she's even going to hit me with a shoe choice as well. A girl can dream.

I open the message and realise it's not Morgan, it's Walker.

. . .

Walker: I think I've finally figured out what your name is.

He just does not quit. I haven't got time for his antics. I've still got to do my hair and makeup, and then get over to Morgan's by three. It's time to give the man what he wants. Maybe that will be what it takes to shut him up.

Elly: Fine. I'll bite. What is it?
  Walker: It would have been a controversial choice by your folks.

I wait for his guess, but it doesn't come, so I'm forced to prompt him, which I hate, but if I thought I could ignore him and he'd go quietly, I'd be wrong.

Elly: …?
  Walker: Are you ready?
  Elly: As I'll ever be.
  Walker: Is it… Elephant?

I really and truly hope that he's taking the piss, but with this man, I just cannot be sure.

•   •   •

Elly: You don't even have two brain cells to rub together, do you?

Walker: You're telling me your birth name isn't Elephant?

Elly: Shockingly, no.

Walker: And I was so sure this time.

Walker: Are you going to tell me what it is?

Elly: If I do, will you PROMISE not to message me again for at least 24 hours?

Walker: That's a lot of hours. But I do really want to know… hmm… okay… deal.

Elly: Eleanor Daisy Johnson. Yes, it's an old lady name. Yes, I was named after a family member. And yes, I will arrange to have you taken out if you so much as think about calling me Eleanor.

Walker: It's no fun when you take away all my feedback.

Elly: Good. I hope you have a miserable rest of your morning.

Walker: See you real soon, Elly-May.

That fills me with dread, but as much as I hate myself for it, it gives me a hit of excitement too. I'd really rather not feel that way – but that's not how feelings work, I guess.

I shove my phone under my blanket and head back into my closet.

After trying on every skirt and sweater combo I have, I finally settle on a black leather mini and a white sweater. I look decent. My boots give me some height – as much height as I can get without wearing stilts.

I'm going to look ridiculous next to Morgan anyway, not to mention her gorgeous tall friends and all those giant NBA players, I don't even know why I bother worrying about my height.

I've done what I can. I've kept my hair and makeup simple. The best I can realistically hope for today is to blend in, and I'm not going to be able to do that with winged liner or a smoky eye anyway.

I look myself up and down again in the mirror.

I can't help but wish I was taller, sometimes I wish I suited being a blonde. Nothing ever looks as good on me as it does on the model in the photos.

I sigh. *Maybe I should change my top…*

I was meant to be in the waiting car ten minutes ago, but I'm still not convinced by what I've got on.

I'm about to pull off my sweater when my phone beeps again. I dig it out from under the mess on my bed and I can't help but laugh when I see the message. She really does know me too well.

Morgan: You look hot. Get in the car.

I roll my eyes, toss my phone in my bag, and head for the door.

WALKER

"Ma, have you got another beer?" I call out from the living room.

"Don't give him another one, we don't need a repeat of last season," Tom yells into the kitchen.

I fire a remote control at his head, but he catches it swiftly and sends it back my way. I guess they don't rank him as the best player in the NBA because he's out here fumbling.

"Asshole."

I hear Ma fluffing around in the kitchen, but she doesn't respond. She's likely ignoring both of us.

Thirty-two years of our combined bullshit has made her immune to our constant stream of nonsense.

"Last season was fun," I argue.

He laughs. "Last season nearly cost me three endorsement deals."

"I think the fact that you're a clown who runs his mouth had something to do with that."

"And you cracking onto that CEO's wife was irrelevant," he drawls.

I'd forgotten about that. *Good times.*

I chuckle. "Maybe I could take responsibility for one, but the other two were all you."

"If you want to believe that."

"Life's short, gotta keep things interesting."

"No one could accuse you of not meeting that goal."

I shrug my shoulders and glance at the replay of the Bulls game from a few weeks back. "I'm an over-achiever, bro, you're lucky you have such a dedicated member of staff."

"Count my blessings daily, cupcake." He blows me a kiss.

I catch it and pretend to use it to jerk off.

Both of us are cracking up. I don't know what it is about being with my brother in our parents' house, but we revert back to being immature teenagers. It's funny as fuck. At least *we* think it is. Ma rolls her eyes a lot. I bet Grace is glad she doesn't live around here anymore. No one got more fed up with our shit as kids than our little sister. Maybe that's why we only see her once a year these days.

She's cool with us now, but when we're all together she still looks like she could murder us both.

Dad is sitting in the corner with his headphones on, analysing last week's game so he can give Tom pointers before he goes to meet the team for tonight's game, ignoring us entirely.

Everything is exactly as it always is.

I think that's why I find it so comforting here. No matter how famous Tom might be, or how many NBA finals he wins, no matter how many world-famous pop stars appear on his arm, or how many followers he has on social media, here, at home, in the house we grew up in, Ma treats us the way she always has.

Tommy's just her baby boy, and I'm her favourite child.

She's never changed. She'll still tell him off for not taking his shoes off at the door. She doesn't care if I'm dating a supermodel, or if a million people follow me on Twitter, she'll clip me round the ear if I dare stick my finger in the sauce she's making.

And Dad, he's as unbothered by anything other than basketball as he's ever been.

He doesn't come to the games. No time for all that 'chit chat and socialising'. He watches every game on the TV at home. Needs the quiet to help him think; apparently, live games are just a distraction.

I think he's just too nervous to watch Tom in person. Although he does hate making small talk with people, so maybe there is some truth to his excuses. Whatever it is, there's *nothing* that will get him to a game in the flesh.

Tommy's NBA Finals victory with the Bears – he watched them from his comfortable chair, in his underwear, with a beer from the fridge in one hand and a packet of BBQ chips in the other.

He doesn't say much, but we both know how proud he is of both of us. Grace too. He's a good man. I owe him a lot. We all do.

"Can you look after Morgan at the game today? She's got her friends, and Ma will be there, but just keep an eye on her?"

There he is with all that nervous energy again. Dude has got it bad.

"Already told you I would."

"Just making sure," he mutters.

I pull my attention from the TV and raise a brow at him. "Awfully protective of this girl, princess."

He flips me off.

"You leave him alone; he's being a good man. And she's a lovely girl. I like her," Ma chimes in from the kitchen.

I guess the old bird is paying more attention to us than I thought.

"I was just saying, Ma, I don't think she needs babying – she's a strong, independent woman."

I refrain from doing sassy finger snaps to go with my statement, but it's definitely implied.

"You just behave yourself."

Tommy cracks an invisible whip. I flip him off.

Ma saying she likes Morgan is both a good and a bad thing. It's nice she approves, but it's kind of icky that we're lying to her about it all. I guess what she doesn't know, can't hurt her. It makes me feel better at least.

"Don't you have places to be?" I ask Tom as I glance at my watch. "Team meets in thirty."

"Sure. Yeah," he replies absently.

"You got this, bro. Victory backflip."

"All day," he replies, nodding.

I can't remember when it became a *thing*, but every

time his team wins, he busts out a backflip. And not just some lame little half-ass move; the guy has some serious skills. I've never seen a guy his size backflip so flawlessly.

The fans love it. Everyone loves a good show.

The NBA is a bit of a production. Playing the game is only half the fun. The boys get celebrated like the super stars they are.

He disappears down the hall, and I presume into the bedroom that used to be his. He's back within a minute and tosses me a jersey.

"What's this for?"

I hold it up, and once I see the size of it, I already know.

"Can you give it to Morgan?"

Well, isn't that just too fucking cute? Old mate super star wants his girlfriend to wear his number.

The big red twenty-two stands out on the blue jersey.

"Shut up," he says quickly, before I can even reply.

I just laugh. The boy is in well over his head here.

"I'll give it to her." I chuckle. "I'm hurt you don't want me to wear your number though, I'm not going to lie."

"You're not my type, sorry."

"Hurtful."

"I'm not into facial hair."

"I could shave."

He huffs out a laugh. "Catch you later, bro."

I shake his hand as he walks past to say goodbye to dad, who does his usual 'give em hell, boy' pep talk, and Ma who looks like she could burst into tears, she's so proud.

I follow not far behind him. I've got time for a run, and shower and maybe even a wank before this thing kicks off.

I've got an interesting afternoon and evening ahead of me, might be wise to unload the gun before I leave the house.

I arrive in the suite after Morgan and her celebrity posse, and as beautiful as they are, surprisingly they're not who my eyes are drawn to.

Elly-May.

She's a tiny little thing, not only short, but small overall. Even with her fuck me boots on, I reckon I could tuck her under my arm. She's slim, but the rack and ass on her is flawless.

I'd never noticed before, but then she's never looked like *this* before either.

Damn.

Little miss uptight has got it going on.

I wonder how much shit I'd get in with Tommy if I screwed the crew.

I chuckle. The woman can't stand me, so I'm counting my chickens long before they've hatched on that one. If I did somehow manage to win her over, I don't think my brother would stand in my way. As long as no one is trying to get in between him and his precious little songbird, he'll be a happy man.

I've got Tommy boy's basketball jersey clutched in my hand as I cross the room, heading for Morgan.

She's got a drink in her hand and she's laughing with her friends. She looks so totally at ease here; I can see why the world believes this so completely. I'd believe it too if I didn't know better.

The way her eyes keep sweeping out to the court, looking for Tom, the way she catches eyes with Ma and smiles so genuine and wide.

Maybe she should have been an actress.

I don't wait for a good moment to approach her, or bother being polite and patient, if she's going to date my brother, she's going to get the real me, the unfiltered version.

"Morgan!" I boom her name.

She grins when she sees me and breaks away from the group to hug me. "Walker!" she squeaks as we embrace each other.

"I got something for ya."

She pulls back to look at me curiously. "Fingers crossed it's not contagious."

I chuckle and pass her the jersey. "Hand-picked it myself."

She holds it up and smiles at the number on it. "Nothing to do with Tom at all, huh?"

I shake my head. "Honestly it was kind of awkward. I showed him it and told him it was for you; he was pretty embarrassed he didn't think of it himself."

She nods, playing along. "That *is* embarrassing."

"Not all men are as considerate as I am though, Morgs, I don't know what to tell you."

She hugs the jersey to her chest like it's a prized possession. "Come meet my friends."

She leads me towards her friends, who also happen to be gorgeous A list celebrities.

I'm not a total stranger to rubbing shoulders with the rich and famous, but this is a lot.

I kind of wish I'd worn more expensive clothes.

"This is Camryn and Adam." I shake hands with what is quite possibly the hottest couple alive – like seriously, she is so beautiful it's hard to look right at her, and he could make even the straightest man think he might be gay. "And this is Olivia and Jones." Two more insanely stunning girls.

"I'm Walker Brooks, I don't know if you've met my slightly more famous brother, Thomas?"

"The name sounds sort of familiar," Camryn jokes.

"He plays basketball or something. You probably won't find him very interesting to talk to, but he's pretty to look at," I assure her.

"My kind of man," she teases, catching eyes with her husband.

"And you obviously already know Elly." Morgan gestures towards her PR manager extraordinaire.

"Haven't stopped thinking about her since the moment we met," I reply, being nothing but honest, but letting it sound like a joke.

Morgan does a cheeky little snort laugh and exchanges a look with Elly, who if I had to guess, is seething under the surface.

I get the feeling these ladies have been talking about me. It's probably nothing good, but you know what they say, any attention is good attention.

"How have you been sleeping, Elly-May?"

She narrows those bright green eyes at me. "With my phone on silent," she replies, quick as a whip.

That amuses me.

"Can I get you a beer?"

"I figure that's the least you could do."

I can see Morgan out of the corner of my eye. She's involved in a conversation with some other people, but she's watching mine and Elly's interaction with a curious intensity.

I don't blame her. There's something electric in the air between us.

It could be the hate vibes she's practically shooting at me out of her eyeballs, or the fact that she'd likely light me on fire if she thought she could get away with it, but I don't know, there's something there.

I disappear to go and grab a couple of beers, checking in with Ma, who's already got her hands on a brandy.

She's in her happy place here. Everybody loves her in the basketball world, people have huge respect for her, and she treats all the boys like they were her own.

It's something pretty special.

I make it back to the front of the suite just in time for the players to run out onto the court.

I hand Elly her beer as I take a seat a row behind her, and she actually smiles and says thank you.

God she's pretty. She's so delicate. She's like the

size of one of my legs. I could pick her up and throw her across a room onto a bed without using barely any effort at all.

The thought turns me on. I'd have a hard-on by now if I hadn't emptied the tank before I came out.

"Number twenty-two, Tom Daniels!" the announcers booming voice comes over the speaker and the suite goes crazy, pulling me from my filthy little daydream.

Shit man, I've got to get laid soon.

Morgan, Elly and their crew are cheering and hollering. I glance over at the big screen and sure enough, the camera crew have focused in on Morgan as she cheers for her man. She notices her face splashed across the huge screens and laughs and waves.

The crowd goes even crazier. At this point I'm convinced her fans have bought half the seats in this place, just for the chance to see her.

"That's my boy!" I yell.

Elly turns back to me, half her beer already gone. "It's crazy to think that Morgan's sold-out venues over four times this size, all on her own."

Well *shit*, I didn't actually know that, and it *is* impressive, I won't lie, but I'm more impressed by Elly and her not so subtle brag. What a power move.

"Tom won the NBA Final here. He's the top ranked player in the whole league right now. Top points scorer for the season so far too."

She takes a slow sip of her beer, peering at me with a playful glint in her eye.

"Come talk to me when he's filled the stands all on his own."

I don't know who the guy sitting next to her is, but a laugh escapes him when she replies.

I raise my brows at him, and he's suddenly very interested in watching the last of the players run out onto the court.

I don't even have a comeback for that, but she's started a war now, and I'll find a way to bring it.

She crosses her legs, and I can't help the way my focus goes to the rising hem of her short skirt. She's got soft, smooth-looking skin. Her little black mini skirt leaves little to the imagination, and it hugs her ass in all the right places. The white fitted jumper she's got on looks good on her.

She's far sexier than her bland work clothes gave her credit for.

She's far sexier than *I* gave her credit for.

Pestering her might have started out as a fun little game, but looking at her now, I want her for real.

As if she can read my thoughts, she half turns, giving me the side eye for only a second, before turning back to the game.

I grin at the back of her head. Long dark waves trail down past her waist, and I bet they're soft as hell to touch.

I stop myself from running my fingers through the strands, she'd probably tip her drink on me if I did. I only *just* have the self-control to stop myself from finding out.

Everyone around me starts cheering and yelling,

and I realise I haven't watched a single second of the game so far. I glance at the clock, and I can't fathom how so much time has passed already.

She's like a vortex I've been sucked into. I've got to focus.

Tom's on the court. He receives the ball from Lenny and sends it up for the basket, from the top of the key. It sails through with a swish for three points.

Nothin' but net.

The crowd goes crazy. Morgan goes crazy. Her big-time celeb mates go crazy.

Fuck it, I go crazy too. I've always been the type to match energy.

Even Elly is on her feet clapping.

She looks good when she's celebrating, but I need to find a way to get closer to her. Basketball is cool and all, but clearly my focus is divided.

I lean forward and talk into her ear.

"I've got an idea."

She shivers.

"Is that a first for you?" She only half turns to look at me. It's giving *I don't give a fuck* energy.

I chuckle. "Are you a gambling woman?"

"Are you planning to elaborate further?"

"I think you and me should make a little wager."

I straighten up and take my seat, she sits too, but twists around to fully look at me with a suspicious look on her face.

Cute as a fucking button.

She crosses her arms across her chest. "What'd you have in mind?"

"The Bears win, and you have to do something for me."

She scowls. "No way, they're the favourites, I want them to win too."

"Something else then."

"You'll have to be more specific about what it is you want from me. I'm not stupid enough to agree to just anything."

I nod. "Fair enough."

She arches a brow at me, waiting.

"Alright, what about if Tom scores five three pointers?"

She shrugs. "What if he does?"

"You let me buy you a drink."

Her eyes widen slightly, but other than that, she doesn't give anything away. I think it's a harmless enough deal, but clearly she thinks otherwise.

"You already bought me a drink." She points at the half-empty beer in her hand.

"That was free, corporate perks. Doesn't count. And we're not alone. It only counts if we're alone."

She fidgets, looking nervous. "Buy me a drink *when?*"

"Whenever I want."

I watch her slowly swallow.

"Ominous. And if he *doesn't* make the five? What do *I* get?"

I think about it for half a second before I come up with the perfect suggestion. "I won't call you Elly-May ever again."

Her hand is out in front of her before I've even finished my sentence. "Deal."

I reach out and take it in mine. It's so tiny, my hand swallows hers up.

"Deal, Elly-May."

I wasn't expecting it to be that easy. Now all I need is Tommy to come through with the goods and I'll have won myself a date.

CHAPTER FIVE

ELLY

I know a bad idea when I see one, and making a deal with the devil himself definitely counts as a bad idea.

I don't know what I'm thinking.

Tom Daniels is the top point scorer in the whole league. He's bound to come through with that many three-point shots today. The odds are all kinds of against me.

Walker's played me like a fiddle, and I've let him.

I've still got my hand in his, but a deal is a deal, even a hastily made one, and I can't take it back now.

"Do you want to tell me your drink of choice now? Or later?"

The deal has only *just* been done and I already regret it. I also don't appreciate how big and warm his hand feels, wrapped around mine. I feel all tingly and stupid.

I pull my arm back. I need to put some serious distance between me and this big oaf.

He's grinning wide again, like the fucker doesn't have a care in the world. He's grinning like a man who's already won.

I turn away from him to find Morgan half turned in her seat to look at me. I meet her stare and she mouths the words 'what the hell?' at me.

I probably look like a deer in headlights, and a blushing one at that.

I shrug. I don't know what to tell her. I don't even know what to tell myself. But I do know one thing, if I never have to hear the name *Elly-May* again, it will have all been worth it.

I don't like my chances of that happening, but a girl can dream.

Morgan gestures for me to come over to her, and I sigh. I feel an interrogation coming. I can smell it in the air.

I go, because even on my forced day off, she's still the boss.

She's only a couple of seats away, so I crouch behind her, between her and Camryn – no small feat in a skirt this short.

"Don't start with me," I tell her quickly, my voice hushed.

She's still looking forward, towards the court, but she speaks into my ear quietly. "Um what's with all the sexual tension?"

I scoff. "There *isn't* any sexual tension."

I'm only half lying. I'm attracted to that man, at least physically. He doesn't shut up long enough for it to stick though. But there's no way it's reciprocated.

Walker likes tall, thin woman. Google said so.

Morgan is his type. Camryn and Jones are his type. Not me.

She leans around me to exchange a look with Cam. The two women look at me like I'm an idiot.

"Honey, that man wants to fuck the brains right out of your pretty little head," Cam tells me.

Morgan nods her head in agreement. "What she said."

No way.

All three of us look over to where Walker is laughing loudly.

He catches us staring and gives us a girly little wave, wiggling his fingertips.

The girls crack up laughing, but I'm too shocked by their suggestion to react.

"Why do you think he just made a bet to try and get you to go on a date with him?" Morgan asks.

I shake my head. "It's not a date, it's just a drink."

"*Please*. That's the same thing."

"And to try and drive me insane, I guess? Seems to be his goal in life right now," I carry on, exasperated.

"You know, sometimes I think I have you working too much; you're sheltered and naïve. We need to get you educated about the real world. I'm going to make you take more time off."

"So you can drag me to more sporting events?" I reply dryly.

"Maybe we could get you a hot baller too, really make Walker crazy," Morgan says excitedly.

I shake my head and get to my feet. "I think that's enough crazy talk for one day."

The girls giggle and whisper to each other as I go back to my seat, and I hear Morgan say to Camryn, "Poor girl doesn't even know when a hot guy is trying to bone her."

I shake my head in disbelief. They're crazy.

Walker Brooks is absolutely not trying to get into my pants.

Guys like *him* don't go for girls like *me*. And girls like *me* are too smart to have a problem with that fact.

"Did you see that play?" he asks me, grinning.

I glance back out at the court, to the game I've forgotten in my internal panic.

The Bears are leading the Blazers forty-seven to forty-three.

"He's got that look in his eye, Elly-May. It looks like he wants to put some points on the board."

I roll my eyes. "He's got his back to us, you big dummy, you can't see his eyes."

"It's brotherly telepathy. I can *sense* it."

"Do you ever stop and think… *I sound like an absolute idiot,* or do you like the sound of your own voice so much it really doesn't matter?"

He smirks, and oh gosh, my stomach flips; it's so unnecessarily sexy.

"I think you like the sound of my voice too, Elly-May. You haven't hung up on me yet."

I scowl at him. There's no logic to that statement. "You know, it's like sense has chased after you your *entire* life, but you've always been just fast enough to get away from it."

I watch as he processes what I've just said, and then he laughs big and loud.

I don't even know what else to say. He is so mind-blowingly maddening. You can't argue with stupid.

If only I *could* hang up on him in person, it would have been done the minute he opened that big dumb mouth of his.

I look away, suddenly paying close attention to the game that I don't care the outcome of anymore, outside of this bet.

He chuckles, clearly amused by my reaction.

Dick head.

The Bears do score off the next play, and it's all Tom, putting three more points on the board, bringing his three-point shot count to two for this game.

Shit.

The game ticks on for another thirty minutes, with the Bears leading the entire time. The Blazers are hanging in there, but they just can't seem to get the edge.

It's the longest game of my life.

Tom has scored a total of twenty-four points, and four of those have been from behind the three-point line, which is a bit of a problem for me.

He only needs one more.

The whole section is aware of mine and Walker's wager now – the gossip spread back through the rows, which is just *great*, but has made for entertaining banter, if I'm being honest.

I've been informed that Tom's three-point average per game is four baskets. So I'm hopeful that he's done for the night.

I've downed another few beers, and coincidentally, Walker seems slightly less annoying with each one. Maybe that's the key to tolerating him – get a little tipsy.

Morgan looks every part the glowing basketball girlfriend. She's waved to fans across the court, talked to supporters around her and cheered like a crazy person every time the Bears get the ball.

I'm going to have to have a word to her about preserving her voice; her vocal coach isn't going to be impressed.

She looks so happy and giddy, it's nice to see, even if it might not be totally authentic.

There's hardly any time left on the clock, but if I know one thing about basketball, it's that a few minutes can take ten times longer to actually play out in this game.

"Time's running out, slick, you might have to kiss that nickname goodbye."

"It's not over until it's over, Elly-May." He smirks, still cocky and confident as hell.

"That's it, get them all out of your system now," I taunt him. "Might be the last time you get to call me that."

A few people next to Walker laugh.

"Vodka cranberry?" he asks me.

He's been sporadically guessing my favourite drink all night. He's also been wrong so far.

"Do I look like I have a UTI?"

He's shocked for half a second before he loses it laughing. I'm tipsy enough to join in.

"I can safely say I've never been asked *that* question before," he says when he finally regains his composure.

There's a first time for everything. This whole experience is certainly a first time for me.

The game is *so* close to being over and Tom is yet to find a home for another long-range shot. I smirk at Walker, all confident and sassy as time ticks down.

It's short lived. I really should have known better than to get cocky.

The Blazers have the ball, and they're only trailing by one point currently, so they're looking to score and take the game in the last few seconds. They're passing the ball around the court, trying to run down the clock.

We're all on our feet, screaming and yelling. The home crowd is chanting 'DE-FENCE" over and over.

The Blazers players are starting to piss me off now.

"Just take the shot!" I scream.

Walker looks at me in amusement, but also yells out, "Yeah, take the shot, you pussies!"

One guy makes a pass to another, but it's just a fraction too slow, Zayn comes flying through for an intercept and as though Tom had a premonition of it happening, he's right there with him, sprinting down the court.

There's a matter of seconds left.

Zayn flicks the ball to Tom, who's well back from the circle. The final buzzer sounds as the ball leaves his hands.

The shot sails effortlessly through the air, up towards the basket.

The whole stadium is watching the ball as it moves in what feels like slow motion.

It sails through the net with a whooshing sound, and time speeds up again.

Game over. Bears win. Tom wins. *Walker* wins.

"What a play by Zayn Reynolds and Tom Daniels! Bears win by four!" the announcer cries.

Everyone around me goes bat shit crazy. The screaming is so loud I can't even hear myself think well enough to register the despair I should feel about losing this bet.

I can't even be mad. I just witnessed firsthand a display of why these players are two of the best in the game.

Unreal.

And I don't even really like basketball.

Walker is yahooing and air punching, celebrating yet another victory for his super star brother.

I sigh heavily.

"*Well, well, well...*" he drawls as he faces me, his expression the smuggest I've ever seen it.

I click my tongue. I've got nothing to say. He won fair and square. You wouldn't read about it though. Last play of the game. I think I missed the victory backflip too, damn it all. I do love me a hot guy pulling tricks.

Walker leans in close, and my heart starts racing.

"Can't account for the improv of those two, Elly-May, they're unpredictable, it's what makes them the best."

One positive thing I will say for Walker, is that he seems genuinely thrilled for his brother. There's no jealousy, negativity or resentment that I can see. He's happy that his younger, more successful sibling is thriving, and it's not something you see every day.

Humans are jealous by nature. People resent other people, especially the ones doing well. For every person celebrating their hero's win, there's another ready to criticize and tear them down.

It's refreshing to witness Walker be so authentically in Tom's corner. It makes me dislike him a little less.

"You win, Walker."

"I'll let you know when I want to cash in my prize, Elly-May."

"And I'll pretend not to hate that nickname with every fibre of my being every time you use it."

If I thought he was laying it on a little heavy prior to this, I'm sure I'm in for a treat from this point onwards.

"Unlucky, Elly-May," one of Tom's mates teases me as he leaves his seat.

"Don't *you* start," I warn him.

Walker looks so fucking pleased with himself.

"You owe me a date," he boasts.

I point a finger at him. "I owe you my presence for *one* drink."

He chuckles. "You just wait, when it comes to me, one is never enough."

I don't know if it's the beers I drank during the game, or the excitement of the high from the win, but watching Walker pretend the ESPN and Sports Illustrated reporters are waiting for *him* outside the VIP suite, has got me in stitches.

He just told Hillary Frank that she shouldn't talk to Tom because he's not much to look at and has a personality to match.

The man is a menace.

They're all laughing, so I can only assume these kinds of antics are a common occurrence with these brothers.

I also don't know if it was intentional or not, but the scene he's causing flexing his biceps and showing off – which is giving me Spike from *Notting Hill* vibes – has given Tom and Morgan the opportunity to slip out the back, right by the few select paparazzi I pre-arranged, and off to the club.

Walker is telling jokes now, and everyone has fallen victim to his shenanigans.

He's either a mastermind or a blithering idiot.

Maybe he's both.

He looks over his shoulder and sees it's just me waiting back here now, and winks at me.

I shake my head, in disbelief or amusement, I'm not sure which. I still can't quite figure him out. He's brash, rude and loud, but he's also passionate, loyal and proud. He's a family man through and through, and the sweet interactions between him and his ma that I saw today were unexpected and adorable.

I like to think of myself as an observant person, and I saw a lot more than the game today.

I watched Morgan win him over completely. I could tell from our initial meetings that he wasn't entirely convinced by her. I get it, she's a mega star. She's insanely wealthy and there's probably not a place on earth you could go where someone didn't know her name. But she's one of the few celebrities who has managed to remain humble and kind amongst the chaos. She's authentically herself all of the time.

She understands that the craziness is the price you pay for fame, and not only that, but she's grateful for it. All of it. She's got everything she ever wanted, and she's managed to have the sense to appreciate every part that comes with that.

She's a good person. A little loopy at times, but you've got to be at least a little sideways to live this life, I think.

She's my closest friend, and it's a privilege to be able to call her that.

Right now, it's a curse, because it means I'm stuck here, waiting for trouble.

"Alright, *Miss Clampett*, we're outta here." Walker's voice is at my ear, making me jump.

He chuckles as I leap half a foot in the air.

Miss Clampett. I don't even want to engage. *I will not engage*, I coach myself. It'll only make him do it more.

I swat at his big broad chest. "You gave me a fright."

"The reporters got tired of me, and I think they realised Tommy made a sneaky getaway out back.

And you pack about as much punch as a tiny cat, just FYI."

Douche.

Wish I could have escaped with Tom and Morgan.

If it wouldn't have killed the vibe of the media and fan photos, I would have. Shit, I'd have gone home with the cleaning crew if it would've gotten me out of getting in a car alone with Walker, but here we are. Just the two of us left together. So cosy.

"It's so nice that they can just be done with you when they've had enough." I glance up at him, ignoring the cat comment. "Wish I was that fortunate."

Gosh, I don't remember him being *so* tall. I feel like a little kid standing next to him. Sitting down it's far less outrageous. I'm used to being shorter than most, but this is just silly. I'm even wearing my highest heel boots, but it's not helping me.

He's *hugely* tall. In fact, he's just a massive guy in general. I think he could pick me up and carry me like a handbag if he wanted to. Maybe tuck me under his arm like a basketball.

His grin is so wide and easy, it's impossible not to smile back at him, as much as I don't want to.

Hate that for me.

He looks me slowly up and down, for far too long, and I feel so self-conscious.

His gaze lingers on my face, like he's probing my eyes for something, it's too intense and it makes me very, very nervous. He's looking at me like a puzzle he can't solve.

"What?" I demand.

A chuckle escapes him as he shakes his head. "Nothing. Don't go getting all riled up."

Sure as hell didn't feel like nothing, felt like he was reaching into my soul.

"When you're ready." He gestures for me to go ahead.

I want to come back with some rebuttal, but now is not the time and this is certainly not the place.

I start to weave through the crowds, heading for the exit. A lot of the other players are still here being interviewed, waiting to go into the official press conference, and be screamed at by fans. It's nothing on what Morgan puts up with, or what I've endured with her, but it's enough, and it's packed to the point of being uncomfortable.

I don't expect to see Walker when I look back, he's so bulky, I don't know how he could have squeezed through those tight gaps, but surprisingly, he's right there behind me, his hand outstretched like it's going to rest on my lower back, but never actually making contact with me. Like it's there just in case. His eyes find mine and he raises his brows in what I assume is a question to check if I'm all good.

I nod and turn back quickly so he doesn't see the colour on my cheeks. I don't even know why I'm blushing. It's pretty embarrassing that my body is betraying me like this because his hand is *near* my back and he bothered to check on me.

I need to get some chill.

I hear him talking to people, there's a bit of banter and some nickname calling, but I don't catch most of it, and I can feel him right behind me, so I know he hasn't stopped to chat.

We make it to the far side of the room, and he opens the door for me. It's a relief to step out into the empty corridor. It's colder here too, I was almost sweating inside there.

"You good, kitten?"

I close my eyes for a moment, trying to talk myself through being the bigger person, but I'm tiny, not a big person at all, and I'm about to act like it.

I spin on my heel to glare up at him. "Look, *Shrek*, you need to cut this nickname crap. Under no circumstances are you going to call me *kitten*. No small cat jokes, no more Elly-May for the night, no *Beverly Hillbillies* references. Take a day off, *okay*?"

He bursts into laughter and just keeps on walking like I didn't just make the scene of my life. I have to rush along to keep up with his much bigger strides, even while he's virtually doubled over in laughter.

I poke my finger into his side, and it only makes him laugh harder.

"I knew you got the *Beverly Hillbillies* reference. That was quite the tantrum too. You're just the cutest little thing I've ever seen."

Urgh.

I might look cute, but I'm blind with rage. No thirty-year-old woman wants to be called *cute*. I want to be sexy or beautiful. I want to be witty or smart. Babies are cute. Puppies are cute.

The man is making me want to see the world burn.

I huff out a breath and walk faster so I'm ahead of him.

He follows along, letting me lead, still laughing his thick skull off.

All traces of the amusement I had for his nonsense earlier, are *long* gone. I don't know how he does that – uses up every last ounce of my patience in an instant. *Just when I was beginning to find a way to tolerate him.*

I push through the door at the end of the corridor and step out into the cool night air. It's drizzling a little, and it feels refreshing on my skin. I'm glad we didn't have to use the main exit.

I look up at the sky and take a deep breath. It helps calm me down.

I don't know which car we're taking, so unfortunately, I can't take off without him. I'm going to have to talk to the big dummy.

I brace myself, and mentally prepare my brain cells for the ordeal.

"You comin'?" he asks, beating me to it.

He's standing a few feet away, watching me closely.

I don't like the way he watches me. It's like I can *feel* it. His gaze touches my skin somehow and it makes me feel… *something*. I don't know what, but the fact that it has any affect at all is not good. I look down and file that puzzle away for later, when I'm alone, and can think straight.

He leads me over to a modest black sedan and opens the back door for me, gesturing for me to go ahead.

It's things like this that make him even more of a mystery. He's such a dick to me most of the time, but then he holds the door for me like a gentleman and it messes with the cocky image I have of him in my head.

The best I can do is try not to think about it.

I get in, and he slides in after me, confirms with the driver where to take us, and then we're driving the streets in silence.

I don't really want to go to the after party, but I promised Morgan I would. She'd have dragged me along with her, to keep me in her sights and stop me from ghosting, but she knows she had a role to play.

A role she's playing a little too well, if you ask me. I'm starting to think that maybe this is becoming real for her. I just hope she doesn't get her feelings hurt.

I glance at the driver. He doesn't look like he's paying attention to the two of us in his back seat; he's humming along to a song on the radio, but that doesn't mean anything.

I want to ask Walker about his take on everything between Morgan and Tom, but I can't do that with an audience. Even one who's probably signed an NDA. It's a risk we can't take.

I glance over at Walker, and he makes his eyes go cross-eyed.

I want to refrain from laughing, but it's the beer, I swear, it's made me live, laugh, lose the plot.

His face lifts into a smile, but it's not the cocky grin he wears so well, it's a genuine smile. It's like the one he wore when he was talking to his ma. It makes him look like a different person; he smiles with his eyes... with his whole face.

This is an inherently more dangerous smile.

The back seat of this car feels very small all of a

sudden. His big thighs are spread wide across the seat, so close one is almost touching my leg.

He leans forward to say something to the driver about where to park, and his jean-clad leg brushes my skin.

He glances at me over his shoulder, his gaze travelling from my face, down my body to my exposed leg. He lingers there for a few moments and then turns to listen to whatever the hell the driver is saying.

Little goosebumps break out on my skin, and I release the breath that got stuck in my lungs while he fixed me with his stare.

Shit. How many beers have I had… I feel like I'm in a vortex. I need to get a grip.

I slip my leg away from his, crossing it over the other in an attempt to appear casual and composed. I'm sure I fail miserably.

Walker leans back in his seat again, the picture of control, and lets his hand fall to the seat in between us in a move that feels very deliberate.

He's not even touching me, and I can feel the heat coming off his big palm. I don't know how a hand can be sexy, but his are.

He's so infuriatingly attractive.

He squeezes his fingers together and his exposed forearm bulges, the muscles tightening and then relaxing.

Jesus.

I think I'm going to hyperventilate if I don't get out of this car soon.

The *intensity* of this eye contact.

He's looking at me like I'm a snack. Or like he wants to wear my skin.

No sooner has the thought crossed my mind, the car pulls to a stop. I peek out the window and see that we're here, thank goodness. I don't think I could take any more of that.

I've never been to this club even though I live somewhat nearby.

I haven't been to many clubs. All I really do is work, sleep, eat and work out. Then work some more. I'm a slave to my job but I wouldn't have it any other way.

Walker looks at me expectantly. "Here we are."

CHAPTER
SIX

WALKER

Oh yeah. That girl wants me. She just doesn't know it yet.

Her eyes, her mouth, *fuck* even her legs are giving me the signs, but she's got one hell of a brain on her and that's still firmly in control of this evolving situation.

Not like some of the women I've dated over the years – not so much brain going on there.

Elly is different. She's not like anyone I'm used to.

She's not at all my type, but somehow, she's the sexiest woman in the room.

She can't stand me, but she's drawn to me in a way she can't make sense of.

She's knee-high to a grasshopper, but she can control a room of men twice her size without batting an eyelid.

All sounds like fun and games to me, but I need to try and keep my head. This is my co-worker. My brother's celebrity girlfriend's PR manager. She's not mine to take.

I almost laugh at myself. Since when has professionalism been my first concern?

I'm good at my job, but I do it my way and if people don't like it then they're free to leave.

I take another sip of beer and watch Elly across the room. I can't seem to stop myself from finding her constantly. She's dancing with some of the other girls up the front of the club's stage. Everyone is engrossed in the woman with the mic.

It's not every day you get to listen to Morgan Rhodes sing karaoke.

You could sell tickets to this thing for thousands of dollars, and those crazy-ass fans of hers would sell it out in seconds, no matter the price tag.

Hell, I'm pretty sure some of her fans have her signature tattooed on them; these women would stop at nothing for an experience like this.

I see Tom come up next to me out of the corner of my eye.

"The girl can sing," I remark.

"You'd think the nine Grammys would have already given you that impression."

"I reserve the right to form my own opinion for anyone carrying less than ten. That's when the real quality control starts."

He shakes his head in amusement and takes a pull from his bottle of beer.

He won't be drinking too much tonight, not with

another game in a few days. He's in the zone right now. A couple of drinks to unwind and that'll be it. He's the life of the party without alcohol anyway. Most of the team is here with their partners and friends, and they'll all follow his lead.

The Bears rented the whole back of the place out so everyone could enjoy a chill night without having to risk the bullshit that goes with hanging out in a venue open to the public. Tom insisted on it.

He's a smart man. He's also a protective one, and this move is as new on the scene as the pop princess is.

Another interesting 'coincidence'.

"I hear you had the whole suite on the edge of their seats, making bets with a certain little brunette." He chuckles.

I smirk. What a night.

"Yeah, you really came through for me at the end there. I owe you. I was starting to think I was going to look like a loser."

"You do look like a loser."

"At least I'm a winner on the inside."

Morgan belts out a chorus, and I watch the corners of the fan boy's mouth lift even higher. He's got hearts in his eyes for fuck's sake.

"Do you really think this is going to work?" I ask him.

I have my doubts. Seems like a suicide mission to me, but hey, they're not my feelings that are going to get all fucked up.

"I don't know what you're talking about."

"Yeah, and I look good in a dress."

"Why don't you just worry about your own love life?"

"Well thanks to that three pointer, it's off to a good start," I reply smugly.

"Morgan told me Elly thinks you're a douche bag." He laughs. "And that she hates your sunglasses – she thinks they make you look like a tool."

I chuckle. This is hardly a surprise to me. "She's a smart woman, but she has to go out on a date with me now, she's got no choice. And what's wrong with my sunglasses?"

"I thought it was just a drink. And she's right... they make you look like a douche."

Harsh but fair.

"It was. It *is*. I just don't plan on letting her escape so quickly afterwards."

"It's giving kidnapping vibes. Most people frown upon holding hostages, but you do you, boo."

"Tom Daniels, get up here!"

We both look towards the stage at the sound of his name. Morgan is pointing a finger at Tommy, ordering him up next to her.

All his teammates are hollering and barking, making a show of it.

"That's my cue, bro," he says with a grin as he prowls towards the stage. That's the only way I can describe it. The nerves of having this chick around seem to be long gone right now. He's strutting around like king dick now.

I'm like a proud dad. The guy is about six foot four, but I still treat him like my kid brother.

He climbs up onto the stage and she hands him a

mic. Some *High School Musical* shit is about to go down and I'm so here for it.

I make a beeline for where Elly and the others are waiting for the next performance.

"Get it, Troy Bolton!" I yell out.

Elly glances up at me in surprise. I'm expecting her to give me shit, but instead she grins. "Go Wild Cats."

"We're up next," I inform her, the idea hitting me in that moment.

She balks. "I don't sing."

"Sure you do."

"No but *really*. Think cat wailing."

"I bet it suits you."

Spicy little kitten that she is.

Tom must have heard me yell out, because the intro for 'Start of Something New' starts to play and I *lose* it, big time. We watched the shit out of those movies when we were younger, and I'm not even embarrassed to admit it. Baller life.

Tom always did have a soft spot for Zac Effron.

"Oh my god." Elly laughs. "They *didn't*."

Oh, but they did.

Absolutely classic.

I hope someone is filming this. It's not every day you get to watch two huge names sing a song from your favourite teenage movie.

What a time to be alive.

It would have been funnier if they couldn't sing for shit, but that's not the case here. Morgan sounds like an angel, and Tom is one of those guys who pisses everyone off because they're good at anything and everything.

He's got rhythm. And swag. He can carry a tune well enough.

They belt out the chorus, and while I don't think he'll be joining her on stage for a duet any time soon, they've got everyone singing along.

It's a jam.

The song comes to an end, and I catch eyes with Morgan. *This is my chance.*

I point at Elly and myself and then the stage. Hopefully she'll pick up what I'm putting down. Morgan smiles knowingly.

She speaks into the mic. "Next up is the extremely gorgeous Elly Johnson and the real winner of the night, Walker Brooks."

Elly gasps. I chuckle.

I lean down to talk close to her, so she'll hear me. "Can't argue with her, beautiful, she's in charge."

Everyone is looking at us, waiting; there's no getting out of this now. Elly must realise the same, because she lets me lead her to the front and even accepts my hand to climb onto the stage.

I think she might be in shock. I've never seen her be this accepting of her fate.

I gesture to the screen with the song choices and her eyes widen.

"I don't even know where to start."

Morgan whispers something to her as she leaves the stage, and Elly relaxes a bit, and then grins at me.

I don't know what just happened, but it can't be good for the likes of me. It feels an awful lot like she's just taken back control of the situation.

I feel like they've got some secret karaoke past I'm not aware of.

Elly messes around for a few seconds and then hands me a mic. "I hope you do a good Pitbull impression," she says innocently as the music starts.

There's a lot of skills I could put on a resume, but my Pitbull impersonation is not one of them.

Everyone erupts into cheers of approval as *Fireball* starts playing.

I'm fucking impressed with the way she's turned the tables. That's well played. Props to her, this is a classic stitch up, but I've never been one to shy away from a challenge.

I've got minimal skills, but even less shame.

Let's do it.

I shimmy my shoulders, channel my inner bald rapper, and get to work.

Everyone is vibing. Elly is cracking up laughing and dancing around the stage. She looks thrilled that I'm getting into it.

She does the John Ryan part. She's no Morgan Rhodes, but the girl isn't half bad.

Half the boys have formed a conga line around the room. It's classic.

I can't remember the last time I had quite this much fun.

Tom and Morgan are in a dance battle in the middle now, and like the rap legend I am, I haven't missed a beat.

It's a lie – I've fucked up about twenty times, but the vibes are immaculate.

I grab Elly's hand on the instrumental and spin her around, her long dark hair fans out around her.

God, she really is beautiful.

I can't remember why I've never gone for dark-haired girls.

I bust a move; I'm not as smooth as Tommy, but I'm no chump either.

She matches me, swaying her hips and shaking her arms. It's one of those songs you dance to whether you want to or not.

I can't believe this is the same chick who found the most polite, professional way to tell a news station to *fuck off* a couple of days ago. Or the one who has stayed put together and composed as I've pushed her to the point of insanity.

It's unreal to see her let loose. I didn't know she had it in her.

The song finishes and everyone is cheering and clapping for us. We're just standing there like a couple of goofs, grinning at each other.

Elly-May… full of surprises.

"I'll walk you up."

She raises her brows at me. "That's *really* not necessary."

"A gentleman would."

A laugh escapes her. "Who gave you the impression that you were a gentleman? That's a wild accusation if I ever heard one."

"You're a tough woman to impress, you know that?"

She flashes me a knowing smile. "There's no fun in making things easy though, is there?"

I couldn't agree more. I'm a reward driven man.

She turns the handle and opens her door. I ignore her protests and climb out my side, rushing around to pull her door open the rest of the way.

She rolls her eyes at my deliberate chivalry.

I even offer her my hand as she climbs out.

I lean back into the car to speak to the driver. "You can come back for me in the morning, Joey."

"Ah, I don't think so. He leaves and you're going to be living up to that name of yours and *walking* home." She corrects me quickly, before leaning in to talk to Joey herself. "Don't you dare go anywhere."

"Oh, come on, Joe, help a lad out. At least go get lost for half an hour."

Elly glares at me. "Well, you have fun hanging around out here while you wait for him, because *I* am going inside, and *you* are not."

I see Joey shaking with laughter from inside the car.

I grin at him, and by the time I turn around she's already headed off up towards the door of her building.

"A thirty-minute estimate isn't exactly the way to tempt a girl either, just so you know," she calls back to me.

"I prefer to under promise and over deliver." I jog after her.

She's at the door now.

"Wait." I push my hand against it, stopping her in her tracks.

She turns around and shoots me a look that screams 'get the hell out of my way'.

"I need to talk to you about work."

"Bullshit." She sets her hands on her hips.

I edge a bit closer to her and it doesn't escape her attention.

"I really do. Me and Tom have a radio interview in a few days, and I want you to come."

"You do realise I'm not either of your PR managers, right?"

"*Right,* but I already know it's going to be all about Morgan and their relationship. ESPN, the NBA, all the major news stations are hyping this thing up big time. They haven't even kissed for the cameras yet, and they're already adjusting everything we know about the promo of the games to accommodate her and her fans."

She knows I'm right about that. They've changed their social media bios, made TikToks, every highlight reel has one of Morgan's songs as the backing track. It's out of control and they're laughing all the way to the bank.

I'm pretty sure I even heard that one of the sports show hosts spent fifteen minutes before the game basically running through basketball for dummies for all of Morgan's fans who don't know jack shit about the sport.

"I have a tendency to run my mouth and –"

"You don't say," she interrupts me.

I smirk. "*And* Tommy is a smart ass. You get the two of us on a roll and you never know what might come out. We *need* you there to keep us under control. Be the voice of reason. *Please.*"

"It pains me to admit that I agree. You can't be trusted."

"I'm a liability," I reply smugly. "So, you'll come?"

"Email me the details. I'll check my schedule."

"While you're being so agreeable, can I get a good-night kiss?" I move in a little closer, and surprisingly, she doesn't back up.

"Not in your wildest dreams, slick."

Her mouth is saying one thing, but her eyes are telling another story. She wants to explore this chemistry as much as I do, she's just got far more restraint.

She just batted her lashes. She's basically putty in my hands.

I reach out to rest my hand on the door behind her. My arm is caging her in on one side and I dip forward to get closer to her face.

She looks up at me with big, wide eyes, the picture of purity.

"How would I go about getting that approved?"

She shrugs her shoulders, playing on the whole 'I'm so innocent' vibe. "I don't know. I guess you better hope your brother has a few more tricks up his sleeve."

I groan and let my head fall back. "You're telling me that my ability to score *off* the court is directly related to his ability to score *on* it?"

"Seems like a fair deal to me."

"Is there some kind of credit system I can use for the points he's already scored this season?"

"Absolutely not."

"You drive a hard bargain."

She shrugs. "If you don't like it, go play somewhere else."

I shake my head. "Nah, think I'll stick around and try to drive something hard into you."

I can't even keep a straight face while I deliver that crass line.

"My *god*. You really consider *that* to be a pickup line?" She looks truly horrified.

I said it for effect and I'm not disappointed with the outcome.

"Anything can be a pickup line if you believe in yourself."

"It *really* can't," she tells me.

She glances over her shoulder towards the door. "Guess I better head up to bed."

"Weird way to propose, but okay."

She rolls her eyes but doesn't move right away. She's looking up at me like she wants me to kiss her, even though she wouldn't admit it.

It'd be so easy. She's right there. What's the worst that could happen... even if she punched me, it's not like it'd hurt.

I lean in a fraction closer.

A car toots as it drives by, and she snaps out of the trance and turns away.

"Have a good night, Walker," she says, a smug smirk on her pretty face.

She pulls the door open, and I catch it, holding it open as she crosses the lobby.

"Hey, Elly... since when can you stand me anyway?"

She stops, turns and raises one brow, all attitude and sass. "I don't know what has mislead you into thinking that's the case."

I grin wide. "I'll be in touch about our date."

"I'll pin my every last hope and dream on it," she replies sarcastically.

I watch her go until she turns the corner and I can't see her anymore.

ELLY

His cell goes to voicemail again and I have to take a deep breath in my nose and out my mouth to stop myself from throwing my phone across the room.

The one time I actually need him for something and he's not picking up.

He can call me in the middle of the night, but business hours are a no go.

"Did she mention you by name?" I ask Morgan, my rage flaring again.

"She sure did. *And* dragged my fans through the mud. She said I'm a stupid little girl and my fans are crazy."

"*Far out*, did her PR manager just hand her the shovel to bury herself?" I mutter.

"I think she must be helping her dig the hole."

Morgan seems like she finds this whole thing

amusing, which is all good and well, but in my experience, where there's smoke, there's fire, and I don't have time to be putting out fires.

"I need to watch the whole thing."

She hands me the phone and I hit play.

It's pretty much just fifteen minutes of this trash bag talking shit about Tom and his family, and their break-up, which she insists was all her idea, even though she's saltier than fucking sea water. She then goes on to dog Morgan and her fans, but then swears she's a 'girl's girl', and that she's just trying to warn Morgan of what she's in for.

What a freaking idiot. We had an idea this was coming, and there will be more, this is just a spoiler clip, but I didn't think she'd be able to make herself sound quite this stupid doing it.

It's really not *that* terrible – she'll probably come out of this looking worse than anyone else, but girls like that are unpredictable.

The main issue is that there's talk she's hinting at accusing Tom of being a cheating, abusive, pig. Which I don't believe in the first place, not to mention that it's not my job to protect his reputation, but *his* reputation is directly tied to Morgan's right now, and *that* makes it my business.

If I could get hold of Walker, I could make it *his* issue to fix, but it seems like he's taken the liberty of sleeping in today.

"It's not that bad. Everyone online is telling her she sounds petty and ridiculous and like a jealous ex."

"She does sound petty and ridiculous. And she is a jealous ex."

"Exactly."

"But that's not the point. People on the internet are too good at sleuthing. They get a whiff of a scandal, and if it's there, they'll sniff it out, no matter how well buried it is. I need to make sure Walker has their shit locked down tight."

"There's nothing to lock down," she says simply.

I respect her unwavering faith in the guy, but she's the type to see the glass half full, even if everyone else sees it as half empty. She sees the good in everybody, and while I love that about her, it leaves her vulnerable to be taken advantage of.

"That might be the case, but you don't know him that well yet, Morgs. We don't know what his past looks like."

She lifts one shoulder. "I bet you it's all crap. He's a sweet guy who loves basketball and his family. He's not a narcissist. He's definitely not a cheat."

I hope she's right. An unearthed mistress won't be a good look.

"I'll ask his brother… if he ever bothers to call me back."

She smiles at my obvious agitation. "What's the deal with the two of you? What happened when he gave you a ride home the other night?"

"*Nothing*. He's a flirt and he knows he gets under my skin. That's all it is."

She looks at me sceptically. "You know what Tom thinks?"

"I'm sure you're going to tell me."

"He thinks that Walker really likes you. Says he's never seen him act so giddy and smitten."

"Oh *please*." I roll my eyes. "Let's not have two fictitious romances going on at once. Walker is a *player*. I'm not saying he wouldn't sleep with me if he got the chance, I'm a female with a pulse – but trust me, that man has *no* genuine interest in me, other than driving me absolutely insane."

She's going to argue, but I carry on. "He's certainly succeeding at it this morning."

She sighs. "Tom can't get hold of him either, but he had to go to practice so I haven't talked to him for about an hour."

Dammit.

I could file a defamation suit, but until the full interview comes out and I know what else this bimbo has to say, it's not going to stick. She hasn't said enough about Morgan. She's run her mouth plenty about Tom though, so Walker will be able to handle that.

My phone rings and I almost drop it in surprise.

"Finally," I mumble as I swipe the screen to answer. "About time, slick, we've got a problem."

He laughs, and I can hear that I'm on hands free in his car. Guess he's not in bed after all.

"Don't worry your pretty little head, Elly-May, I already know, and I've got it handled."

I narrow my eyes as I look out the window of the apartment that Morgan keeps in the inner city. It's one hell of a view, but I'm looking at it through sceptical eyes.

I'll admit, I'm surprised he seems to be totally aware of what's going on. That's something at least.

"How exactly have you got it handled?"

He chuckles. "You really have no faith in me, do you?"

"With the greatest respect – which I have very little of – I'm not sure how I'm meant to answer that without hurting your feelings." I grind out the words.

It winds me up to no end that he keeps laughing when I insult him. Maybe he's a masochist or something.

"Tell me something, Elly-May, when you first considered this little scheme of yours, you researched not only Tommy, but me as well, correct?"

I don't even bother denying it. Of course I did. "Correct."

There's not a morsel of legitimate information available on the internet about either of them that I haven't been made aware of. I had my team do a total sweep.

"And did you find any evidence of trouble?"

I pause for a second. "No," I admit. "Not really."

"No bad blood, no pregnant side chicks, no arrests."

"No."

"Tom is squeaky clean, right?"

"Right."

"Now don't get me wrong, there *isn't* a knocked-up chick, and that one arrest was just a misunderstanding, but the point is that I know how to make things go away."

I'll have to come back to that one arrest when I'm not dealing with a semi crisis. I peer over at Morgan in the kitchen and ask my next question quietly, so she doesn't hear.

"Just give it to me straight... *Is he* a cheating narcissist?"

I really hope he's not. I know his brother isn't the best person to ask this question; I'm sure Walker would lie for his own flesh and blood if he needed to, but oddly, I trust him to give me an honest answer. Saying exactly what is on his mind seems to be one of the only things I can rely on him for.

Either way, I need to know.

For Morgan's sake, I *need* Tom to not be the worst kind of guy.

"He's never cheated on a woman in his life, and if he's a narcissist, then every man on earth is. There's nothing to find because there was never anything to tell."

He sounds a little pissed at my question. That's probably fair enough I guess, I am insinuating negative things about his brother's character.

"Okay. Good." I nod. "I'm sorry for asking."

"You're forgiven. Now do you care to tell me why you needed to call me fifteen times?"

"Because you didn't answer the first time."

"Impatient little thing, aren't you? I was busy doing that job you think I'm terrible at."

I sigh. "Fine. I'm sorry for that too, now can you please just tell me what's going on?"

"I already told you, it's handled."

"But the rest of the interview doesn't come out until tomorrow."

"There won't be a 'rest of the interview'," he assures me. "She signed an NDA when her and Walker started dating. He insists on it to protect his family and teammates, and she signed it all too willingly. I've been down to Studio Nineteen this morning, shown them the signed paperwork, and threatened to take them to court and sue them for all they're worth if they air that crap. They pulled it on the spot."

"*Wow*. Okay. You really *do* have it handled."

"Your total lack of faith in my abilities is extremely insulting."

"I can admit I underestimated you, I'm sorry."

I seem to be apologising a lot in this conversation.

"Apology accepted. I've got thick skin, and I think *I'm* still underestimating *you* anyway."

This is possibly the most genuine interaction we've ever had. I don't know what to make of it.

"What are your plans tonight?" His abrupt change of subject catches me off guard.

"Nothing. Why?"

"I'm taking you out. You owe me a date."

"I owe you a *drink*. That you're paying for," I correct him.

"Dress it down any way you like, Elly-May. I'll pick you up at seven."

I curse the fact that he knows where I live.

"I'll still be working at seven."

"No, you won't. I cleared it with the boss. You're taking the evening off. She says you work too much."

I spin around to glare at Morgan, who is watching me with far too much interest for an innocent party.

They're working together, damn it all.

"Gin and tonic?" he questions, continuing this drink guessing saga.

"You're still going with this?" I groan.

"I am."

"*Great.*"

"See you at seven, Elly-May."

I don't even get a chance to argue, he plays me at my own game and ends the call.

I glare at Morgan.

"So… I'm giving you the night off." She grins.

I think it's time I just gave in and accepted my fate. Everyone else has.

"You got a *limo*?" I gape.

I'm starting to become quite concerned about what I've got myself into with this man.

He's gone all out. He looks so handsome, like the kind of handsome you don't see in real life. He's almost *too* good looking. He's dressed up, and the bunch of flowers he gave me are up in my apartment in water. I have to admit, I feel like he's made a sincere effort to try and impress me.

Maybe he's just trying to prove that he *can* be a gentleman – he totally seems like the type to need to prove a point.

"Technically it's Tom's limo, but it's the thought that counts, right?"

I laugh. "At least you're honest. We're not leaving him without a ride, are we?"

He shakes his head and opens the door for me. "She didn't tell you?"

"Tell me what?"

"Tom is going over to Morgan's to watch a movie tonight. They're staying in."

I smile knowingly to myself.

"I should have organised a pap to get a shot of him going into the building."

"Took care of it." He smirks.

"A man after my own heart," I reply dramatically.

"You could just say thank you." He grins.

I bat my lashes at him and pout my lips as I put on my best bimbo voice. "Thank you, Walker."

He blinks a couple of times like he's momentarily stunned, and then slowly grins before laughing. "You scare me."

I flick my hair over my shoulder and climb into the back of the limo.

It's not the first time I've been in a limo, Morgan takes them a lot, but this is the first time it's been for *me*. No date I've ever had has picked me up in a car like this.

He climbs in behind me, his huge frame having trouble with the space.

I expect him to sit across from me, but instead he plonks himself down next to me, stretching his long legs out in front of him.

"Champagne?" He produces a bottle from in the door.

"Are we just going to have a drink while we circle the block and then you're dropping me back home?"

He chuckles. "This doesn't count. I paid for it

before the date. The drink you owe me has to be purchased in a licensed establishment."

He hands me a glass and I take it. Fuck it, may as well make the most of this and enjoy some expensive champagne.

"I'm going to read the fine print before I make another deal with you, there seems to be a lot of rules I wasn't made aware of."

He fills my glass and smirks at me. "A real oversight on your behalf. I expected more from a trained professional."

He's got an answer ready for everything.

Tom is the same. Witty, cheeky and quick with a comeback. Their poor parents must have had their hands full with them as teenagers.

I don't envy their mother, but I do envy her patience.

He clinks his glass against mine. "To us."

"To having better luck with bets," I reply dryly.

He chuckles. "There's no way Tommy wasn't going to get those points on the board, not with her there watching again. The kid was sweating bullets all day."

"That's pretty cute."

"But enough about them. We've got the night off. I don't want to talk about work, I want you to tell me everything about you."

"My whole life is work," I admit sheepishly. "I don't have much else to tell."

"We'll kick off with the cliché favourite colour and whether or not you have any siblings then," he replies, undeterred.

"Yellow. And yeah. A brother and a sister. They're

eight and eleven years older than me though, so we've never been close. I was a surprise baby that no one saw coming. They still live in New York."

"You grew up there?"

"Yeah mostly. My parents are Australian; we were all born there, and we moved to Albany when I was about two. My dad still lives there in the same house I was raised."

"That explains your weird accent." He grins. "What about your mum? Where's she?"

It hurts my heart to say it, but I'm getting better at talking about her. "She got real sick a couple of years ago and passed away."

His eyes soften and it looks like he might tear up. "I'm sorry."

"Me too." I shrug. "She was a good woman who lived a full life. It took her quickly, and I'm grateful for that. She didn't suffer for long."

He lays his free hand on top of mine and gives it a squeeze. It feels nice, it's warm and comforting.

"So yeah, once she was gone, I moved out here to San Fransisco to be closer to Morgan – makes life easier not having to go back and forth so much, and I travel with her a lot now. She's got a beautiful home in Los Angeles and a penthouse in New York that we frequent as well, so we spend time all over."

"But you mostly live here?"

I nod. "Yeah. I own my apartment here, and I spend probably eighty percent of the year here. Sometimes I work from here while she travels, sometimes I go with her. It really just depends on how everything is going."

"Do you like it here?"

"Yeah, I do. I didn't think I would. Morgan had been trying to get me to move for months, and I was adamant I'd never buy here, but I was wrong. It's home now."

"I always thought I'd move out of state when I got older."

"You did?"

He drains the last of his glass and nods his head. It's funny seeing such a delicate little wine flute in his big manly hands.

"Yeah. I planned to go out of state permanently to play ball after college. I went out and played that one season with the 89ers, and then after my injury took me off the court, I eventually moved back home. Tommy got signed here with the team we'd supported our whole lives and it didn't make sense to leave. So, I got my own place, been here ever since. My sister got married to her high school sweetheart and they moved to Canada for his work a few years back, so we don't see her much. There's no bad blood, but she's just drifted away from us. I try to call her once a week to catch up."

I knew he had a sister, but I've never heard him or Tom speak of her.

"Do you travel with Tom a lot?"

"All the time during the season. Ma sometimes comes too. I'm working a lot on the trips, so sometimes I only see the hotel and the stadium."

"You go to every game?"

"Not all of them. Just when I can. It's a long season, even I don't want to sit through eighty odd games plus playoffs. Ma never misses a home game. I think she's getting superstitious in her old age."

"Do you wish it were different? That you were out there playing all the time too?"

"Sometimes. It broke my heart for a while, and then I started working with Tommy and I've never really looked back. I get to enjoy the game in a different way, and Tom is a super star. Getting to see every moment of his rise to greatness has been unreal. I'd have missed so much if I'd still had my own career. I don't think I'd have become half the player he has."

He's a good brother. Seeing their close bond makes me jealous that I'm not closer to my siblings.

"Sometimes things work out for the best even if it doesn't feel that way at the time."

He looks at me like there's something he wants to say, but for the first time since I've met him, he holds back.

"So, where are you taking me?"

"You'll see."

We drive across town and get dropped outside a building I've never been into before. He leads me through the entry and up the stairs, where we're greeted by a hostess who takes his name and gestures for us to follow after her.

I assume we're going into the bar, or the dining room, but she leads us past both and out to a glass door that she opens.

She holds it open for us but doesn't follow us out. *Weird.*

Walker rests his hand on my arm to direct me out in front of him and across the empty patio.

"It's not very busy," I whisper.

His chest moves with laughter at the joke I don't get.

"Exactly how thirsty are you?" he asks me as he stops at one of the smaller tables in the middle of the outdoor patio and pulls out my chair for me to take a seat. "Have you had enough hydration today?"

"Umm I'm *moderately* hydrated I guess?" I furrow my brow in confusion to his question. I doubt my pee would be bright yellow, but it probably wouldn't be completely clear either. I'd also be willing to bet that telling him that would be entirely too much information.

He sits down opposite me, still grinning. I'd be sick of the smug routine by now if I wasn't so totally intrigued about what the heck is going on. It doesn't hurt that *smug* looks pretty good on him.

The server drops a thick blanket off for each of us and then disappears again without a word.

I've never been here before, but it seems odd to me that we've been seated here alone and that no one has said fuck all to either of us. Maybe it's one of those weird no talking places.

Walker can clearly tell that I'm a little confused, and it seems to amuse him that I've got no idea what's happening.

I'm about to ask him what the heck is going on here, but another server appears with a gigantic tray of drinks in his hands.

My eyes bulge as he starts unloading them *all* onto the table in front of me.

"What did you do?" I demand, looking around the liquid dinner to glare at Walker.

There has to be at least fifteen drinks here, all of them different, and all of them in front of me.

"You wouldn't tell me which one you wanted to drink… so I got them all."

My jaw falls slack. I look at all the different options. These are all his guesses. Every last one.

This man is unhinged.

The server places a single bottle of beer in front of Walker before turning and disappearing, leaving us all alone out here again.

"You've got to be taking the piss."

"I'm nothing if not thorough." He smirks.

"You're *something*, alright," I muse. "You don't seriously expect me to drink all these, do you?"

"I assumed you'd just pick your poison, but if you want to take a run at it…"

"Not if you'd like me to remain conscious."

"I much prefer my women responsive," he replies suggestively.

I look over the drinks. I don't know what to do here. This is outrageous.

"The suspense is killing me, is your favourite even here?"

I raise a brow at him. "On this table?"

He nods.

"Yip." I smirk.

"You're destroying me."

"You really want to know what my pick would be?"

He nods eagerly, all golden retriever energy.

I shrug my shoulders, stand, reach over past the crystal glasses and fancy cocktails and take the bottle of beer from in front of him.

He's in disbelief as he watches me bring it up to my mouth and take a long drink.

"You're *kidding*."

I laugh at his reaction. I can tell he's wild with himself for not thinking of it sooner.

"Beer?!" He palms his forehead. "*How* did I *not* guess beer?"

"I don't know what to tell you."

"You'd really rather a beer than any of these?" He's in disbelief. I guess he's used to fruity cocktail girls – not that I've ever turned down a fruity cocktail, but it's not my first choice.

"I mean… I'd drink pretty much anything, but you can't beat a cold beer."

"I've misjudged you," he mutters, more to himself than to me, and reaches across to pick up what I think is a bourbon and coke that was to my right. I guess he's accepted he's not going to see his beer again.

"Cheers to surprises," he tells me, raising the glass.

I touch the lip of the bottle to his glass.

"And to mixing drinks," I add with a laugh.

He runs his hand through his hair and shoots me a guilty look. "Yeah… it was a better idea in my head."

Weirdly, it's a sweet gesture, and very unexpected.

"I think it was a good idea, a little excessive and ultimately wasteful, but I appreciate your dedication to the cause."

The corners of his mouth turn up into a cheeky

grin, and there is something about that smile that makes me feel weak.

He's so freaking hot.

The world might be going crazy for his brother right now – and that's valid – he's one hell of a man, but Walker is just as handsome, just as tall, ripped *and* gorgeous. Seems like maybe he might be just as thoughtful and charming too – at least when his main focus isn't on being painful as hell.

It's worrying. I'm losing control of this situation at a rapid rate of knots.

I look up at the sky. This all might be a bit strange, but it's undoubtedly beautiful out here. And not what I expected from Walker. I thought he'd have taken us to some exclusive VIP bar where he could show off the fact that he knows the bouncer and doesn't have to wait in line to get in. Some place with sweaty bodies grinding and a hint of sex in the air, and a bartender he's fucked at least once. *That's* what I was prepared for. That would have been easy to be unimpressed by, it would have confirmed that we're two people with nothing in common. *This*, though, this is perfect.

This is a problem.

"Did I tell you how beautiful you look tonight?"

"You did actually." I blush. "*Twice.*"

He smiles, the genuine one that makes my stomach flutter.

"Do you want to hear it again?"

"I don't really know what to do with compliments."

"Well… you better figure out how to get used to them."

God. I don't know what to say to that.

"You're seriously stunning, Elly."

"Thank you," I whisper.

I know I'm never going to be the most beautiful woman in the world, but he really does think I'm stunning tonight. I can hear the authenticity in his tone, see it in his eyes.

This annoyingly gorgeous man thinks *I'm* beautiful.

I guess I can find a way to live with that.

CHAPTER
EIGHT

WALKER

"Okay but seriously, why is there no one else here? It's *weird*. Maybe the food is bad." She says the last part in a hushed whisper.

God she's adorable. She's also clueless. I'm going to have to spell it out for her.

"I booked the whole patio, Elly. We're alone out here because that's how I planned it."

Her jaw almost hits the table. "What? *Why*? How?"

I can't believe she didn't figure that out already, the indoor dining room is so full it's almost overflowing, there's no way we managed to luck out and find the patio completely vacant. It cost me a lot of money *and* several promises of tickets to games to get this space to ourselves, but it was worth it.

She's waiting for her answer.

"I didn't want to share you with anyone else," I reply simply.

Her full pink lips part as she whispers a soft, "Oh."

"Yeah, *oh*." I chuckle.

"I think maybe I didn't quite realise how serious you were about this drink."

There's a light blush on her cheeks as we just stare at each other, seeing each other in a new light.

I know she came into my life because of Morgan and Tommy, but this isn't about them anymore. Right now, I don't care about their public image, I don't care about the career I've spent years building. I care about making this night one that she'll never forget.

"I know we've been pushed together to benefit the happy couple, but don't for a second think that you're here right now for anybody other than *me*, Elly."

I can practically see her heart thumping in her chest. She looks lost for words.

I'm glad she seems to understand just how serious I am about this – about her.

The server comes back, with two others in tow, loaded plates of food in all of their hands.

I had no idea what she liked to eat, and Morgan wasn't much help, stating that Elly 'will eat anything'. She did tell me to make sure there was a lot – apparently, she eats like a horse, which I took to be a joke since she's so tiny, but I wasn't willing to risk it, so I over ordered anyway, making sure I covered all the bases.

"Woah." Elly's eyes are wide as the plates are set in front of us.

"Um, we didn't order food," she tells one of them.

"Definitely not that much." She looks to me for support.

"*I* ordered it," I tell her.

She gives me an 'of course you did' look. "And did you order *everything* on the menu?"

I laugh and lean back in my chair. "I couldn't ask you what you wanted, because I already knew you'd tell me that the bet was a drink, *not* a dinner. So, I just ordered what I thought sounded good. You're not a savage, you're not going to let good food go to waste just to prove a point, right?"

"A man with a plan. Very resourceful, Mr. Brooks."

"Is it working?"

"If you're asking me if I'm going to let this all go to waste out of spite, then *no*… I'm stubborn, but I'm not stupid. It looks *amazing*."

She's already reaching for a fork.

That was far easier than I anticipated. I make a mental note that the way to her heart could be through her stomach.

She takes a bite of the lamb and moans. "Oh my god this is *so* good. You're a genius, you have to try this."

She holds out the fork for me to taste it.

I moan as soon as the flavour touches my tongue. Only thing that would taste better than this is her.

"Right?" she agrees. "*So* good."

We carry on like that, her tasting everything first and then offering me a bite. I don't know when exactly I turned into a total wet wipe, but here I am, getting my kicks from watching a pretty girl eat.

What the fuck is happening to me?

I might be counting my chickens before they hatch, but I think Elly is enjoying herself here with me tonight.

I think she made up her mind about me the moment we met, long before this date, but I'm wearing her down – proving her wrong. I'll do whatever it takes to show her that there's more to me than banter and the obvious raw sex appeal.

Morgan really wasn't kidding when she said Elly likes to eat. I'm a big guy, and she gave me a run for my money. I don't know where she put it all. I doubt either of us could have eaten another bite, and there was still enough left over to feed me for the rest of the week. I'll have to order like a normal person next time.

I can appreciate it's presumptuous of me to assume there will be a next time, but I'm not sure I could accept no for an answer. Not when I know she wouldn't mean it.

We're both on our third drink; she went for a margarita and a gin and tonic after her stolen beer, and I've had a cosmo and a lemon drop to wash down the bourbon and coke, like the manly man I am.

I can feel the headache I'll have tomorrow already.

We moved from the table to the lounge setting in the corner that faces the huge block wall with a projector screen about half an hour ago. They're playing some foreign film that neither of us is really paying attention to. I can't imagine anything interesting enough to take my focus tonight.

She's just finished telling me about the time she went back to Australia as a teenager to visit her extended family and she went for a hike over her grandparents property without telling anyone what she was doing. She got lost and when she finally made it back, they'd all assumed she'd been bitten by a snake or slaughtered by one of the hundreds of things that lurk around waiting to kill you in that country. Apparently, her grandma nearly had a heart attack. Sweet little Elly-May hadn't remembered that Australia even had snakes. Bless her innocent little heart.

She's heard about how I managed to break both arms and one of my legs when I was six, and how Tommy cracked open his skull when he was eight, and I thought he was dead.

Real nice first date kind of stuff.

I don't recall consciously doing it, or seeing her move, but we're so close to one another now, it's like we're magnets that have been drawn together.

I want to kiss her so badly.

"Want to make another bet, Elly-May?"

She doesn't answer right away.

"What's the prize?"

I'm momentarily distracted by the exposed skin on her legs as she crosses one leg over the other, leaning her body in even closer towards mine.

My gaze travels over her legs, up her body to her pretty face. She raises an eyebrow in question.

"You."

"Me?" I don't know if she's outraged or intrigued.

"Yeah. You. Just a kiss… for now at least."

"Okay," she whispers.

The air feels heavy around us, like we're in a bubble and it's getting smaller – pushing us closer together.

"Aren't you going to ask what you get if *you* win?" I murmur.

She shakes her head as I lean in closer. "I have a pretty strong feeling I'm going to lose."

"Yeah?" My voice is barely audible, and thick with desire.

We're so close now, a tilt of my head and our lips will touch.

She nods, her eyes wide. "I'm on a losing streak."

"Can't argue with that."

I close the gap and brush my lips against hers. She sighs heavily as I pull back, it's only for a moment and I'm kissing her again.

My hands have a mind of their own; one is gripping her jaw and the other is on her thigh without my thoughts giving them permission. I can't decide which has the better deal.

She's clinging onto my arm and kissing me back with the passion of a woman who's just won a bet, not lost one.

She's so warm and soft and irresistible.

I don't know how to keep my cool with a woman like this. One look from her and I swear to God, I'll fall in love.

I'm six foot four, worried about protecting myself from a five-foot three woman. I almost laugh.

Her nails sink into my arm as I sweep my tongue into her mouth. I have to hold back a groan. That's seriously hot, I hope she leaves a mark.

I don't care that we're in a public restaurant, I don't care that staff or other diners could probably see us over here if they really wanted to, it's just her and me as far as I'm concerned. I'm only human, and the noises she's making are sending me over the edge.

She's so tiny, I've got her laid back beneath me with as much as a flick of my wrist.

This couch isn't exactly built for a frame the size of mine, too much enthusiasm and I'll be buying the place a new one.

It'd be worth it.

I smile against her lips as I think about having to explain my way out of that one.

"What's so funny?" she asks, her lips not leaving mine.

"Thinking about this couch meeting an unfortunate end if I decided to really have my way with you out here."

She must like the sound of that, she pulls my face back to hers.

I slide my hand up her thigh, to her hip, and then to cup her waist. She leans into my touch, and that's all the encouragement I need to go higher.

I only lightly brush her boob before common sense flickers in the back of my mind and I'm reminded of the fact that while I couldn't care less who might see me, I *do* care who sees her.

I pull away and rest my hand on the couch next to her head, I'm holding up all my body weight off her – I'd probably crack her ribs if I didn't. She's breathing heavy and her eyes are bright and wide.

"That's about all the self-restraint I've got," I warn her.

I can tell that pleases her. She so fucking sexy, those green eyes absolutely ruin me. Her dark hair is fanned around her face, all messed up and gorgeous.

"Hell of a kiss, Elly-May." I grin.

"Not too bad from you either, slick," she teases.

I peck her lips and then her forehead before peeling myself off her body and dragging her up with me.

She straightens out her clothes and drags her fingers through her hair, trying to tame the mess.

Fuck, I can't wait to see what she looks like when she's just been fucked. It's lucky I chose a pair of jeans, or I'd be pitching a tent in my pants right now.

A man only has so much self-control and mine is maxed out.

"That was unexpected." I chuckle.

"You thought I was going to play hard to get, huh?"

"You said it, not me."

"Turns out when it comes to you, I'm incredibly easy to get." I think she's blushing, but it's hard to tell out here with only the little fairy lights above us.

I'm certainly not complaining about her finally letting her guard down. The thrill of the chase is fun and all, but the reward sure is sweet.

We half watch the rest of the movie with her

tucked into my side. I'm sure the place must be close to closing up for the night, but neither of us are in a hurry to leave.

It's nice. The conversation is easy, and the silences are comfortable. We empty a few more of the various glasses that were served to us, and I know I'm definitely going to be a little dusty in the morning, but I don't give a shit. It was worth it to see the look on her face when they all got put in front of her.

This feels different to any date I've ever been on. I don't need to show off or pull flashy shit to impress her. I can just be myself.

She's not impressed by nice things. She's probably seen more luxury than I ever will. If I'm going to impress her, it's going to be with what comes out of my mouth, not my wallet.

The movie finishes and I think we both know it's time to leave. It gives me a thrill that she seems as reluctant for this to end as I do. We walk hand in hand out of the restaurant and into the waiting limo.

I'm a little tipsy. Mixing drinks like that wasn't my smartest move.

We don't talk the whole drive back to her apartment. Her head is resting on my shoulder and my hand is on her leg.

All too soon, we pull up to her building, and I have to pretend to be a gentleman who isn't desperately keen to take her home to my bed.

I sigh and open the door before helping her out.

I take her hand again and we stroll along with our arms swinging between us.

"I'm glad you're shit at winning bets."

"Me too. This wasn't entirely unpleasant," she teases.

"That might be the nicest thing you've ever said to me."

She laughs, it's sweet and girly. She's fidgeting a lot, like she's nervous. "But seriously. I had a really good time. Thank you for the drink."

"I'm going to take you somewhere totally different on our next date."

Her eyes flash back to mine. "Our next date?" She's trying her best to play it cool, but her eyes just lit up like a tree at Christmas.

She's got a terrible poker face.

"Yeah. I think we'll be going outdoorsy."

She's not saying anything, just standing there with a funny look on her face.

"You're not one of those girls that hates going outside, are you?"

She shakes her head quickly. "*No*, it's not that. I love being out in nature."

I'm glad to hear it, but there's something she still isn't saying.

I lean in and cup the side of her face in my hand, bringing her head up to look me in the eyes. "Then what is it?"

"I just wasn't expecting you to want to take me out again."

She looks vulnerable. It's the sweetest fucking thing. Bless her naïve little heart.

Elly Johnson is *mine*. She just doesn't know it yet.

"I've been telling myself that you just like the thrill of the chase," she explains. "You like to win. You won the bet; you got me to go out with you. I didn't think it was anything more than that. I thought you were just a bad-boy player."

"You think too much."

She smiles. "Oh, I know."

I tuck a strand of dark hair behind her ear. "I *do* like the thrill of the chase." I move closer to her. "I *do* like to win." I dip my head lower. "But I also, really, really like *you*, Elly-May."

She rolls her eyes at the nickname, but its half-hearted.

"I don't think you have any idea just how irresistible you are."

"I bet you say that to all the girls."

I chuckle and close the gap between us, kissing her lips softly. I planned to leave it there for the night, but her hands wind up to my neck and pull me down for another kiss.

She doesn't fool me; she's got as much invested in this as I do. I'm almost completely confident that little miss Elly-May has caught a few feelings of her own.

This kiss is hotter, more urgent, and I welcome it. She's a delicate little thing, but she's full of fire on the inside.

She sure as fuck knows how to kiss.

I'm the one who pulls away. It takes every ounce of my self-control not to pick her up, chuck her over my shoulder and carry her up to her apartment to show her how bad I can really be.

I kiss her once more, on the tip of her nose.

"Thank you again," she says as she heads for the door.

"It was all my pleasure, trust me."

"I guess I'll see you tomorrow," she says, pausing at the door.

It's only a few hours away, but it seems like too many. I want her with me so badly, but I remind myself that she's different. She's special. And I need to at least try to take things slow. She looks like she's battling the same thoughts.

I like that.

I smirk. "I'll see you tomorrow."

CHAPTER
NINE

"I feel incredibly uneasy about this."

Walker flashes me a huge grin. He's like a little kid heading off to school and you just know the teacher is going to have their hands full with him all day long.

He's in one of those shit-stirring moods.

The radio presenters are all too aware, it was pretty obvious he was trouble when he walked in, and this isn't their first time hosting these brothers – they know what they're in for.

I made the mistake this morning of listening to the last interview they did together, it was a PR manager's worst nightmare. That shit will keep me awake at night for a long time.

Both Walker and Tom went to school with one of the guy's hosting – Blake – and the woman – Christina – is cheeky and confrontational, she'll ask *anything*.

The boys are too relaxed around them, and when they're relaxed, they say more than they intend to. They treat these interviews like they're catching up with mates over a beer.

It's a dangerous game.

Morgan is one hundred times better media trained than either of these two. In fact, she makes them look like clapping monkeys. They're lucky they have a special knack for making their hot mess antics come across as endearing. Good looks and status is funny like that.

I wish I'd lied and said I couldn't make it – now that I'm here, I feel like I'm responsible for keeping them in line. The hangover I'm sporting isn't helping in the slightest. Mixing those drinks was a terrible idea.

"Don't stress it, Elly-May. We've been doing this for years."

That's what concerns me. They've been behaving like this for a long time, they're not about to start acting right all of a sudden.

"He hasn't been dating the most famous singer in the world for years, though," I mutter. Walker doesn't seem to understand just how much the stakes have changed.

"That's what you're here for, beautiful."

As much as I appreciate him calling me beautiful, I don't want to be the one in charge of keeping either of them in check. I don't need that failure on my conscious. I'm also not going to storm in there mid-interview and stop either of them from opening their mouths, I'm just going to be the first to witness it.

"Can you just behave, and maybe watch your mouth?" I beg.

He shocks the absolute life out of me when he leans down and kisses me, just once on the lips. "I make no promises." He chuckles.

He's in the studio before my shock wears off. I don't imagine that anyone missed that. I'll have to run my own PR campaign next. Walker is no Tom Daniels, but he's a popular guy. He's had a pro career, he's always photographed with Tom and the Bears, and is mates with heaps of them, so he's got his own following. About quarter of a million people give a shit about what he posts and who he dates.

It's a far cry from the five hundred followers I have on my private account. I had to make a new account a few years back, Morgan made the mistake of following my old one and I was getting thousands of follow requests every day from people who would come via her profile. She only follows about twenty people, so the fans were all over that like a rash. I'm not cut out for that life.

"I'll at least *try* and behave," Tom tells me, a grin the same as his brothers on his face. I've never really thought they looked all that similar, other than their size, but right now they've got identical matching grins. It'd be adorable if it wasn't so concerning.

"Yeah *thanks*," I reply with a roll of my eyes. "Filling me with confidence."

He squeezes my shoulder and follows his brother in, I watch as they take their seats and get headphones on, and mics settled at the right height on the table in front of them.

"These are for you." Ashley – one of the producers I was introduced to earlier – hands me a headset and gestures to a chair I can sit in, in the producer's booth.

I've always hated live radio interviews; they seemed so risky, but now that Morgan is selling out huge venues for her tours, and going on live television interviews all the time, radio should be the least of my worries.

I think I have some old unresolved trauma from the early days.

I sit patiently through the intro, watching Walker. He's totally at ease. The picture of relaxation.

"We're back now with Tom Daniels and Walker Brooks. Always a good time, lads. How's everything been going since we last saw you?"

There's some back and forth, a bit of banter, some chat about who the boys think will make the playoffs this year, bit of talk about new coaching structures and defensive plays.

It's all very civilised, it's also bound to be too good to last.

"I don't mean to be a girl about it, and basketball is great and all, buuuuuut," Christina says after the talk of last game dies down. "I think there's a question the listeners really want us to ask."

Tom chuckles. "I can't imagine where you're going with this."

"I don't know if whispers of a certain pop star might be able to give you a hint?"

He smiles even wider, looking like the cat that got the cream. You can't fake a smile like that, I don't care what anyone says.

"Yeah, we can talk about Morgan. Talking about Morgan is one of my favourite things to do."

Lord, I can almost hear all the women in the world swooning from their homes.

Hell, maybe I'm even feeling a little faint. The way his eyes light up when he mentions her name, it has to be real. No one can fake those kinds of emotions.

"We couldn't help but notice her presence at the past two games."

"Was she there? I wasn't aware," Walker jokes.

Tom laughs. "It was great to have her come out and support. She got the fans hyped; she got *me* hyped. It was good. Might have to get her a season pass."

"I couldn't help but notice that you brought Morgan's PR manager with you here today too. *Hey, Elly.*"

They all turn to look out the glass window and wave at me.

"Oh my god," I mumble, blushing. I give them a half-ass wave and pray that the floor might be willing to swallow me whole.

"Are you not allowed out without supervision these days?" Blake jokes.

"I shouldn't even be allowed to take a piss without supervision," Walker answers. "But in all seriousness, I'm here to keep Tommy in line, and Elly is here to keep me in line."

"I bet that's a job that doesn't pay enough." Christina smirks.

"Not a salary in the world that could keep you two out of trouble." Blake laughs.

That's a man who knows exactly what I'm up against.

Walker is a professional, he knows what he's doing, but he doesn't care about protocol, he's got his own way of doing things and the reigns are looser than my aunt Belinda after a few red wines.

"Tommy, I couldn't help but notice that you've had your highest scoring game of the season when you had Morgan watching courtside."

Tom just grins like an idiot. It's pretty sweet really. I can tell he's genuinely thrilled by the fact she's been there supporting him.

"Had to show her what I could do." Tom smirks.

"She's the most famous female musician in the world and he's a *big* fan. The whole world was watching her watch him. It's perform, or die trying," Walker chimes in.

"And then you played exceptionally well again this past weekend," Blake replies. "Some might even say you've got yourself a lucky charm."

"That one was for Walker," Tom replies. "He had a lot riding on me getting the ball through the hoop."

They're grinning at each other.

"I'm intrigued." Christina is looking backwards and forwards between the two of them, waiting for the rest of the story.

Walker shakes his head at Tom, but he's still smirking.

"Can't get dates without his help." Walker chuckles. "I had a bet with a beautiful woman that if the golden boy here made a few three pointers, I got to take her out on a date," he explains.

"And he came through for you. What a guy. I hope you got that date."

"I did. We'll see if the rest is history."

His eyes find mine for a few beats before he looks back to the two people interviewing him. The look doesn't go unnoticed.

I don't even know what the point in worrying about it is. It's not like you can fly under the radar with a guy like that. If I'm going to go on another date with him, then I need to accept people are going to notice.

I can't stop thinking about last night. He's consuming far too much space in my head right now.

"But I'm pretty sure you'd rather hear about how Tom here is set to be the subject of a pop album one day," Walker says.

"You planning on being the subject of a break-up ballad, Tommy boy?"

"I was thinking more along the lines of the happily ever after album," Tom corrects him.

Walker relaxes back in his chair having successfully redirected the conversation.

I shake my head at him, my cheeks still heated. God, I really don't like being the focus of too much attention, even just for a little bit. I don't know how these celebrities do it.

They start talking about how Tom is finding his newfound A-list fame, and being followed by paparazzi everywhere he goes.

"Are you aware her fans call her their 'Queen', and they've already crowned you as their 'King'?"

Tom laughs and nods. "It's been brought to my attention.

It's all over TikTok, the *Rhode Runners* have taken over basketball-tok and are making their presence felt. Tom's comment section has been overrun by Morgan's fans saying things like 'our King doing King things', 'King behaviour', 'Royal treatment', 'our Queen chose well'.

It's getting a little out of hand considering most of these people had probably never watched a game of basketball until two weeks ago, but it's such positive, harmless energy.

That's one thing about her fans – they're intense, but they're kind and considerate. They're respectful of Morgan – protective even. I think who they are as a group is a reflection of who *she* is.

My phone rings, it's a member of my team, so I slip off the head set and duck out of the booth to take it.

By the time I get back, they're wrapping up the interview. Maybe now I can breathe a little easier.

Ashley plays me back what I missed and it's not too bad, all things considered.

As it turns out, I shouldn't have worried about this interview. Tom *did* say too much, but it was all so genuine and complimentary it'd be impossible to be mad with him about it, it painted Morgan in nothing but a positive light. If the world didn't believe they were madly in love before, they will now.

Even the craziness of her life didn't seem to faze him.

He's the first guy she's dated that seems to

completely understand he's with *the Morgan Rhodes*, and not just a girl who happens to be able to sing.

Some of the boyfriends she's had have been the absolute worst. They've loved the idea of her, but the reality of her life has been nothing but a burden to them.

They don't understand that you can't have one without the other.

Tom seems to get it. King behaviour after all. I guess it's easy when it's not one hundred percent real, and you know it's not likely to be the rest of your life, but I really don't think that's his mindset. It all feels very genuine from him.

This interview today has pretty much confirmed my suspicions. I truly believe that guy is in *big time* love with Morgan.

I'm starting to think that it's never been pretend for him. I think he's orchestrated this whole thing to get closer to her.

He knew he wanted her, and he did what he had to do to give him the best shot at making it happen. If I'm right, then he's a genius with some of the best luck I've ever seen.

He's making one hell of a play.

"*More* flowers?" Morgan stops strumming her guitar to look at me as I carry yet another delivery of flowers into the room.

"I know. Third bunch today. My apartment is going to look like a meadow. He's out of control." My words sound like I'm scolding him, but really my stomach is filled with butterflies every time I see the bunches of beautiful flowers. This one has a note saying, '*I can't wait for date #2.*'.

"I know what you mean. Tom is going to make me gain so much weight if he doesn't stop sending me treats every day."

"We need to thank those boys' parents. They've raised them to know how to treat a woman right."

I read the note again and find myself smiling.

"You guys are so cute together."

I roll my eyes. "We're not *together*. We had *one* date."

She strums a few cords, notes something in the book in front of her and then fixes me with her stare again.

"Have you seen the photos yet?"

"*What photos?*" I ask quickly. That's not something any public relations manager wants to hear. I know Morgan hasn't done anything to paint herself in a bad light, but whatever these pictures are, if she feels they're worth me seeing, then I should already know of their existence. That's my job.

We pay off a good percentage of the paparazzi for the chance to veto what they sell, but there's always a few rogue ones who aren't willing to take the regular cash. They're waiting for their big break and even bigger pay day. I just have to hope that it arrives from some other celebrity.

"I wasn't shown any new photos of you in the team meeting this morning." I'm crossing the room with my hand out, waiting for her to show me what the damage is.

She smirks. "Well, that's because they're not of *me*."

I frown. "Tom?"

She shakes her head and bites her lip to stop from laughing as she picks up her phone and taps the screen a few times. I take it from her outstretched hand and my mouth falls open as I see the images on the screen.

It's Walker and me, leaving the restaurant hand in hand last night. I had no idea that anyone even took a photo of us, nor would I ever have imagined that anyone would bother, but that's not what shocks me most about it.

"Oh my *god*. I look like a *child* standing next to him. Is he dropping me off at pre-school or taking me on a date?"

"He's a big man," Morgan agrees. "And you're a small woman."

"He could wear me like a backpack," I deadpan.

"I think you look good together. You guys look like a real couple."

"We look *ridiculous*, and you know it. You were laughing before you showed me. I can't believe someone cared enough to take these, and then some site cared enough to pay for it. I'm not a celebrity. People need to get a grip."

"I was laughing because you were spinning out

into another dimension at the mere mention of a photo. And I might have been laughing a little bit because that's *drunk Elly* in those photos."

"He gave me about twenty-five different types of alcohol!" I try to defend myself as I flick through them all.

"How's the head?"

"Pounding," I admit as I hand her phone back. I've seen enough.

"Why don't you go home? It sounds like the radio interview went well. The internet can have that for today, they don't need anything else. Go take a nap."

"I'll survive, I can't leave early for a date *and* take an afternoon off for a nap, people will talk."

"No one would know that you 'took the evening off', given that the workday ends at five and everyone respects that. All you did was actually work business hours for once. What a wild concept. And besides, you're the boss. Do what you want."

"I think you might be the only person in the world who is upset that someone wants to do *too much* work."

"As the person benefitting from that hard work, I'm thrilled. As your friend, I'm horrified. I want you to have a life, Elly. It's passing you by while you answer phone calls and emails and waste *all* of your precious time making *me* look good. Do something for yourself. Do Walker. *Literally.*"

I know I work too much. I have a whole team beneath me, I built this business from the ground up, and I still don't fully trust the people I carefully selected to support me. Maybe it's time I learnt how to loosen up. It's a scary concept, to put your trust in other people. Nobody cares about this company more than I do. Nobody cares about Morgan's public image as much as I do. But that doesn't mean they won't do their jobs. I just have to figure out how to let them.

I trust them with our other, less famous clients that I've taken on along the way, in fact, I barely have anything to do with those accounts, but Morgan's *my* client. I've been with her from the start, back when it was just the two of us, and I don't know if I can let go of that.

"Like seriously, if you don't climb that man, I'm going to start playing up in public. I can make a real scene if I want to."

"He kissed me," I blurt out.

She looks at me with an expression so outraged I'm almost worried she's going to fire me on the spot.

"Why didn't you lead with that?!"

"We're lucky no one decided to pull a phone out and capture that little moment," I add on, mortified.

"Oh my god, was it hot? It was hot, wasn't it?"

"It was very, *very* hot," I confirm.

"Tell me *everything*," she demands.

She's my boss, I *have* to do what she says, so I launch into a detailed play by play of how the night led to us making out on the couch under the stars. It's nice to have something to contribute to these kinds of girl talk conversations for once. I've been severely lacking in that department for a long time.

"That's so cuuuuute!"

I'm not sure that having about two hundred pounds of smoking hot man on top of you is best described as 'cute', but she's a romantic, so I'll let her have it.

"He was a lot more chivalrous than I was expecting. He's pretty charming, in his own way." I can't help but smile when I think about the fact that he not only remembered every drink guess, but actually ordered them all too.

"I think those brothers are charming in *every* way, and that's half the problem."

"That's the *whole* problem." I yawn. "I don't know about you, but I'm defenceless to quick wit and banter, especially when it's coming out of a guy who looks like *that*."

"Go home. Take a nap. You deserve it. Taming a hot bachelor is hard work."

I shouldn't, but a nap does sound good right about now.

"Maybe I will. And there's definitely no taming that man… but I think I like that about him."

"I think I agree." She smiles.

"The radio interview really did go well, by the way. Tom handled it like a pro and said some really sweet things about you. He confessed far too much, but it came across well."

"He's a big teddy bear." Her voice is full of affection.

"Everyone seems to love him. He's managed to win over millions of people simultaneously."

None more so than the woman in front of me by the looks of things.

"I feel bad for him, every post-game press conference is turning into an attempt at a gossip magazine tell all exclusive about our relationship."

"Do you really think it bothers him?"

I *know* it doesn't. If anything, he seems to love it. The attention, the jokes, the admiration. He can't seem to get enough. I don't think he was joking around when he said that his favourite thing to talk about is Morgan, he certainly doesn't shy away from it.

He's unapologetically smitten.

His whole face lights up at the mere mention of her name. The man looks as excited as if he'd just won the Championship Final for the second time.

She shrugs. "It doesn't seem to. I know he's not sharing his true feelings about dealing with all this, but it seems like he really gets it. If only it was real, huh."

She's right. He does get it, or at the very least he accepts it and welcomes it as part of the package.

I think that's all Morgan has ever really wanted – for someone to believe that being with her is worth the trouble.

As for it being real, I think she'll get her chance at that too.

"When are you seeing him again?" I ask her.

We've got plans for them to step out publicly together for lunch tomorrow, but I'd be willing to bet that he won't be able to wait that long. He heads away with the team day after tomorrow for a game, and I have a feeling he's going to be having some Morgan withdrawals.

"He's cooking me dinner at his place tonight."

She's picking away at the strings on her guitar, avoiding my eyes.

"Romantic dinner for two, huh?" I question.

"I know it isn't part of the plan, but we're having fun, so what's the harm, right?"

She looks up at me and her eyes are begging me to tell her that it's okay.

It's really time she opened her eyes and stopped being so blind, but it's not a conversation I'm willing to have right now.

I'm a little hungover, and while I'm confident that Tom is the real deal, I want to know with absolute certainty that he is, before I encourage her to involve her feelings.

Unfortunately for Tom, that's going to mean that he's going to have to put *his* feelings on the line some time and risk getting shot down, but he's a solid dude, one who knows what he wants, and I'm sure that'll be a risk he's willing to take.

"You're meant to be a couple. Of course you should do couple things," I reassure her.

"I'm starting to feel a little bad that we're lying to all our friends and families. My mum loves him. All his friends are telling him to marry me."

I can understand feeling guilty about that. It can't be easy to lie to everybody in your life – but the thing is, I don't really think either of them is lying at all. I have a feeling this is all going to wind up working out, but even if it doesn't, no one will ever know. No harm done.

"Just enjoy getting to know his people, and him, yours. We don't know exactly how this is all going to play out, but that doesn't mean you can't make genuine connections, Morgs. You're allowed to have real feelings."

I'm not talking about his friends and family anymore; I'm talking about *him*. Whether or not she picks up what I'm putting down is up to her.

"You're right. Tom is a great guy. There's no reason we can't all stay close."

Never mind the fact that he's in love with her and would probably take his friends advice and marry her if he could.

"Exactly. Stop worrying so much and just enjoy yourself, you're hot and famous. *He's* hot and famous. You're the most talked about couple in the world right now, just have some fun with it."

"I've had more fun with him in the past two weeks than I had with Liam in four years," she admits.

I'd tell her that that's possibly got more to do with the fact that Liam was a total wet blanket than anything else, but I don't bother. He's out of her life now and I don't think anybody is happier about that than I am.

"Good. Let your hair down and relax."

She focuses for a second, scribbles a few words in her notebook and then looks up at me again. "Got it."

"Don't forget that we're hoping for a kiss for the cameras tomorrow if it's possible. Hand holding, all that good stuff. This is the real hard launch part, okay?"

She nods. "He holds my hand all the time anyway."

I bet he does.

"We don't need a huge PDA, just a little peck will do the job. Even on the cheek if that feels more natural. We just need the world to see that you're undoubtably more than friends."

She nods. "It'll be good. We've got it."

"Call me if you need me, okay?"

"I will. Now go home and get some rest, you kind of look like shit."

I laugh at her brutal honestly. "Thanks, I love you too."

WALKER

Walker: In case you haven't noticed, I'm mad at you.

Elly-May: What? I saw you in the office five minutes ago and you couldn't stop smiling.

Walker: It wore off when you were out of sight.

Elly-May: Do you need me to buy you some binoculars?

Walker: Better not. I'd stalk the hell out of you.

Elly-May: Okay, *Joe Goldberg*. Seems like the kind of thing you should think internally but not say out loud…

Walker: Technically, I typed it in a message, I didn't say it out loud.

Elly-May: Good luck making that hold up in court.

Walker: Stop changing the subject, I want you to apologise to me.

Elly-May: Do I get the privilege of knowing what I'm saying sorry for? Or am I just expected to say it regardless?

Walker: I'm insulted you don't already know.

Elly-May: What can I say? I'm not very bright. Maybe you could point me in the right direction...

Walker: Do you recall the conversation we had the other day about you having siblings and your favourite colour being yellow?

Elly-May: You remembered. I hate that that impresses me.

Walker: This isn't about you, beautiful, try and focus.

Elly-May: I recall the conversation, smart ass. What about it?

Walker: What's MY favourite colour Elly?

Her messages have been coming through quickly, barely seconds after I hit send, but this time it takes a while. I wait nearly three full minutes and when it finally beeps, I nearly fumble it out of my hand like a total rookie. I slide the screen open and grin at the two words on my screen.

Elly-May: I'm sorry.

Walker: I'll accept gifts and grovelling.

Another long wait.

. . .

Elly-May: How about a second date?

Now she's just playing me at my own game, and I'm here for it. I'm down for whatever if it gets her to go out with me again. She's not getting off that easily though. I'll see her offer and raise it.

Walker: How about a weekend away?

Elly-May: Oh, come on, it's not like I forgot your birthday.

Walker: It hurts the same.

Elly-May: It does not. I can't go on a weekend away with you, I barely know you. You barely know me.

Walker: I know enough.

Elly-May: And what if I don't know enough about you?

Walker: Then I can think of the perfect way for you to catch up. A whole uninterrupted weekend with the man of your dreams.

Elly-May: Really? When do I get to meet him?

I chuckle. She's such a savage.

Walker: Stone cold.

Elly-May: It's bold of you to assume you know my type, you know.

•   •   •

It *would* be bold of me to assume given that my thorough search of her dating history came up completely empty. But that doesn't matter. I don't care if she's never been on a single date in her life. Her type is *me* now. She better get used to it.

Walker: I'm sure my multiple personalities have it covered one way or another.

Elly-May: I feel like we're getting wildly off track here.

Walker: You're right. I'll book us somewhere to stay next weekend. Problem solved. Misgivings forgiven.

Elly: Oh my god, you're insane. And relentless.

Walker: Let go. Live a little, maybe you'll enjoy yourself.

Elly-May: I'm worried about enjoying myself too much.

I smirk. There's my girl.

Walker: So you'll come?

Another long wait for a reply.

Elly-May: I guess I could...

· · ·

Fuck yes. It's not like she can't summon Morgan's private plane or car to come save her if she needed to, but I'm not about to put ideas in her head.

Walker: Where do you want to go?
Elly-May: I think the less I know, the better.
Walker: Got it. I'm on it. Leave it with me.
Elly-May: That sentence fills me with worry.
Walker: I think you should go to sleep. You've got a big weekend coming up.
Elly-May: If you make me hike for a whole day or something stupid like that, you're going to end up carrying me on your back – just a warning.

I've taken shits that were bigger than her. I can't imagine that'd be a problem. Not that I plan on spending all my precious time with her, walking up hills.

Walker: I'll keep that in mind. Good night, beautiful x
Elly-May: Walker?
Walker: Yeah, Elly-May?
Elly-May: What is your favourite colour?

I grin at my phone. Sweet little Elly-May.

• • •

Walker: Green.

I don't elaborate that my favourite shade of green is the exact same one as her eyes. She's only just agreed to spend a whole weekend with me, I don't need to scare her off with heavy shit.

Elly-May: Nice choice. Good night, slick x

You've got to feel bad for Morgan's ex. The guy must be absolutely spewing whenever he goes online.

From what I hear, he's a tool, but he's got to be having a rough time at the moment, and I've got at least a little bit of empathy for that.

The photos of Tommy and Morgan necking have just hit the media, and it's blowing up big time.

It wouldn't matter if the guy wasn't an NBA fan – which I already know he is – short of going bush and living in a cave, he still wouldn't be able to hide from this story.

The fans are going *crazy*.

They wasted no time comparing pics of Tom and Morgan kissing, and what looks like Morgan trying to give her ex a kiss and him trying to hide.

There couldn't be a starker difference. When she's with my brother she looks happy and free. Those old pictures make her look worn down and embarrassed.

I flick through a few more of the photos that were posted to TMZ only a few minutes ago.

"Pretty cute snaps, bro." I make a kissy face, puckering my lips at Tom as he flops down onto the couch with a protein shake in his hand.

"What can I say? This face is made for it. The camera loves me."

"It's all you, man. She's just an NPC."

He chuckles. "Yeah, Morgan who?"

"Did you guys get swamped?"

"Not too bad going in. Elly had tipped off most of the paps that were there waiting, so then it was just random fans that happened to see us, but coming out was pretty crazy, I swear those women can multiply with a click of their fucking fingers. Never seen anything like it."

"It's fucked up huh, I don't know how she lives like that."

"She's so sweet to them all too. Takes the time to say hi, wave… she's grateful for the love, doesn't care how inconvenient it is."

She does seem pretty genuine. For someone who is worth hundreds of millions of dollars, she hasn't forgotten about the loyalty that got her there.

"You're so smitten with her. Looks like quite the kiss too."

"Bit rich coming from you, big guy, I've been hearing all about you trying to charm your way into

Elly's pants." He's grinning wide. "Very romantic, bro, dinner under the stars. Anyone would think you'd been reading romance books for tips."

I forgot how much women talk.

I shrug and lean back, relaxed. He can give me shit all he likes; it doesn't bother me. He's hardly in a position to talk anyway, he's got romance flowing in his veins.

"I'm not embarrassed about knowing how to treat a woman right." I shrug.

"Fuck, you actually really like her."

He sits up and takes notice.

"Yeah, I do," I admit. "You've met her. I'm not about to fumble that."

He looks blown away. Maybe I've let this whole playboy bachelor vibe go on too long. I'm thirty-three years old, acting like a frat boy isn't charming at this age. It's been about two and half years since I had a proper girlfriend. I'm surprised Ma hasn't started hassling me about grandkids yet.

"Fuck I'm good," he boasts.

"How's that?"

"Wingman extraordinaire. I've managed to get Morgan Rhodes to date me, *and* she came as a package deal with your dream girl. I've got a very particular set of skills."

"Yeah, you're a real champ, someone should give you a medal."

"When are you taking her out again?"

"We're going away for the weekend. We're leaving early Friday so I can be back to fly out for the game on Sunday."

He laughs and runs his hand through his hair. "Weekend away. Credit where credit's due, Walk, you go after what you want."

"No one is going to accuse me of not coming on strong enough."

"They're certainly not," he mutters. "Where are you taking her?"

"Called in a favour with a buddy of mine down in Santa Cruz – he's got a place on the beach there and I didn't want to go too far. Road trips are cool and all, but I can think of better things to do than sit in a car."

"How have you always got a buddy in every town?"

"I'm a likable guy. You wouldn't know about that."

He flips me off. "Mint place?"

I groan in appreciation. "It's crazy. Got the sickest pool overlooking the shore. He barely uses it. Met him in college, he's a big name in advertising now. Probably only sees the place twice a year."

"I'll have to remember that."

I chuckle. "Bro, your girlfriend owns more property than you've got pairs of shoes."

"I dunno man, she's loaded, but I've got a lot of kicks."

I respect the hell out of how secure he is. He's not intimidated or emasculated by the fact that Morgan is far wealthier and more successful than he is, and probably ever will be. He's unfazed by anything like that.

"Speaking of shoes, what the hell were you wearing before the game last week?"

He grins. "You saw the fit."

"*The fit* hurt my eyes. You looked like the guy who

gets hired by a drug cartel to sweet talk the cops for them."

"That's very specific."

"It was a very specific fashion choice."

He's got that stupid grin on his face again. It's one I know well. He's a pesky menace.

I still can't figure out if he dresses the way he does because he thinks it's funny, or if he genuinely thinks it looks good.

Personally, I think he looks like he rolled around in a suitcase of our grandparent's old clothes and then took a walk, but the internet is going crazy for it.

The man can dress like a shower curtain and still do no wrong.

"I liked it."

"Who dressed you the game before?"

"My stylist."

"Your stylist deserves a minimum of two life sentences. You looked like a pimp."

"Thank you."

I huff out a laugh. "Only you would think that was a compliment."

"Morgan likes it." He smirks at me.

"Morgan might need to get her eyes tested."

He chugs back half of his shake in one go and stretches out his calf.

He's been trying to play it off as nothing, but I know he's got a niggle. He left training early yesterday to see the physiotherapist.

"When do you leave for Cali?"

"This afternoon."

"Will you be able to manage a few days without your girl?"

The question is a joke, but his response is real.

"She's going to fly out for the game."

Well, well, well. That's interesting.

"Maybe I'll hitch a ride with her." I mull it over. I was going to fly anyway, surely Elly would be willing to sweet talk the pop princess into letting me jump on board. "I wonder if Elly will come too."

"The poor girl will probably be dying to get away from you by then. A whole weekend with your cocky attitude."

"By Sunday afternoon she'll be in love with me," I joke. "You just wait."

He turns more serious. "I know how important Elly is to Morgan. Can you do me a favour and just *try* not to fuck her over. We both know you can be a bit of a dick every now and then… *no offence*. But just… don't be this time."

I know better than to be offended. He's right, I've been a dick lately. Actually, I've been a dick for a while now – especially to women.

It's all been fun and games, but this feels different. The games aren't fun anymore. Being real is. Being with her is.

I want her.

And not just in my bed, I want her in my *life*. I want her sitting next to me on the couch and at the games. I want her shit cluttering up my bathroom, and the kind of food she likes in the fridge. I just want her near me, and that's pretty much the opposite of the tap and gap attitude I've been running this past year or so.

"Elly's safe with me. You can trust me."

He must believe me, because he just nods, pulls out his phone and starts watching TikToks about himself at full volume.

CHAPTER
ELEVEN

ELLY

I can't believe I'm doing this.

Who even am I?

I don't have a spontaneous bone in my body. I consider going to the grocery store without a list to be a risky endeavour.

I thrive on organisation, structure and routine. My work life can be so unpredictable, I usually try and keep total control in my personal life.

That concept has gone completely out the window since meeting Walker.

There is no control *whatsoever* where he's concerned. He's erratic. It feels like anything could happen with him around.

A prime example is what's about to happen now. A weekend away with a man that's basically a total stranger.

It's not too late to back out. I tell myself.

I stuff another dress into my bag and shake my head. I don't know why I'm bothering to pretend I have options. I know as well as he does that I'm going on this trip. I'm no quitter, but more than that, and as much as it pains me, I *want* to go.

I'm dying to see him again, to see if my memory serves me right.

No one could possibly be as good looking as the image of that man that exists inside my head. He can't be as charming, as sweet and as wildly inappropriate as I remember him. Every time I see him, I expect to be disappointed, but I never am. I might end up somewhat infuriated, but at this point I'm starting to think it's all part of the charm.

And of course, he's a good kisser. *Great* kisser. I'm thirty, and I'm sitting here daydreaming about a kiss like a teenage girl. That guy finds his way into my knickers and I'm going to be in serious trouble.

I glance at my phone but resist picking it up to check my emails. I'm under strict instruction from Morgan to 'not touch the fucking thing'. In fact, she threatened to drop me 'from a great height' if I so much as answered a work call in the next couple of days.

I'm fairly confident she sweet talked someone at my office to divert my calls or at the very least filter them, but I can't be sure.

She's demanded I enjoy my weekend without interruption. It's the most diva behaviour I've ever seen from her. Given that the media is going insane right now after her and Tom's very public display of affection at lunch, it's not ideal timing, but she's insisted. Apparently, she 'has it handled'. Whatever that means.

I think it's safe to say she approves of the company I'm keeping.

I look at my packed bag and sigh. I don't know what's possessed me to pack ten pairs of underwear and three outfits that I've never worn in my life, but you just never know what you might need – or if you might shit your pants three times a day.

Can't be too careful.

I zip up the bag and swing it over my shoulder. I try to take deep breaths as I walk across my apartment and out the door, desperately trying to settle my racing heart, but I'm too nervous for it to work.

I'm *freaking out*.

I fidget as the elevator takes me down to the ground floor. I'm sweating and it's got nothing to do with the temperature.

I'm *so* nervous.

I haven't dated in *so* long; I've forgotten what it's like to feel hopeful over some guy. In my experience, they all let you down somewhere along the line, but so far Walker is nothing like any guy I've dated before, so I've stupidly allowed myself hope that this time it might be different.

This is the part I hate. The part where you have to let your guard down and allow yourself to be vulnerable. You have to give someone else the power to hurt you, and just hope like hell that they won't.

I don't have complete faith in Walker yet, but I've put more trust in him than I have in anyone else in a long time and that's enough to make my palms sweat.

The doors open with a ding, and I steady myself.

I can do this. I can be brave and impulsive. I *am* brave and impulsive; I just have to let go of the protective shield I keep in place to control that side of myself.

I cross the lobby and push through the front door.

I look up the street and then down, and there he is. Leaning against the side of a shiny red convertible.

Only this man would turn up in a car like *that*.

It looks expensive. It's only then that it occurs to me that I have no idea of his wealth.

We haven't discussed anything like that, outside of knowing we both own a piece of property.

I'm sure he does well for himself. He's a smart guy and he would have been paid well for the time he did do in the NBA.

I don't do too badly for myself. I struggle to have a proper grip on the reality of how well I do, really. It's hard when the most regular company I keep is with a multi-millionaire.

I own my apartment and a house back in New York that I rent out. I don't bother keeping a car, I can send for Morgan's any time, so it isn't worth having my own. I have a successful investment portfolio and could probably afford to quit work and travel the world for a few years if I wanted to. I wouldn't do that though, I love my job, and it takes me wherever I want to go anyway, but the point is that I *could*.

"Hey there, beautiful." His eyes light up when he sees me.

He strides towards me, kissing me on the cheek and taking the bag from my hands in one swoop.

"I was starting to think you were going to stand me up."

"Were you planning to scale the side of the building, or come in through the front door and drag me out kicking and screaming?"

He slings his big arm around my shoulders and tucks me into his side.

"I was thinking of starting with calling every thirty seconds, can't be jumping straight into *Spiderman* mode. The neighbours would talk, and I hear kidnapping is frowned upon so snatching you would be a last resort."

"I'd hate to have to deal with the media if you got arrested."

He leads me to the passenger door, opens it for me and gestures with his hand for me to get in. "And you accused me of not being a gentleman." He scoffs as I take my seat. He shuts my door, winks at me and goes around back to put my duffel into the trunk.

I don't know how he manages to get his big body and long legs into the driver's seat, but he does, and then the engine is roaring to life.

There is going to be absolutely no missing us in this thing. It's loud, ostentatious and bright red. At least I know he's not embarrassed to be seen with me.

"Is this your car?" I ask him. I can't really imagine him owning this car, but I don't know all that much about him when it comes down to it.

"Nah, Tommy gave it to Ma for her birthday a couple of years back. She barely uses it. Dad reckons it'll come in handy for a midlife crisis one day, but it pretty much just sits in the garage."

"Oh my god." I laugh.

"No better way to enjoy a coastal road trip than with the top down if you ask me. Even if it's ridiculous and over the top."

"You're lucky I didn't spend hours doing my hair this morning," I tease.

He leans across me and opens the glove box, pulls out two Bears caps and presses one onto my head.

I wiggle it into place and look at myself in the wing mirror.

"It suits you," he tells me.

"Go sports," I reply dryly.

He chuckles, puts his own hat on, and pulls out into the street.

No backing out now.

"Do you want to stop up here for a bit?"

I nod eagerly. When I was younger and we went on road trips, my parents always just wanted to get to where we were going as fast as we could. My college boyfriend was the same way. That guy was about as adventurous as a paper bag.

I always saw things I wanted to stop and look at, and I was never allowed.

He pulls off to the side of the road and kills the engine.

It's so quiet without the roar of the car and his random playlist. He's kept me guessing with every new song that played. It was never what I expected.

We've had everything from The Spice Girls to Marilyn Manson.

I waste no time climbing out and stretching my legs.

We've been driving for about forty-five minutes, so we can't have too much longer to go.

I'm glad we're delaying our arrival for a little bit, the fact that all too soon we'll be pulling up to a house – one with beds and total privacy – is a little scary to me. It's been a long time since I've been alone like that with a man, and this will be the first time I've ever been alone with a man like *this* one.

I watch him as he strolls towards the grassy bank that lines the coast. The cliff face drops away down to the rocky coastal beach below.

It's beautiful, but even the stunning scenery can't distract me from the real view in front of me.

He stretches his arms above his head and the hem of his t-shirt rides up, exposing a sliver of his toned stomach.

I'm such a goner. The thighs and ass on the guy are *exceptional*. I'm not surprised he's a cocky prick, who can really blame him when he looks like that?

He looks back at me and grins, then, true to character, pretends to slip near the edge of the cliff.

My heart rate speeds up so fast it feels like it misses a beat.

"Can you not fall and die? I don't know how to drive a stick."

He chuckles and stands up straight, farther away from the edge. That throaty chuckle of his does fucked up things to me.

"Come over here." He holds his hand out to me.

I raise a brow at him. "So you can take me over the side with you? I think not."

I take a couple of steps in his direction but stop a few feet short of where he's standing. I don't like heights, and I certainly don't like heights with a prankster nearby.

He shakes his head in amusement. "You really think I'd let you fall?"

He pins me with his stare, and I forget how to breathe for a few seconds.

He closes the gap between us and wraps his arms around me. It's so comfortable and easy. It feels like we've been doing this together for years.

He's big and warm and he smells *so* good.

That's probably a weird thing to think about, but it should be illegal to smell as delicious as this man does.

I cuddle into his chest and run my palms up and down his back. "This shirt feels nice."

"That's because it's made of boyfriend material," he replies, without missing a beat.

"Oh my *god*." I groan. "I'm both impressed *and* disgusted by that line."

His laughter shakes his body against mine. It's embarrassing how much it turns me on.

"Boyfriend material," I mutter.

His hand leaves my back and finds its way under

my chin, he tips my face up towards his and leans down to kiss me so casually, I forget that this is something totally new to us.

The way he handles me… it's so confident and sure… He takes control and I surrender it willingly. He doesn't hesitate, doesn't give me time to overthink every little thing the way I normally do.

Like the way I spent the majority of what should have been my sleeping hours last night. Thinking, re-thinking, *worrying*. Thinking some more.

"When was the last time you had a boyfriend, Elly-May?"

I don't really want to admit to him just how much of a lonely loser I am, but I think he's probably got his suspicions already. It's so obvious, I may as well be wearing one of those big tacky sandwich boards with the words *eternally single* written across it.

"It's been a while," I admit. "I've only had one since I've been working with Morgan. I thought he was a stand-up guy, but it turned out he was just some crazed fan who pretended he'd never heard of her. He got close to me to get close to her. It was gross. Ended with a restraining order. Good times. Swore never again after that."

"What the fuck?" he growls. "That's insane."

"You don't need to convince me; I know *exactly* how crazy it was."

He looks into my eyes. "You've really never dated since?"

I shrug. "I've had a couple of dates. I was seeing a guy for a little while, but he had no idea what I did for a job. It wasn't sustainable."

He looks like he feels sorry for me.

"I don't really mind," I tell him. "I just poured myself into work."

"Do you ever see yourself getting married?"

His question surprises me. I wouldn't have expected him to think about things like marriage.

"Yeah." I nod. "I'd love to have a husband one day. Someone to grow old with and all that. Start a family…"

"I wonder what our children will look like," he muses, his smart-ass grin back in full force.

I roll my eyes. "You could always ask AI to figure it out."

He smirks. "That's alright. I'll just wait and see for myself."

My god, this man is too much. I don't know how to handle myself when he plays like this. I decide it's probably safest to just go along with it.

"How many children are we having?"

"Two. Both boys. They'll be the future of the NBA."

"Naturally."

"They'll out-do their uncle's legacy – it'll break his heart a little bit, but he'll put on a brave face."

"I hope I have a c-section." I grimace. Even just the idea of birthing a fictional baby that shares Walker's DNA makes me want to cross my legs.

It'd probably come out the same size as me.

"We'd make aunty Morgs shout us the best obstetrician in the biz."

"Oh, you think Aunt Morgs and Uncle Tommy will still be a thing by then, do you?"

He looks a little sheepish, like maybe he's said too much.

"In my story they fall in love and live happily ever after. It'd suit me to have a celebrity for a sister-in-law and it's all about me, *obviously*."

I don't press him, but I have a feeling he knows more than he's saying – which further confirms my theory about Tom's true motives.

These Daniels men are tricky. They need to be well supervised.

"Can I ask you something?"

We're still standing together, locked in an embrace, me straining my neck to look up at him, and him straining his to look down at me. We're both going to wind up with spinal issues at this rate, but I've still got no desire to move.

"Always."

"Why do you go by the name Brooks, when your legal name is Daniels?"

He shifts his weight from one foot to the other.

"My last name was Brooks when I was born, and after Tommy was born and my parents were married, we changed it to Daniels so we could all be the same. My name has been Walker Daniels for most of my life, but when Tom cracked it in the NBA and hired me in a professional capacity, I decided I wanted to go back to Brooks, just for work."

I nod. That makes sense.

"Pretty much everyone knows we're brothers, and we don't hide the fact, but sometimes it just works better for business deals and stuff if we're not immediately identified as family. People tend to speak a bit freer if they don't know they're speaking about a guy's little brother."

"Fair call. That's actually really smart."

"You sound surprised."

He's not insulted, but he probably should be. I've made some unfair assumptions about him and his intelligence.

"Honestly… when we met, I was convinced there was not a single thought behind those pretty eyes."

He laughs. "All blues, no clues."

"But you're actually really intelligent. Especially for a wannabe jock – sorry to stereotype, but most of the guys I knew who played ball in college didn't give a shit about getting their degrees. The game was life, and the rest was just a technicality, but I can tell you had a plan for more, even before your injury."

"Yeah… I mean, those guys are boneheads. There's no guarantees in the game. Every guy on that court is just one injury away from their career being over as I so aptly demonstrated. Even Tommy got his degree. I dragged his ass through it, but he graduated."

I've seen footage online of Walker playing basketball. He was good. Fast. Especially for his size. Ironically, he was one hell of a track runner in college too.

It's nice to know there's more to him than just sports.

"So, the basketball dream ended, and Walker Brooks was born again, huh?"

"He was, and I haven't looked back, not professionally at least."

I've been wanting to ask him about his mother, but we've spent so little time together in person, and it didn't feel like the type of conversation to have over the phone.

"Will you tell me about your birth mum? I know she left when you were young and your dad raised you, but I don't know all the details."

His shoulders drop a little, but it's a such a subtle movement, I can't be sure I didn't imagine it.

"There's not much to tell. She was kinda young I guess, but old enough to know better. Dad was a few years older. They got pregnant and decided to go through with the pregnancy and raise the baby together even though they hadn't been a couple that long. It only lasted a few hours after I was born. She left the hospital without me the next day, and dad was left holding the baby – literally. He told me once that he thinks she planned to leave all along and was just playing along so she wasn't pressured into a termination."

Oh woah.

"I can't imagine how hard that must have been for him."

"That's the only reason I ever get emotional about it. I feel for Dad. It must have been terrifying to be handed a newborn baby and have to process that, *and* the end of your relationship with no notice. He told me when I was older that there's no way they'd have made it as long as they did if it weren't for her falling pregnant, so maybe there wasn't much of a relation-ship to mourn."

"Still. I'm sure he never planned to do any of that alone. He must be a very strong man."

"He is. He's the best man I know. He's a little

quirky, a little different as time has gone on and he's got older, but we could rely on him for anything growing up. Still can now. He's not a lot like me or Tommy – but he says we're like his father was. I think the sporting gene skipped a generation."

"I look forward to meeting him one day."

"He'd love that. I'm surprised he hasn't broken his tradition of avoiding the stadiums just for the chance to meet Morgan; he's a bit of a fan. I'll take you around to the house some time."

"You admire him a lot."

It's not a question – the answer is obvious; I can hear in his voice how much he respects his father.

"More than anyone I've ever met. To be strong enough to do what he did… I don't know many men who would step up like that."

"He sounds incredible," I agree.

We exchange a long look.

"So, you're a newborn, he's raising you on his own… and then he met your ma?"

"Yeah, I was just a baby when they fell in love. They didn't waste any time. Tommy came along soon after, and Grace after him and we've always been a family. Sandra never treated me like I was any less than her own flesh and blood. She's been my ma for as long as I can remember. Her and dad, they've taught me what love is. Given me something to strive for."

I squeeze him a little tighter. He seems like he's totally fine – like this hasn't impacted his life in a negative way, but something about this story makes me want to hug him.

I can't imagine knowing that my mum looked at

me after growing me inside her body for nine months and just turned and walked away without even knowing what would come of me. It was probably for the best, she was obviously not ready to be a mother, but it's still a difficult concept to understand.

"Do you ever think about trying to find her?"

"I talked about it when I was about sixteen, thought I might want to know something about her. What she looks like even. I thought maybe I could meet her once, and show her what she'd missed out on…"

"You didn't go through with it?"

He shakes his head. "Nah. I thought about it for a little bit. Ma and Dad told me they'd support whatever I wanted to do, and then it just occurred to me one day while I was sitting in the kitchen eating a bowl of Fruit Loops, that it didn't matter who *she* was, or what *she* missed out on, because *I* hadn't missed out on anything. I had a mother and a father, a brother, a sister and a whole life that I loved and appreciated. There was nothing some stranger whose DNA I shared could offer me. I never gave her much thought after that."

"Wow. That's… pretty profound for a sixteen-year-old boy."

"What can I say? I've always been mature for my age," he says with a smirk.

I roll my eyes. Now *that* is a total lie.

"Maybe that's why I've never really settled down though. I've probably got a few abandonment issues buried deep in there somewhere."

"I don't think so. You seem like you've got it

together. Maybe you just haven't met the right person yet."

He doesn't say anything more, not with words anyway, but those eyes – they sure as hell have a lot to say.

"We should get back on the road," he announces. He gives me one more quick kiss, takes my hand in his and leads me back to the car.

WALKER

"What a beautiful house," Elly breathes as she watches the waves crashing against the shore, not far from the pool she's standing next to.

"I hope you brought your bikini."

"I brought six," she admits sheepishly, giving me the side eye.

I chuckle. "You know we're only here for two nights, right?"

"I'm under no illusion that it's ridiculously excessive. I couldn't pick."

"You could always swim naked."

She turns to me and raises an eyebrow as she fights the smile trying to make its way onto her face.

"You think so, do you? Wouldn't that make all the options even more ridiculous?"

I shrug and saunter towards her. "Yeah... but if

you're still having trouble choosing which to wear… I'd hate for you to be stressed about it. Might be easier to just wear nothing."

She throws her arms around my neck as I reach her.

"That's so thoughtful of you, Walker."

"I'm nothing if not considerate."

She's looking at me like she wants me to kiss her.

Those soft pouty lips of hers are begging for me to claim them.

I reach down and scoop her up, lifting her into my arms so our faces are level.

She gasps, her grip around my neck tightening, but I don't give her any time to react, I crash my mouth to hers.

She moans against my lips, and it makes me even crazier.

She's so fucking sexy, I don't know how I'm meant to keep my hands off her all weekend. Not here, with total privacy and no interruptions. Once we reach that bedroom, *if* we reach the bedroom, I can't imagine we'll leave it in a hurry.

She drags her teeth over my bottom lip, and that's it. I'm screwed.

"*Jesus*, Elly. I'm going to throw you over my shoulder and carry you to the bed if you're going to do things like that."

Her hands, which are wound into my hair, tighten their grip. "Maybe I'd be okay with that."

Fuck.

I've been coaching myself since she agreed to this trip, to *not* rush it with her. We've known each other a while now, talked multiple times nearly every day, but that was mostly work. We've only had *one* official date. I want to do right by her, no matter how much she doesn't seem to care about the formalities.

"*Fuck*," I growl as she kisses me again. I can feel my dick getting hard. "We need to stop before I can't."

She giggles and rests her forehead against mine. I'm still holding her up and she's so fucking tiny I could do it all day. What a dangerous game.

"What if I don't want you to stop?"

I groan. "I need you to let me anyway." I sound like I'm begging.

Truthfully, I *am* begging. I might be holding her entire bodyweight in my arms, but she's the one in control. She's holding what's left of my willpower in the palm of her hand.

"I want to show you that there's more to me than a big dick and incredible sex." I manage to get the words out with a straight face.

She throws her head back and laughs louder than I've ever heard her. "You are seriously something else."

"You're saying that now, wait until you've experienced the full package."

"I look forward to seeing your full package."

I place a kiss on her jaw, and she arches her neck, exposing her throat to me.

Such a pretty throat. It'll look even better with my hand wrapped around it.

Fuck, my mind can't stay out of the gutter. I need to put some space between us and see if my brain can still function.

"I'm taking you on our date," I announce, setting her down on the ground.

Fuck, she looks so gorgeous staring up at me with her cheeks flushed and her pretty eyes wide.

"Where are we going?" she asks brightly, none of her former arguing this time.

Somewhere without access to a bed.

"It's a surprise. Bring a sweater just in case."

"Roger that."

I reach out to grab her, but she dances out of the way, giggling.

I watch her disappear inside the house and resist the urge to say *fuck it* to this date plan, and just have my way with her now.

I hadn't anticipated her being so eager. She's let her hair down and relaxed, and she's all too willing it would seem.

I give myself a mental slap. This isn't just *some* woman. This could be *the* woman.

If I'm right about her, then I'll have all the time in the world to do wicked things to her. I can be patient for now. I don't want to have to tell my grandchildren one day that I ploughed their grandmother the first chance I got. I'd rather they hear all about a dramatic build up – really scar them for life.

I head inside and into the kitchen. I ordered a full spread picnic to be delivered here this morning before we arrived, and I've got a blanket in the trunk of the car.

I find the labelled containers in the fridge next to a bottle of wine, and the picnic basket in the scullery. I pack it all up quickly and run out to the car to grab the blanket before she comes back down.

"Walker?" she calls from somewhere outside the kitchen.

"*Coming*," I reply. Ironically, that's probably what I'd be doing right now if we'd carried on the way we were headed.

I scoop up the basket and head out to meet her.

Her eyes light up when she sees what I have. "You made us a picnic?"

"Technically I paid someone else to make us a picnic, but it's the thought that counts, right?"

"Did the thought extend to champagne and straw-berries?" she asks hopefully.

"The thought did."

She sighs. "You're good."

She doesn't even know the half of it yet.

I usher her out of the door and across the patio.

"Where are we eating it?"

"There's a path down there, it'll take us onto a little beach."

She looks pleased. That is, until she sees the 'path' – apparently, she really is scared of heights, and this is a 'death trap'.

It takes me about ten minutes to convince her that she'll be fine, and another five minutes to get her to move. I'm just grateful that it's been upgraded to include a handrail; the last time I was here, it was just a goat track where you basically picked your way down the cliff face at random. At least now it's a goat track with a handrail.

Some of the neighbours got together and put it up

– I'll have to thank them all personally. Elly would have lost her shit if I'd asked her to go down *that* as it was.

I stay close by her, holding her hand and reassuring her the whole way. Thank fuck it only takes a few minutes to get down, she looks wildly uncomfortable.

"Thank god," she breathes as her feet hit the sand.

"Well, I learnt something new about you today."

"Yeah, that's embarrassing, I'm sorry I'm such a baby."

"Don't apologise for things you don't need to be sorry for."

"Okay. Sorry," she replies, smirking.

I shake my head at her. She keeps being such a smart ass and I'm going to have to put her over my knee. "So, you're afraid of heights, but you live in a twentieth-floor apartment?"

"Ironic, I know. I try not to go near the edges of the balcony." She laughs at herself, so I figure it's okay if I do the same.

"What about planes?"

She shrugs and kind of looks at me like it's a silly question. "They're fine. If I'm enclosed, I'm good. I'm not going to fall off the edge of a plane, you know? It might crash and burn, but that's another fear to unlock at a later date."

I chuckle at her logic.

"Riiiight. Okay, so just nothing you can fall off?"

She nods. "*Exactly*. It's not actually the heights that I find scary, it's the chance I might fall to a tragic death that really bothers me."

"Both slightly irrational and totally logical."

"I felt better about it when you were holding my hand," she says as she gives my hand a squeeze before letting it go again.

"I'll sleep a little easier tonight then," I tease her.

Truthfully, knowing that she feels safer with her hand in mine, blows my ego up to three times the size it was at the top of that hill.

Makes me feel like a man. Nothing a man loves more than being made to feel like one.

She stops to pick something up off the sand, and I feel something less than ideal happen.

I grimace as I realise that she's downwind from me. *Whoops.*

"I'm going to need you to walk faster," I tell her.

"What? *Why?*" she's got a shell in her hand and she's looking at me with a confused expression on her face.

"Quick, hurry. I've just unintentionally crop dusted you."

She rushes forward and then stops and stares at me when the words really register. She blinks twice. "You just farted in the air space in front of me?"

"Yeah..."

"Why?!"

I can't hold in my laugh. "I didn't do it on purpose. It wasn't pre-planned. It slipped out."

"My mouth could have been open."

I'm almost doubled over laughing as she sticks out her tongue, looking disgusted, but at least a little amused.

"I'm sorry."

"Oh, you *will* be," she replies.

"I'll be sure to fart downwind from now on. Or wait until your mouth is closed, at least."

She shakes her head and does her best to glare at me, but she can't stop her lips from curving up into a smile.

"You can laugh, Elly-May, farts are funny." I grin.

"Maybe if you're a five-year-old," she offers. "I can't say that potential pink eye gets the same giggles out of me these days."

I can't stop laughing. I can't believe I just farted on our second date. What a guy. Talk about romance.

"Just when you thought I couldn't get any better." I wink at her.

"You sure showed me," she replies dryly.

She turns around in circles slowly, checking out the view around us.

"This place is so pretty."

It's got nothing on her, but I can appreciate that it's easy on the eye.

She picks out a nice flat spot for us and I lay down the blanket and start to unpack the food. It looks *so* good; my stomach is growling. We pop the cork and I insist on feeding her a strawberry, much to her disgust.

It's all picture-perfect coupley romance kind of stuff. I hope I'm getting it right – rogue fart aside.

This is all new to me. It's not as though I haven't done sweet things for a woman before, but I haven't tried *this* hard until now. People are free to take me as I am, women included. I don't pretend to be someone I'm not, and while I'm still one hundred percent me when I'm with Elly, I'm somehow better. I want to put in extra effort. Like I'm being one hundred and fifty percent me somehow.

Me with a system upgrade.

"I could get used to this, you know," she tells me softly.

She sips her glass of champagne and smiles shyly when she catches me watching her. She's *so* pretty. I bet she's the kind of girl who wakes up looking beautiful, if not a little blind.

"Why are you looking at me like that?" she asks, blushing.

"I was just thinking how gorgeous you are."

She glances away, embarrassed. "Stop it, I am not."

"I think you are."

Her eyes snap back to mine. She'd have to be deaf and stupid to doubt the sincerity of my statement.

She blushes. "Well thank you, I still think you're wrong, but I like that you think that."

"Anyone with eyes would think that, Elly, you're *beautiful.*"

I can tell she's uncomfortable accepting compliments.

"I'm not used to being the centre of anyone's attention."

"Well, you're the centre of mine."

She likes the sound of that – I can see it in those stunning eyes.

She bites her lip and looks at me in a way that I don't think I've ever seen a woman look at me.

"What are you doing to me?" I breathe as she slides herself across the blanket, closing the distance between us and snuggling into my chest. I stroke her head and kiss her hair.

"I don't know, but if it makes you feel any better, I think it's the same thing you're doing to me," she confesses.

Neither of us say anything else, but the silence is speaking for itself.

We're falling. Both of us.

What a feeling.

I've never felt so confident and so terrified at the same time.

"I know you want to wine and dine me and make me feel special and respected and all of that, but I swear, if you don't take me upstairs and disrespect me real soon, I'm going to go insane."

Elly-May. What a bad, bad girl.

Why is it always the ones who you think would be the most innocent…

I like a woman who knows what she wants. Even better is *this* woman, and her knowing that what she wants is *me*.

We've been back from the beach for a couple of hours, but we're just doing more of the same; eating, drinking and talking. Apparently, that's enough of that now though. She's done with the talking.

She raises a dark brow at me, waiting for my answer.

Abso-fucking-lutely.

I'm a strong-willed man, and I had a plan, but right now, with her looking at me like that, saying what she's saying, my only plan is to get her between the sheets as quickly as possible.

"It'd be my pleasure to disrespect every single inch of you."

I pick her up in one swoop, and head for the bedroom.

She moans, a breathless, sensual moan, and I'm completely fucked from that sound alone.

I stride into the room and toss her onto the bed. The sharp intake of her breath draws my attention to that sexy mouth of hers.

Jesus, I want those plump lips wrapped around my cock so badly it's like my life depends on it. But not yet. I haven't got the self-control for that right now. I need to be inside her, everything else can wait.

I'm betting there will be time for that later.

I tug off my shirt and throw it to the ground and then I'm unbuttoning my shorts.

"Take it all off," I order her.

Her eyes widen and then she's moving, pulling her dress over her head and dropping it onto the bed.

The only sound in the room is my laboured breathing as I take her in.

She's wearing a matching set of white lacy underwear, which really does prove that *she's* the one who initiated this.

"Lose the bra."

She pushes up to rest on her elbows and reaches behind her to unhook the bra, dropping it on top of her dress.

She's got one hell of a rack for such a petite little thing. So fucking hot.

"Touch yourself."

I watch as she reaches down between her legs and slips her hand underneath her underwear to touch herself.

Jesus. This isn't going to last long. I hope I don't embarrass myself.

I tug off my shorts and add them to the pile of her clothes before doing the same with my boxer briefs so I'm totally naked in front of her.

She swallows hard as her gaze travels to my rock-hard length.

"See what you do to me?" I growl as I stroke myself from base to tip.

She licks her lips like the dirty little devil it seems she is. *Fucking hell,* I'm definitely going to have to have those lips on my dick before the night is done.

I snag a condom from my shorts pocket and tear the foil packet open, the sound the only noise in the room. She's watching me eagerly – *hungrily* as I roll it on.

I drop down to hover over her, resting my elbows on either side of her head, and kiss her hard showing her just how desperately I want her.

"*Walker,*" she moans, and it's just like in every one of my fantasies – and there have been *plenty*.

"Yeah, Elly-May?" I ask in between placing kisses to her neck.

"Please don't stop."

I chuckle. No worries there. I've got absolutely no intention of stopping. Not now, not tonight, not ever.

I pull back so I'm up on my knees again, looking down at the flawlessness that is the woman in front of me.

I hook my thumbs into the sides of her tiny little panties and drag them slowly down her legs, and off over her feet with her cute little pink painted toenails.

I don't even have a thing for feet, but somehow, hers are sexy.

She's writhing beneath me as I look down at her, committing every single inch to memory.

Fuck it, I can't wait any longer. I nudge the head of my cock at her entrance, slowly at first and then as I feel how wet she is, I drive in hard.

She's so ready for me and I haven't even touched her.

She moans in my ear, and it spurs me into action. I start moving, burying myself deep, right to the hilt with each thrust.

This isn't going to be sweet and gentle. This is going to be hard, primal and fast.

"Walker," she breathes as I hitch her leg up and pound into her.

She grips onto my shoulders, her nails sinking into my flesh.

It's so fucking hot. "Scratch me," I demand.

She does what she's told, her nails skating down my back, digging into my skin. I can feel the trail she's leaving behind. I hope it leaves a mark.

I keep up a relentless pace, her moans becoming louder and louder with every passing second.

So fucking hot.

Her hands find my head and grip onto my hair, pulling and tugging as I bring her to the brink. I grip her hips as I feel her body start to tense.

She starts to wriggle, and I hold her tighter, not allowing her any escape from the intense orgasm I know is building inside her.

"Show me how good it feels," I growl.

She whimpers. "Oh my god." She cries, "I'm going to come."

"Come all over my cock like the good little girl you are."

She falls apart beneath me, her body going limp as I keep up my pace, draining every last moan out of her until I feel myself fall over the edge with her.

I've been responsible for my own releases for a little while now, but that doesn't even come close to how good this feels.

No amount of jerking off will ever satisfy me after this.

I fall forward, trying not to crush her under my weight, but I'm so drained I can't hold myself up any longer.

"I knew you weren't kidding about the big dick and the incredible sex, but I didn't think you were *that* serious either," she says.

Her voice is husky and light as she tries to settle her breathing back down to normal.

I laugh and she joins me, and the feeling of my dick still inside her almost gets me hard again.

Jesus. This girl is going to kill me.

I roll and ease myself out of her. She comes with me, cuddling into my side, her finger skating gently over my chest.

I kiss her forehead and she looks up at me with lazy eyes.

"That was… *wow.*"

It was fucking wow alright. It was so much more than I was expecting, I don't know how we're ever meant to leave the bed if that's what's waiting for us.

"We're going to have to go out to eat."

"What?" she laughs at my random statement.

I nod my head. "You heard me. If we stay here in this house all night, the only thing I'm going to eat, is you."

"Dinner out, dessert at home," she offers.

Deal of the century.

CHAPTER
THIRTEEN

We come across a local sports bar and decide that a hearty pub meal is exactly what we need to refuel after all the sex.

Walker holds the door open for me, and then takes my hand in his as we walk towards the bar.

I try not to think about the fact he makes me look like *Dora the explorer* out for a walk with a yeti.

The place is mainly filled with men, but there are a few women in here, and every single one of them do a double take when they see Walker.

I don't blame them. He's worth a double take, if not a triple.

He's insanely hot, and now that I know how good he is in the sack, it's only made him even hotter.

"Two for dinner?" Walker asks the guy behind the bar.

He hands us a couple of menus and tells us to sit wherever we want. It's all super chill and I'm grateful for that.

Walker chooses a booth down the back, with only one occupied table near it. Two slightly older guys are watching the basketball on the TV on the wall. When I get closer, I see it's a replay of the Bears game from last week.

"Reynolds is on some form, I'm keen to see how they go against the Sharks next game."

"He's on fire. Him and Daniels are playing like they share a brain."

Walker raises his brows and tips his head towards the table, making sure I'm listening too.

I'm definitely listening. I love it when I hear things in the wild. It's so interesting to me to see how the public perceive things. I'm also pathologically nosey, I love myself a good eavesdrop.

"Oh hell, there she is again, I've lost count of how many times they showed that new woman of his."

"Tell me about it. This is basketball, not a singing contest.

'Morgan Rhodes – nine-time grammy winner.' Pops up on the screen as they flash back to a shot of Morgan sitting with Tommy's people, right up front. I see myself on the side of the shot.

"Nine-time grammy winner," the other guys reads it aloud. "Get back to the game, boys."

They make a few comments between themselves that I don't catch, but I think I hear something about 'nice legs'.

A woman comes out of the bathroom and joins

them, sitting down opposite the two men, her back to the screen.

"You missed more of that Morgan Rhodes than you did of the actual game," one of the men tells her.

She pouts. "That's all most of us are watching for these days."

The two men exchange a look, although I can't see their faces, I can guess what it symbolizes. They're classic men's men. They don't care for all this romance bullshit.

"Yeah, all of us real ball fans are just going *crazy* for her," one replies sarcastically. "I don't know why they're making such a big fuss. This isn't a chick-flick, it's basketball. They need to stop giving her airtime. This isn't about boosting her career."

The woman snort laughs. "She has a bigger audience than the whole NBA anyway, so it's not like she's the one gaining anything here."

"You think she has a bigger following than the *National Basketball Association*?" one asks, his outrage obvious.

"I don't *think*, I know. Look on any social media. She's a *way* bigger deal."

One of the guys goes to get out his phone but the other shakes his head at him. I think he knows that she's right, he just doesn't want to admit it.

"She put Tom Daniels on the map. Luckiest son of a bitch around," she continues, driving the knife deeper.

I bite back a laugh.

At this point I'm convinced this chick is doing everything she can to wind up her table mates, and

I'm all for it, it's entertaining as hell. The guys may as well have smoke coming out of their ears.

"He's the best shooting guard in the game, for fuck's sake. He won the NBA playoffs… some singer in hot pants didn't *put him on the map*… Don't ever say that again. Don't even talk to me."

She's grinning. "I'm not saying he's *not* the best, but the whole world collectively doesn't know about the playoffs, or Tom Daniels, or even the NBA, but they sure as hell know about *her*. They might not like her, but they know her name."

"Wash your mouth out."

"It's just fact. It hurting your big man feelings doesn't make it any less true."

"Maybe *he's* the one putting *her* on the map."

"Classic boy math. Being so threatened by a woman's success that you can't even see it's doing good things for a sport you love."

"Pffft. I don't think a few songs is going to change the game."

"It's not a few songs. It's a newly diverse audience. She's a global phenomenon."

"And he's a millionaire. He's one of the most well-known players ever."

"Yeah, in America he is. Go take a trip to Asia, Europe, Australia, or *New Zealand* and tell me who's more well known. Numbers don't lie. I'm not saying he's not a big deal, but she's a bigger one. It's just the way it is." She points at the screen. "She could sell out that stadium on her own, ten times over. There's like a dozen men kitted up for each team at this game. Make that make sense."

One guy dismisses her with a wave of his hand and the other is suddenly very interested in his beer.

She knows she won. The smug look on her face is very telling. It's also very satisfying.

I laugh quietly. *Slay queen.*

Walker doesn't bother with the quietly part. His loud laugh turns a few heads.

"Some damaged egos at that table." He chuckles.

"Ten bucks says one of them will look up the follower counts before this game ends, hurt their feelings even more."

"I'd say they'll be listening to Morgan's playlist on the drive home… just to see what all the fuss is about," he jokes.

"I should have brought a few signed t-shirts with me. They're clearly big fans."

He laughs again, he's probably imagining them wearing pink 'Rhode Runner' merch.

That gives me a thought.

I rummage around in my bag, hoping that I didn't take them out when I packed for this trip. I usually keep a couple of VIP passes in here, for situations exactly like this one.

One of those passes will get the wearer into *any and all* shows on Morgan's current tour, and not only that, but into the first few rows in front of the stage. These passes are talked about like mythical creatures in the fan chats. You can't buy them – they're handed out by Morgan or those closest to her. Morgan likes to surprise people, and I have no doubt that if she were here right now, she'd want to thank this random woman who has her back.

I feel the hard plastic and pull them out, grinning.

"What have you got there, Elly-May?"

"Magic beans." I smirk.

I set two aside to give to that woman when either of us go to leave, and stuff the other back where I found it. I'll slip them to her quietly. I don't want to answer a bunch of questions, but I do want to make her day.

"They're passes for Morgan's show. I'm going to give her a couple."

"Who do I have to sleep with to get one of those?" Walker teases me.

I pretend to think about it. "I mean, the guy in charge of the ticket sales team would probably enjoy a good blowie."

"I'm not sure I can safely say I'd give a *good* blowie."

"Mediocre blow jobs aren't going to get you VIP tickets, Walker, be reasonable."

He feigns disappointment.

"I'll tell you what, since you did such a good job earlier, I'll hook you up. Just this once."

I pull out the one last pass from in my bag and hand it to him. He grins and puts it around his neck.

"I owe you an orgasm for this."

"You owe me two. If not three."

"I'm going to be the biggest fangirl at her next show."

I giggle at his gleeful expression. "You're not really going to use that, are you?"

"You bet that sweet little ass of yours I am. Better

see if you've got any of those groupie t-shirts in my size, kitten, I want to look the part."

"You're really going to come to Houston?"

"Yee-ha, baby. When is it?"

I can't help but laugh at his antics. "In two weeks."

"Count me in." He shakes his pass at me.

"You better be careful flashing that thing around, someone will rob you."

"Teenage girls pretty big on robbing grown men, are they?"

Ah, poor uneducated, naive Walker. It's not just teenage girls, there are forty-year-old women at these shows, hell, there are forty-year-old men, and they're probably the ones you want to look out for.

Morgan's fans would normally be far too well behaved, but as far as a unicorn pass is concerned, all bets would be off. There would be riots in the street to get hands on one of those.

"The eagle is leaving the nest," Walker hisses at me.

I frown, not understanding, but when I look up, I see the Morgan fan getting up from the table and slinging her bag over her shoulder. "I've got to get home to the kids, Millie and her friends have probably turned the place upside down by now."

They say their goodbyes and the woman starts heading for the exit.

Walker shoves the passes into my hand, and I slip out after her.

I catch her just outside the door. "Excuse me!" I call to her as she turns for the car park.

She turns, unsure if I'm talking to her.

"Sorry," I pant from practically running across the room. "This is going to sound really weird, but I couldn't help but overhear you talking about Morgan, and I wanted you to have these."

She eyes me somewhat warily but walks back towards me.

I hold out the two passes on lanyards for her.

She looks at them, her eyes widening as she realises what she's just been given. "Are these…?"

She's a real fan. She knows exactly what she's just been given. I made the right call with her.

"They'll get you into any shows you want to go to," I tell her. "Right up front."

She gapes at me, totally in shock. "Are you serious?"

I can't help but smile. I see why Morgan loves doing this so much; making someone's day is an amazing feeling.

"Yeah. I ah… work with Morgan. She'd want someone like you there. She's all about girls supporting girls."

"Is this for real?"

"Totally for real. I'm her PR manager. You can google me."

"Oh my god." She jumps up and down on the spot. "My daughter is going to lose her mind."

"That seems to be what happens when Morgan plays live." I giggle.

"I can't believe this." She rushes forward and hugs me. "Thank you, thank you, thank you."

I laugh and hug her back. "You're welcome."

"Oh my god, sorry. Personal space." She pulls away, cheeks bright red.

"That's okay, I'm Elly, by the way."

"Olive," she replies. "I still can't believe this."

"Well, it's real," I promise her. "I've got to get back inside, but enjoy the show, enjoy *all* the shows you like."

"We will," she squeaks.

I laugh again. She looks like she's in shock.

"Tell security that Morgan sent you, they'll look after you," I tell her as I take a few steps backwards, towards the door.

She nods. "Okay, I will."

"And you're right by the way, she's a *way* bigger deal than the NBA."

She laughs. "My brother's an idiot. His friend isn't much better."

"I bet they're looking up her net worth as we speak."

"I hope they're not too upset when you get back in there."

I laugh and turn to go back inside. Poor males and their fragile egos.

"Thank you again, Elly," she calls after me.

I give her one last wave.

It is my absolute pleasure.

"Oh my god."

"*What*?"

"Your brother posted a new photo on Instagram and the caption is a crown."

"Slay," Walker drawls.

I roll my eyes. He doesn't get it.

"I don't get it," he says, mirroring my thoughts.

I sigh, then explain. "He's claiming being *her King*. Her fans are going *crazy*."

"*Oh*." He chuckles. "Yeah, well… the boy's not stupid. He knows how to work a room."

"Oh *wow*." I cackle. "This comment section is chaos. The females are going feral."

We're relaxing on the couch, both of us ate way too much at dinner, and now we're just a couple of beached whales who are wishing they understood the concept of moderation.

"I don't get it. Why does half the population care so much about who some singer they don't even personally know, is dating?"

I shrug. "People love love. They love romance and grand gestures. They love the fantasy that comes with celebrities and their relationships. They love the idea that they could have a love like that. It doesn't matter to them that they're only seeing a tiny part of the big picture. That's all they need to feel good… plus, he's hot – women like hot men."

"Do *you* love all that stuff?"

I feel my cheeks heat, but I ignore it. "Do I like romance and grand gestures? *Sure*, yeah… I mean what girl doesn't want to feel special, right? I'm glad that I'm not the one being watched by the whole world though, that's a bit too much of a grand gesture for me."

"And hot men?" He grins.

"I can appreciate a good-looking man when I see one."

"Tom Daniels flicks your switch, does he?"

I pretend to mull it over. "I mean… he's alright. Between you and me, I've kind of got a thing for his older brother," I tell him in a hushed whisper.

He puffs his chest up. "I have heard he's better in the sack."

I roll my eyes. "Horrendous ego on him, though."

He chuckles.

"So grand gestures that aren't *too* grand and being made to feel special. Got it."

"Don't forget the hot guy," I tease.

"I'll start making notes."

"You do that. Truthfully… I really think most of it comes down to it being the right person. The right time. The right situation. Two people willing to put in the effort. I don't know if I really believe in fate or anything like that."

He nods, thoughtful.

"I believe that fairytale kinda love exists though." I nod. "I *do* want that for myself."

"I think today was a fairytale." He reaches for my hand and strokes his thumb up and down the side of it. He's being intentionally cheesy, but I like cheesy.

And he's right, it *was*. When I think of living my life with that kind of love, I think of Walker. I don't know when that became a thing, but I can't deny that it is.

It terrifies me, the things I feel for this man, so soon.

I've never experienced something like this. I'm usually too conservative to even consider the idea that someone could work their way into my heart the way Walker seems to be doing effortlessly.

I'm not stupid, I can see the way he's looking at me. It's the way that Tom looks at Morgan. These men have big, powerful feelings. I don't know if that makes it more or less terrifying for me.

"I'm scared," I admit.

"Scared of what?" he coaxes, taking both of my hands in his and staring so intently into my eyes it's like he's searching them for the answer.

"Of *us*."

"Don't be. I'm not scared of us," he tells me softly.

He cups my jaw, his big hand almost swallowing up half my face.

He makes me feel so small and delicate.

He makes me feel protected and safe.

I can't guard myself against this – against *him*, and even though it might wind up hurting me, I have to take the risk. Him and his obnoxiously large ego are worth the gamble.

He's given me no reason not to trust him, and unless he does, I'm going to do exactly that. *Trust him*.

"You sure you don't want to hold out for one of Morgan's hot celebrity friends?" I tease. "She rolls with some beautiful women."

"You've got no idea, do you?" he murmurs in my ear as he cups the side of my face in one of his hands – the other finds its way to the curve of my back.

I lean into his touch and hum deep in my throat. His hands on my body feel so good.

"You don't know just how tempting you are, do you, kitten?" His voice is low and raspy as he moves in; he's so close I can feel the warmth of his breath on my skin.

"*Me*?" I whisper, more focused on his lips than his words.

"Beautiful…" he breathes.

He kisses the skin on my neck, and I barely manage to hold back a groan of satisfaction.

"Tempting." His soft lips brush my skin again, just below my ear.

"Irresistible," he mutters before drawing the lobe of my ear into his mouth and sucking it gently.

My body is shaking with desire and I'm not even out of my clothes yet. I like to think I'm a woman who's in control of her sexual urges, but there's something about this man that flicks a switch deep inside me that even I don't know how to turn off.

My lips find his and we make our own rhythm, teasing and taunting each other.

I know the way he's kissing me; it's the way that leads to clothes on the floor and naked bodies grinding against one another.

He pulls back to look at me, and I don't know what story my expressions are telling, but I hear a rumble, right down deep in his chest.

I gasp as he lifts me effortlessly on top of him. He shoves my legs apart and forces his thighs between them, his arms coming down on either side of my hips as I straddle him.

We're pushed so closely together I can feel the pressure from the seam of his jeans pressing against mine. He's hard as a rock under it all.

His hands find the hem of my dress, and it's up and over my head before I know exactly what he's doing.

He's good.

"These sexy little sets are killing me, Elly-May." He groans as he sees the underwear I'm wearing, just for him.

He's wearing a button-up short-sleeve shirt, and my fingers make short work of the buttons, undoing them one by one. I slide my hands under the fabric and push it back so I can look at his perfectly sculpted chest and stomach.

His hands are on my ass, gently rocking me forward and back against his crotch.

I slip my hands down his stomach and undo the button and fly of his jeans. He lifts his hips, allowing me to drag them down his legs enough that he can kick them off.

I've seen some sights in my life, but this man sitting here in his black Calvins with a raging hard-on is pretty up there with one of the best.

"What now, kitten?"

Something about him being totally at my mercy makes me feel invincible.

I skim my fingers up his length to his waist band and pull it down enough to free him.

He watches me as I stroke him slowly, taking my time to tease him.

"Those tiny hands are doing wonders for my confidence, Elly-May."

As if he needs any more of that. He certainly doesn't need small hands to be convinced he's well endowed.

I kiss his neck, moving down his chest to his stomach as I shift out of his grasp and slip down to kneel on the floor between his legs.

He leans back, splaying his arms wide on the back of the couch as he picks up exactly where I'm going with this.

God, he's so hot.

I lick my lips and take him deep into my mouth.

He groans, the sound of approval coming from the back of his throat.

"Fuck that feels so good," he grunts as I bob my head up and down, gripping in my hand what I can't get into my mouth.

He reaches down and runs his hands through my hair, collecting up the mass that surrounds me and holding it back so he can watch as his hips thrust upwards, pushing his cock deeper into my throat.

I slip him out of my mouth and run my tongue from base to tip. He shudders as I lick my way back to the tip. "Fucking hell, Elly."

I smirk, pleased with myself for causing such a reaction in him. I'm not a bad girl, but I want to do all kinds of bad things to him.

I try to take him back into my mouth, but he pulls my hair, forcing my head up to look at him. He looks right into my eyes. "I want you on top."

I don't need to be told twice.

I stand as he lets go of my hair and he gently drags my underwear down my legs, I wouldn't care if he ripped them off me and threw them out the door at this point.

He holds me in place with one hand, sucks on his fingers on the other then slides them between my legs. It doesn't take him long to find the spot that makes me shudder.

I grip his hair as he slips his fingers in and out of me, teasing my clit each time he pulls them out.

"Sit," he tells me.

He grips his dick and slides his hand up and down it as I crawl back into his lap. He reaches for a condom that he seems to have pulled out of thin air, rips it open with his teeth and rolls it on.

He lines himself up at my entrance and holds my hips, guiding me down onto him until I'm so full I feel like I'm going to break in half.

"I want you to ride my dick, and don't stop until you come."

Jesus. Those words alone pretty much get me over the line.

I start moving and it doesn't take long until I'm doing exactly what he demanded. I fall forward, crying out as my orgasm rips through me. He wraps his arms around my shoulders and takes over, lifting his hips and making me feel like I'm going to explode from the intense pleasure. He grunts, "Fuck, I'm going to come."

The sounds he makes when he finishes are ridiculously hot, but he doesn't stop.

I ride it out until I can't take any more. "Oh my god, Walker, *stop*. I can't…"

He stills beneath me, a satisfied smirk on his lips.

My chest is heaving as I gasp for my next breath.

Being vulnerable has never felt so good.

WALKER

It's been a long time since I've had this much sex. I was right about us not leaving the bedroom once we got in there.

I don't even know how we're meant to make the drive home tomorrow without stopping for some action along the way like a couple of horny teens.

I can't keep my hands off her. I just want to be touching her, every second of every day. Now that I know what I've been missing out on, it's going to be serious work to just go about my business without her skin on mine.

She smiles at me like she's thinking the exact same thing.

I guess technically we *have* left the bedroom, we're outside by the pool in the shining sun, but the senti-ment is the same. We're barely dressed and lying on a bed together. The fact that we're outdoors doesn't matter, there's nothing but the ocean to see what we're up to.

I could stay here forever.

"You're coming to the game tomorrow, right?"

"No. I don't have a ticket."

I half grunt, half laugh. "It wasn't really a question, Elly-May, you're coming. I've already talked to Morgan; we'll fly out with her. You're with me, I've got you covered, you don't need to buy a ticket online or something stupid like that."

"And what if I had plans?" She sits up a bit and raises one brow at me.

She's so goddamn sexy, that little green bikini leaves fuck all to the imagination but covers just enough to make me crazy thinking about ripping it off.

I'm so distracted by the way her perky ass is trying to escape her bikini bottoms, that I forget to answer.

She smirks at me, waiting patiently for my answer.

"Sorry, what?" I blink, totally blanking on the question.

"What if I had plans, Walker? What then?"

"Then you change them."

"What if I don't want to change them?"

"Then that's bad luck, you're doing it anyway. But let's be real, you don't have plans."

I love this banter. It gets me going.

"You're bossy."

"I've been called worse."

"I've called you worse." She giggles.

"Have you now?"

I reach out and grab her around the waist, dragging her into me as she shrieks and thrashes around.

She's wasting her time, trying to escape, she's got about as much fight in her as a wet paper bag. I'm not sure she'd win if she took on a toddler.

I pin her hands down next to her head, and it requires about as much strength as I have in my pinky fingers.

"Stop trying to fight me, kitten, you're not going to beat me."

"I don't need to be physically strong to get you to do what I want," she teases me.

She runs her tongue along her lip and fuck me, she's right. I'd do anything she wanted me to do, and I'd do it with a smile.

She could hit me with her car, and I'd probably still say thank you.

She's beautiful, smart, funny, sweet and magnetic. I never stood a chance.

"Quit looking at me like that," she breathes. I can feel her heart beating fast against her rib cage.

I hadn't noticed I was looking at her with so much intensity.

"Looking at you like *what*?"

"Like I'm the answer to all your problems or something."

Because you are – you're the answer to everything.

It's far too early in the piece to be making those kinds of confessions. I need to remember to keep it light.

I smirk at her. "Who said I had problems?"

She rolls her eyes dramatically. "There's two types

of people in the world, Walker, ones with problems, and ones who lie about not having any."

I chuckle. She's not wrong.

That smile on her face... the way it lights up those beautiful eyes. She's so stunning. I feel like I can't breathe right when she's looking at me like that.

"You're looking at me like you can see right into me," she whispers.

I feel like I *can*. I can't describe the feeling of being with her in this way. I've never experienced a connection so deep.

"Can you see right into me too?"

She pulls her bottom lip into her mouth and nods shyly.

I bet she can. I've never been this open before.

"You know you're mine now, right Elly-May?"

Her cheeks pink. "I like the sound of that."

It's hard to believe this weekend is technically just our second date. I don't care about dating rules, or social conventions or any of that bullshit. I'm a big believer in just doing what feels right, and everything about this feels right.

This woman came flying into my life a few months ago, and nothing has been the same since.

"I want the whole world to know you're mine."

"That's very sweet, but I think the world is more interested in your brother." She grins.

"Attention hogging prick. I'm sick of him and his big reputation," I joke.

"I'd steer clear of the internet for a while then."

"Are the *it couple* big news again?"

"What do you mean, *again*? There's been no escaping them since they launched."

That's true. It's been a hell of a ride, and this is just the beginning. I still remember the day that Elly called me and told me who she was, and asked if we could meet.

She had me sign the most airtight NDA known to man before she got to the point.

"Remember when we met, and you couldn't stand me?" I laugh, thinking back.

"Oh, I remember alright. You were a pain in my ass. You still are at least half the time."

"I'm just being my authentic self."

"Lucky for you, it's somehow become endearing."

I chuckle. Annoying to endearing, what a transition.

I let go of her hands and she wraps them around my neck and plays with the hair at the back of my head.

"I never thought this would happen."

"You're telling me you didn't want me from day one?"

"Took a while for me to see your charm." She giggles.

"And now that you have?"

"It's life changing," she teases. "I'll never be the same. I can't sleep, I can't eat."

"I want to be the reason you can't sleep at night."

That didn't sound the way I meant it.

"That came out sounding way more toxic than I intended. I meant because you're excited, not because you're depressed or something," I clarify quickly.

She laughs. "I'd be happy to lose sleep over you, Walker. In the healthiest way possible."

I bury my face in her neck and kiss every patch of skin my lips find.

It's not long before she's writhing underneath me, desperately grinding against the barely restrained bulge in my board shorts.

I don't think a single thought about anything or anyone other than her as I drag her bikini bottoms down her legs.

Not as I push deep inside her.

Not as she calls out my name.

Not as both of us find our release.

Not as I fall off the edge of like and deep into love.

"I think I'll just tag along and fly private from now on, way less mucking around," I muse. It took us fuck all time to get here, no airport lines, no pissing around, no bag collection. Straight in, up in the air, and off again. This is the life.

As gutted as I am that mine and Elly's weekend alone came to an end, I'm back watching what I love, and with her by my side to really sweeten things up.

Not too bad of a deal.

Elly rolls her eyes at me. "I'm sure Morgan will be thrilled to hear she's got a permanent passenger."

"Morgan loves me. She couldn't have asked for a better future brother-in-law."

"Yeah, I bet she's counting her lucky stars," Elly mutters.

We exchange a look that only two people who wish they were alone and naked could understand.

"Want a beer, Elly-May?" I need to keep my hands busy before they get me in trouble.

"You're not going to offer me thirty different beverages this time?"

"I'm a smart man, kitten, I've learned."

"I'm very impressed, a man with the ability to be trained. I'm a lucky girl. And a beer would be great."

I'm holding her hand, so I squeeze it and smile at her before going to check with Ma and Morgan about drinks.

I'm actually pathetic. I make myself a little bit sick, because even now, being just across the room from her, I want to be nearer to her again.

It's like my side feels cold without her next to me.

Fuck, what a wet wipe.

Ma and Morgan are all set so I grab me and Elly a couple of beers and head back to where she's waiting for me right up front. She loves people watching, and she's doing exactly that right now, while we wait for the teams to run out onto the court.

You see some funny shit; I can see why she gets so much enjoyment out of it. It's even more entertaining since Morgan came into the picture. You can play *where's wally* with the crowd and pick out which are her fans that are just here to catch sight of her. It's pretty obvious when someone knows nothing whatsoever about basketball. They're usually the ones yelling 'go sports' or 'go Morgan's boyfriend'.

"Thanks, slick." She takes the beer from me and taps the neck of it against mine, while staring into my eyes. Apparently, you have to make obscene amounts of eye contact when you cheers or it's like ten years of bad sex, or ugly kids or some shit. I've never heard it before but whatever miss Elly-May wants.

"Die-hard Morgan fan." She points halfway down the block of seats in front of us to a youngish girl wearing a sequined dress, with her phone out and pointed up at where Morgan is sitting a few metres away.

"Nicely done."

Not one to be outdone, I start a search of my own and then immediately wish I'd just minded my own business.

"Fuck me, that ancient guy down there wearing the short shorts just bent over and the old flesh chandelier fell right out of the ballroom."

"The flesh *what*?" she demands.

"Oh god, my eyes."

"I have *no* idea what's going on."

I point to the scene of the crime. "His cock and balls, kitten. I just copped an eye full of saggy old-man testicles because he decided to bend over in shorts that look the right size for a ten-year-old."

"Oh my god." She laughs as she spots the guy, who is now, thankfully, vertical again, with all his bits tucked safely back where they should be. "That's hilarious."

"Yeah, my retinas are singing a different tune."

She's almost hysterical.

"Come on, I want you to meet Ma before the game starts." I start towing her away.

"Walker, I've already met your ma."

"Not as my girlfriend you haven't."

"The move from saggy old-man balls to meeting my boyfriend's mother is a dramatic one, give me a second to get myself together."

"If I'd known copping an eye full of balls was going to get this kind of reaction out of you, I'd have stopped wearing underwear and started wearing short shorts a long time ago."

"Don't you dare. And *you* were the one copping an eye full, not me." She playfully smacks my shoulder and rolls her eyes.

Hell, when she rolls her eyes at me like that it makes me want to throw her over my shoulder and take her to the closest bedroom.

I bet that would cause a scene.

She's giving me a devious look and it's not helping stop my imagination from running wild.

I need to get this Ma meeting done and dusted before I lose my composure.

I lead her over to where Ma is talking to one of the old Bears coaches. He exchanges a few pleasantries and a bit of small talk before leaving us to it. He's a cool older fella, but I'm glad to see the back of him. It's been a long time since I've introduced my mother to someone important, and I can honestly say that no one has ever been *this* important, so it's a big deal to me. I'm nervous.

"Ma, I want you to meet Elly."

She hugs Elly and leaving her arm around her, turns back to face me. "Me and sweet little Elly here have already met, Walker. You're a bit behind the eight ball."

I know that Ma met her at the first game she came to – the one where we made the bet, and I've told her all about the little brunette that has been taking up virtually all of the real estate in my head, but I want them to meet properly. As my mother and my girlfriend.

"I know, but I've finally got her to agree to be my girl, so this is the official mother, girlfriend meet."

"*Finally*," Elly scoffs, rolling those damn sexy eyes again.

"And how did you manage that?" Ma asks.

"Paid her off," I joke.

Ma swats at my shoulder. I have to laugh. It's the same action Elly did to me only a few moments ago.

"It's true, Sandra. I'm going to buy myself a yacht when I cash the cheque," Elly tells her, all wide-eyed and innocent.

Ma finds that funny. Probably because she knows I can't afford a yacht in the first place.

"We just spent the weekend down at Chucky's place in Santa Cruz," I tell her.

She starts telling us a story about how her and dad used to go there a lot when me, Tommy and Grace were younger. Sounds like it was their dirty little get away spot when they'd leave us with our grandparents.

Old horn dogs. No one wants to hear about their parents' sexy getaways.

"Glad I didn't have to hear about *that* when I was growing up."

"Pfft." She laughs. "You boys definitely got bigger but I'm not sure that either of you really ever grew up."

Elly laughs along with her, and even though it's at my expense, it makes me feel all warm and fuzzy to see them getting along so well.

"This is nice. Gang up on me why don't you. Next we'll be pulling out the baby albums," I retort.

"Oooh, yes please." Elly looks at Ma with a begging look in her eyes. "I'd pay good money to see him as a little kid."

"Oh honey, I won't charge you. I'll happily do you that service for free. It's a mother's duty," Ma replies, laughing. "How about Friday night, come over for dinner and we'll dig them out."

Elly looks triumphant. I'm struggling to remember why I thought this conversation was ever a good idea in the first place.

Benjee, one of Tommy's college mates claps me on the shoulder then, drawing my attention away from the two scheming females who I very much think need supervision in this moment.

He's chewing my ear off about playoff chances and shooting stats, and I'd love to care, I really would, but I'm having a hard time stopping myself from trying to eavesdrop on Elly-May and Ma. It sounds like they're talking about a time I ate sand. *Lovely.*

"I'll catch you later, man," he says, and I nod absentmindedly. I've really got no idea what he just said to me.

"Yeah, yeah, good seeing ya." I wave him off.

I catch the end of a conversation where Ma seems to be informing Elly about the phase I went through where I refused to wear anything but a Spiderman costume, and decide it's time to intervene. The last thing I need is my new girlfriend thinking about ten-year-old me in a stinky onesie.

"And I think that's enough of that." I put my arm around Elly and pull her out of my mother's grasp. "You better save some embarrassing stories for Friday, by the sounds."

Ma smiles menacingly. "Never mind, dear, your teenage years provided enough material to last a long time."

I laugh as I remember the sideways caps and pimp chains that both Tommy and I thought were a real look.

Can't wait to watch Elly slide off her seat when she sees those pictures.

"Ma, a pleasure," I reply dryly, grinning, as I steer Elly away from the woman who knows more about me than any other.

Elly waves to her.

"Your mum is a sweetheart."

I tug her in closer as we walk back to our spot up front.

She doesn't seem to want to talk about her mum a lot, but I get the feeling she misses her all the time. I'll have to make sure to bring her around Sandra whenever I can – I know better than anyone that she's a great mother even if it's not by blood. She's willing to be there in that role for whoever needs her.

"Ma is the best," I agree before kissing her forehead.

The pregame ritual is underway, and the home team is getting a roaring welcome from their fans.

Elly looks up at me with those big, beautiful eyes, and I feel all weak in the knees.

This damn woman, she's like a drug.

I hope I'm using for the rest of my life.

CHAPTER
FIFTEEN

ELLY

"Walker, you studied marketing, right? What do you think? Is it salvageable?" Morgan holds out her phone for him to take.

He studies the album cover design for a long moment, his eyes narrowing and then widening. He turns it side to side and brings it closer to his face and then holds it back.

He's taking so long I'm almost entirely convinced he's taking the piss now.

"Anything short of a completely new design is just going to be putting lipstick on a pig." He shrugs. "No offence."

Her jaw drops at his brutal honesty. "None taken," she replies.

"I think maybe a *little* taken," I offer.

"No… he hit it with some real honesty. It's refreshing," she reassures him as she takes her phone back from him and regains her composure. "I need people to be honest with me sometimes."

"Hey, *I* was honest." I scowl.

Morgan rolls her eyes. "*You* were polite. Saying 'it's not my favourite' isn't *real* feedback."

She's right, I could have told her it was the ugliest thing I've ever seen, but I thought it was safer to be tactful. I like my job.

"But it *was* technically honest." I laugh.

"Don't worry, babe, I've got enough balls for the both of us." Walker smirks. "And I'm not afraid to use them."

"Please don't bring up your balls in public."

"Save it for the bedroom. Got it." He salutes me.

I don't know why we're having this conversation in a fancy suite at a basketball game, but it's happening.

"Are you guys doing anything after the game?" I ask Morgan.

I know a lot of the time the guys go for dinner or drinks, or some kind of after party, but since we all flew out here and Morgan has to head off for her next show tomorrow, we made plans to fly back tonight sometime after the game.

"Nah, Tom is going to come back with us after the press conferences and stuff is handled. We'll probably stop somewhere and get some food on the way back to the airport, but no other plans. Does that work for you guys?"

She's just the sweetest thing.

Yes, I think flying in your private plane at short notice works just fine for me, thanks for asking.

"Can we get Taco Bell?" Walker asks me, excitedly, like he's a golden retriever with a wildly wagging tail.

"Taco Bell?" I roll my eyes. "Yeah, lets send Morgan in to order."

"We should." He chuckles. "They'd be stoked, their sales would go through the roof."

"I saw Morgan Rhodes with Taco Bell and Pepsi, so *I* got Taco Bell and Pepsi." I snigger.

Morgan is laughing too. "I'll tell you what, you and Tom can decide."

Walker pouts. "He'll want to go to some upmarket steak house or something. He's a fancy fucker."

"You poor dear." I pat him on the back, and he grins.

His hand tightens slightly on my thigh. He's had it sitting there for the better part of the past hour.

It's nice. I've never had someone seem so proud to be with me. He doesn't care who sees us, or what anyone thinks. He's happy if I'm happy.

And I'm certainly happy.

This whole weekend has felt like a dream. It was so much more comfortable than I could have ever imagined it would be.

He feels like someone I've known for years, rather than just a few short months. He's going to drive me insane, the cocky comments, the relentless banter, the never-ending energy… but he's a good man. He's kind, and sweet and caring. He's gentle, and loving and considerate.

He's also absolutely out-of-control smoking-hot. So

even if he were an insufferable piece of work, at least he'd be nice to look at.

"I'm going to hit the head and grab a water, do you want one?"

I nod. I've had too much to drink this weekend. I need a detox or something.

"Yes please." I nod.

He gets to his feet, takes one step away, and then steps back again, kisses the top of my head and heads off for the bathrooms.

I don't even realise I'm staring after him until Morgan slips into Walker's seat and nudges me.

"Oh. My. God. You two are just the cutest thing I think I've ever seen."

"We are pretty cute," I admit. I don't even blush.

I'm getting good at this whole thing.

"He's *so* into you."

"He's a pretty sweet guy."

She looks me over, appraising me. I wish I could hide from her – she's got a good eye. She sees too much.

"It was good sex, wasn't it?" she whispers.

Okay, *now* I'm blushing.

"Morgan!" I hiss, eyes wide.

"What?" she says more loudly. "It's so obvious."

"It is *not*. And be quiet."

She giggles. "Oh, I see, it wasn't just good, it was *amazing*."

I widen my eyes at her, trying to warn her to cut it out.

Apparently today is the day that she's forgotten how to read the room and take a hint.

Lucky me.

She makes an excited squeaky kind of noise and I know it's all so silly, but I can't help getting excited along with her.

I feel like a giddy teenage girl who's just kissed her boyfriend for the first time and needs to spend a solid hour dissecting it with her best friend.

"We had the best time together."

"Honey, that's written all over your face. You're glowing."

I'm not surprised by that. I feel like I'm glowing.

"And he looks like he's won the biggest prize of his life."

"You really think so?"

She looks at me like I'm crazy. "It's the most obvious thing in the world. He's obsessed with you."

I can't help it, I start gushing, telling her all about the whole weekend in hushed whispers. She's eating it up.

"What are you two talking about? Why do I feel like my ears should be burning?" Walker startles us both as he appears behind me.

Morgan shuffles over and Walker takes his seat again. Morgan is giving us knowing looks the whole time.

"Morgan was just asking me about the exceptional sex we've had all weekend," I whisper to him. "She wanted a review of performance."

Gosh, I really hope no one is listening in to this conversation. I'll be mortified.

He nods, agreeing. "Ah, yes, valid questions. I would say quality over quantity, but in all honesty, there was plenty of both," he says loud enough for Morgan to hear.

He winks at Morgan, who is now blushing herself, and I finally feel like maybe I've got the upper hand of this conversation.

The game was fun. I never imagined that I'd enjoy myself so much at sporting events, but I'm getting used to the crowds, the familiar faces that go with Tom and his teammates. It's cool. They're good people.

Having more time with Walker isn't a bad thing either.

We did end up going to a nice dinner, and then Walker insisted we also get Taco Bell afterwards.

He's such a child sometimes.

He ate so much he spent half of the flight home groaning.

Males.

The car ride home from the airport was interesting. Tom and Morgan looked as much a couple as Walker and I. They sat close together and talked quietly in a private conversation. I think they held hands the entire way.

That's definitely not for show.

I need to say something to her. This façade has gone on long enough.

They clearly have feelings for each other. It's time to drop the act and just get on with it.

I figure now is as good of a time as any. We've dropped off the guys and are heading back towards where Morgan and I live. She looks deep in thought.

"Are you all good?"

"Yeah, I'm fine."

I can read her like a book, and right now there is something on her mind. "Just tell me already."

It's not really viable for her and me to have secrets, not if I'm going to do my job well, but more than that, we're friends. Good friends. I trust her and I know she trusts me. She always tells me what's on her mind.

"Tom invited me to come to a wedding with him next year," she finally tells me.

"Is that… a problem?" I pry.

She shakes her head, but she looks confused.

"No. I don't know. It's his teammate, Darren. I've met him and his fiancée a couple of times, but when we were all talking after the game, he told them to mark us down as coming."

"I'm not really understanding what the issue is…"

She sighs. "It's not until next year. The *end* of next year. It's a long time away and I know it's all part of the plan right now, but this is someone's wedding, you know? We'll probably be over by then."

Poor, naive little Morgan.

"Oh, honey, let's be real for a minute, this *isn't* about the plan. I doubt it ever was. He doesn't care about contracts, promotions or money. That man is *so* smitten with you. I'd be willing to bet he's been in love with you from day one. He said yes to that wedding because he wants you to be there with him, forever. He told them you'll be there because he has absolutely no plans to let you go."

"You really think so?"

She's no idiot, she knows this by now, she *has* to – she's just scared of being vulnerable.

"If he's not completely obsessed with you then he needs to forget basketball and take up a career in acting, because he is putting on the performance of a lifetime. You should see the way he talks about you. He's got hearts in his eyes."

I wasn't too sure about Tom when all this started. I hoped for Morgan's sake that it would remain purely platonic – that her heart wouldn't be at risk, but it was obvious quickly, to me at least, that it was never going to be just a PR relationship.

Fake boyfriends don't look at fake girlfriends that way.

This has the potential to make my job a million times harder, but some things are worth the risk. I'm already all over this thing – they may as well make it official.

It'd make Tom a very happy man. He had a sign and a dream.

I'm rooting for him now. I hope he gets the girl, because I'm more and more sure by the day that she feels the exact same way. She might not have gone into this with feelings, but they're there now. I've watched this woman fall in love before, I know it when I see it. Only this time, I think maybe she might have found someone worthy of her heart.

"What if we're reading into it wrong? I'm scared. After last time… being vulnerable is hard."

Preach, sister.

I can completely understand that, but I wouldn't encourage her like this if I didn't think he was worth it or if I had doubts it was real.

"*Kiss him*. Really kiss him when no one's watching. Trust me, you'll see it's not for show."

I've watched him open car doors for her, shield her body with his, I've seen him act more protective of her than the people hired for the job. His hand finds hers like it's meant to be there. He's drawn to her like there are invisible strings.

I think this is it. This is *the one*.

I think she might finally have found a guy who can not only handle her life, but fully embrace it. She doesn't have to hide or sneak around with him. He's so proud to be with her. He wants to show her off like the prize she is.

I think he'd take a bullet for her if it came to it. That's his woman, and he's her man.

The King and Queen.

"You think so?"

"Come on, Morgs, you're smarter than this. You know already."

"I don't know what to think. We've got an agreement, you know? I don't know if he's playing a role or being himself. It's so confusing."

I guess I can understand that. I'd probably be as confused if it were me.

"When you're together, does it feel real?"

"Feels like the most real thing in my life."

"Exactly. So maybe you two should just sit down like adults, have a conversation, and keep this thing going for the rest of forever."

Things can't carry on like this, with them both tiptoeing around real feelings. But I totally understand her hesitation to bring it up. If she does, and he's just doing what we told him to do, then she's going to not only feel silly, but be a little crushed too.

It's a risk. But one she's going to have to take.

I've done what I can. I've watched, I've taken notes, I've come to my own conclusions. I feel pretty confident that I've hit the nail on the head.

The rest is up to them to figure out.

"I'll try and talk to him tomorrow."

I nod. "You do that."

WALKER

I sneak up behind Elly. She's watching Morgan and Tom wrestle on the couch. They've been at it a while. It's all very flirty and cute and shit.

It's also totally behind closed doors. There are no cameras here to capture this sweet little interaction. There's no PR motivation.

"Oh my god, 'just for show' *my ass*… make it official already," she mutters. "You're only lying to yourselves."

"What did you say?"

Elly jumps. She didn't know I'd come up behind her.

"What?" she stutters.

"What did you just say?" I repeat.

"I don't know."

She shoots a look at me over her shoulder, her expression sheepish.

"Do you know something?" I ask her cautiously.

"I don't know what you're talking about."

She turns around to face me fully and I tow her a few steps away, so we're tucked behind a wall.

"You know *something*," I accuse.

She looks like she's panicking. "I – I'm not –"

"You can tell me if you do. I might know something too," I say slowly.

"You tell me what you know, and I'll tell you what I know."

I shouldn't. I promised Tommy, but I will. This has gone on long enough. I said I wouldn't tell Elly when she was just Morgan's PR chick. Things are different now, she's my girl, and I'm sick of keeping this from her.

I'm spilling it all. Promises be damned. This is for the greater good.

"Tom's in love with her. He's been crushing on her for *months*. Made all his dreams come true when you approached us with this contract."

"I *knew* it!" she yells.

"Shhhh."

I look around the corner to see if the love birds heard, but they're too busy being adorable.

It's sickening.

"Sorry, but I *knew it*," she whisper shouts.

"How did you know?"

"You've seen him when he looks at her, right? He goes all dreamy."

She's spot on. The dude looks like a lovesick puppy.

I tried to tell him he wasn't going to be able to keep his feelings out of it.

"Do you think she feels the same way?"

"I know she feels *something*. I don't know if she's quite on his level, but she's into him. She was meant to talk to him days ago, but she's being a chicken shit."

Fuck yeah, Tommy boy. Get the girl.

"Something is better than nothing," I say, deciding in that moment that it's time for everyone to come on out of the closet. Morgan won't have to instigate that conversation – because I'm going to.

I step around Elly to go and get this straightened out, but she grabs me and tries to drag me back.

It's about as effective as a light breeze, but I do what she wants and stop.

"Where are you going?" she demands.

"To get the ball rolling." I tip my head in the direction of where Morgan and Tom are mucking around.

"You're just going to go out there and air their secrets?"

"They're hardly secrets, kitten, there's four of us in this room, and we all know it's a thing. It's just a conversation at this point. I'm sick of tiptoeing around."

She looks like she's going to argue, but then she shrugs, smiles and lets go of my t-shirt. She must feel the same way about this as I do.

I stroll out into the living room, a man on a mission.

"You guys are a bit cute, aren't you?" I say loudly, interrupting their little play fight.

Morgan blushes and tries to sit up, but Tommy hasn't let go of her wrists.

He laughs as she's pulled back half on top of him.

"Looking like a real couple there, you two," I say smugly as I sit down on the couch opposite them.

Tommy gives me a look but doesn't say anything as he lets go of her and she sits up next to where he's laxed back.

"Maybe we should extend this contract for a few years… what do you think? Two? Ten, *twenty*. Maybe you get married and have kids. That'd be good for business."

Morgan eyes me suspiciously.

"You'd have cute kids, and they'd have a mommy and a daddy who really love each other." I smirk. "It's a win all around."

"*Walker*," Tom snaps.

"What? Just calling it how I see it." I feign innocence.

"Go and see it from somewhere else," he warns me.

We exchange a long look. He's almost pleading with me with his eyes. Fuck it. He'll forgive me when he's bagged his dream woman.

"Just tell her already," I say.

His expression goes from murderous to nervous as hell.

He's so fucking soft with this shit. Get him out of the court with a bunch of two-hundred-pound dudes, and he doesn't even flinch, but this girl makes him all kinds of nervous.

"Tell me what?" Morgan asks.

Tommy is being a little bitch, but it's time the cat got out of the bag. This has gone on long enough.

She's looking between the two of us expectantly. She looks hopeful, actually. Elly was right, she's feeling it too, but she needs *him* to say it first. I get that. She's the woman and he's the man. Maybe I'm a cave man, but I think it's the man's job to make his woman feel safe – it's his job to leave himself vulnerable so she can feel comfortable.

"Don't listen to him," Tommy starts.

Little bitch.

Oh well, I gave him a chance. If he's not going to tell her, then I will.

He's up out of his seat and headed my way. I don't know what he thinks he's going to do, but it won't matter. He can't stop me now.

"He's basically in love with you, Morgs. Kid had been crushing on you for months before this whole thing started."

Tommy socks me in the shoulder. "*Bro.*"

"Ow, fuck," I growl, rubbing at my instantly dead arm. "What'd you hit me for?"

"Is that all true?" Morgan asks. "Tom?"

I think he's about to hit me again, but he freezes when he hears her voice.

He turns around slowly to face her.

"Is it?" she presses him.

He doesn't reply. I think he's forgotten how to speak.

"The motorcycle, all the romantic gestures, it's all been him," I interject. "He's got it bad."

I'm still not entirely sure who the real mastermind is here. Was it Tom, showing up to her show with a sign? Was it Morgan spotting him and getting Elly onto it? Was it Elly, seeing an opportunity? Or was it me, for daring him to take the sign in the first place?

"Really?" she whispers, looking at me. I think she's realised that Tom has gone into shock.

"As much as I like taking credit for other people's good ideas, I think it's about time he pulled the trigger."

"Tom?" Her eyes flit back to his face.

Her saying his name again seems to get him to remember how to function as he's spurred back into motion.

"Yeah, Morgs?" The way his voice caresses her name is all the answer she should need. He's in big love.

I look over at Elly and she's watching from just inside the room, her hand on her chest and an 'aw that's so cute' look on her face.

"You can give me the beat down later, bro," I announce, standing. "We're going to bounce… give you two a chance to talk."

Neither of them even acknowledge that I've spoken. They're the only two people in the room as far as they're concerned.

I tow Elly out with me, and we leave them alone to do whatever it is a fake couple that's about to turn real might want to get up to.

I hope for his sake that he gets to show her some more of his ball skills.

"Thank you for doing that. I was going to lose my mind if I had to deal with any more of her anxiety over this thing," Elly tells me as we step outside.

She's not the only one who was ready for all the secret plans to be over.

The world thinks they're together, and if that interaction was anything to go by, I'd say that now they really will be.

It's about time.

I video call him so I can get a real gauge of his reaction. He can lie to me over the phone, but his expressions tell all. He's got no poker face whatsoever.

"What do you want?" he answers. He's back at his place now, I recognise the room.

"Nice pics of your walk of shame this morning, bro."

The paparazzi caught him leaving Morgan's just before midday today, wearing the same gear he was seen walking inside in, last night.

He huffs out a laugh. "What walk of shame? There was no shame there, trust me. That was a strut of success."

I can almost see him puffing up his chest.

"In last night's clothes."

"That's show biz, baby."

I chuckle. "You slept over then?"

He's got the widest grin on his face. "I'm not one to kiss and tell."

That actually is true. I remember when we were younger, having to drag it out of him that he'd lost his virginity. I respect it, but sometimes a guy just wants to hear some tea.

"I take it you two are the real deal now."

His grin is huge. The kid has got it so bad.

"Yeah. We had a good talk after you two left."

"Good. And you're welcome." I smirk.

He flips me off. "I could kill you for that stunt."

"What, the one that got you the girl of your dreams? Yeah, I can see why you'd be mad about that."

He just grins again. He's all bark and no bite in this case.

"You guys invited to Ma and Dad's for dinner tonight?" I ask him.

"Sandra and Paul did extend the invitation, but I've got training and Morgan is in rehearsal with her dancers. So we're far too busy and important, sorry."

"You people bore me."

He chuckles. "Sorry I couldn't be of more entertainment value to you."

"I've come to expect very little of you, in all honesty."

"It's better that way. Will this be the first time Elly meets Dad?"

"Sure will. I told him he had to wear pants."

He laughs. "Bet he's devastated about that."

Nothing that man hates more than wearing a pair of pants around the house. I don't know what it is, but as soon as he's in the door, he's getting rid of them.

Doesn't like the feel of them, he reckons.

"Breaking his heart. I got to go anyway, I just got to Ma's, and Elly's just pulled up behind me."

"You two crazy kids have a good night."

"I'll eat some of Ma's corn nuggets for you."

He blows me a kiss and the screen goes black.

I glance in my rear-view mirror and see Elly climbing out of the back seat of the car. She had the car service drive her over since she was already over the other side of town for a meeting with Morgan's label.

I climb out, rush over to her and scoop her into my arms, lifting her clear off the ground.

"I missed you, kitten."

She giggles as I swing her around in a circle. "I missed you too, but if you don't stop spinning me around, I might get sick."

I stop spinning, but don't let her go.

"You're wearing your glasses."

"Nothing gets by you."

"You look beautiful."

The look on her face makes me think that she hasn't heard those words enough in her life. I'll have to change that.

I set her down, kiss her on the lips and then tow her up towards the house by her hand.

"Why are we moving so quickly?" She laughs.

"Because I'm well aware my parents will have been watching from the window from the second you pulled up, waiting not so patiently." I turn back to grin at her, and she blushes.

"They're excited to have you visit."

She beams up at me. "I'm excited to visit. I feel bad they wouldn't let us bring anything though."

"Don't. You'll get used to it. It's pretty much an insult to Ma if you do. One time I brought a dessert with me, and you'd think I was offering to shit in one of her pot plants. It's just easier for everyone if we do what we're told."

She sniggers. "That was graphic."

"I really wanted to hammer home my point."

I open the front door without bothering to knock. I don't think I've bothered to announce my arrival to this house, ever.

"We're here!" I call out. As though I'm not aware they would have watched our every move from the car to the door.

Ma rushes out, apron on and a smile spread wide across her face.

"Hello, darling." She clucks as she pulls me in for a hug.

"Hey, Ma. Smells good in here."

She dismisses me to the side and hugs Elly. She's fussing over her dress and how it reminds her of one she had when she was younger, or something of the like.

I kick off my shoes and hear Ma tell Elly that she can keep hers on if she likes.

I chuckle. I once got a clip around the ears for not taking my shoes off when I got in the door, but it's more than okay for Elly, apparently.

I walk into the living room with Ma and Elly following behind. I find dad with pants on, and he's even up out of his chair waiting.

So far, so good.

"I love your home. I can't wait to look at all the photos."

Damn Ma and her photo-lined walls. There's not going to be any hiding the embarrassing childhood memories tonight.

"Oh well thank you, sweetheart, it's nothing much but it's home and we love it here. Lots of great memories," Ma replies.

"Elly, this is my dad, Paul," I tell her as she steps up next to me.

She smiles at him and holds out her hand for his to shake.

"Dad, this is Elly."

He takes her hand in both of his and gives it a shake-squeeze. "Well now, you're a pretty little thing aren't ya?"

I can tell he's taken with her already.

"She sure is," I agree before she can argue, wrapping my arm around her shoulders.

"Who wants a drink?" Ma asks, already off on a mission to the fridge. "Elly?"

"I'd love a beer if you have one," Elly replies.

She seems comfortable here already.

ELLY

Walker's parents really are the sweetest.

His dad is a little quirky – as Walker had warned me prior to coming here, but he's a great man and I like his eccentricity. He's a very interesting person.

Odd, but sweet. He's very passionate about the things he loves, and nothing more so than his wife and kids.

He's not much of a blokey kind of man, and I think that goes a long way to explain why Walker and Tom are the way they are. They're not afraid of emotions, or of coming across as what some men would consider weak. It's refreshing to see such healthy masculinity. The world needs more of it.

We've had a great evening. Walker talked pretty much the whole way through dinner about the latest promotion and endorsement deals he's signing Tom up for – he spent a few hours today meeting up with a guy, ironing out the details of a contract, and he's pretty excited about it.

Morgan doesn't really do much in the way of endorsements anymore. I kind of miss those days. It was fun when we'd get endless PR packages sent to the office for sorting. We all got so much free stuff.

I think that's why Morgan put a stop to it. She didn't need fifty different face creams or whatever, and she felt guilty for not sharing it all with her followers when the stuff had been so generously given to her. She donated so much of it to charities.

The fan mail is out of hand enough, without there being box after box of products that she was never going to get to using.

I'm on the couch now with Paul, at Walker's insistence, and I can hear Sandra and Walker talking in the kitchen. Actually, it sounds like they're arguing. But not real arguing; mother and son arguing.

It makes me happy and sad at the same time.

I miss my mum. I wish I could be in the kitchen of her home, helping her clean up after dinner.

I wish I could call her up and tell her about my life.

She was still alive when I started working for Morgan, so I'm sure it'd be no surprise to Mum that she made it to the big time, but I know she'd be proud of me for building my company, and for making such a success of myself too.

I have so much I wish I could tell her.

I'd tell her about my life here in San Francisco.

I'd tell her about Walker.

I'd tell her how safe he makes me feel – how

protected. I'd tell her about how his touch sets me on fire and how I'm falling in love with him.

I know she's not here, and she can't hear me even if I were to say that all out loud, and I don't know what I really believe happens after you die, but I like to think that she somehow still watches over me, the way she always has.

"You much of a ball fan?" Paul asks, pulling me from my thoughts.

I quickly compose myself and smile at him. "I'll admit, I've watched more basketball in the past couple of months than I have in the rest of my life combined."

"Sounds like progress in the right direction if you ask me." He smiles.

I nod in agreement.

"Walker was quite the player in his prime." He tips his head in the direction of the kitchen. "Did he tell you that?"

"I looked up a couple of his 89ers games online," I admit. "And he's not exactly known for being modest, so he has mentioned it a time or twenty."

That seems to make his eyes sparkle. He chuckles, and it's a deep, throaty sound.

It's clear to me that he absolutely adores his children. And not just the boys; he also spent the better part of forty-five minutes earlier showing me photos of Grace and the grandchildren.

It was very sweet.

I need to book a trip out to see my dad sometime soon. It's been too long. Maybe I'll even take Walker with me.

It's an exciting thought. Scary, but exciting. I've never introduced my dad to a boyfriend.

"He's a good player. Shame about that knee. I'm not sure my blood pressure could have handled two boys playing pro ball at the same time anyway, probably the only thing stopping me from having a heart attack before sixty."

"He told me you're pretty passionate about the game."

He nods enthusiastically. "Never really cared much for basketball until the boys were teens. They played all kinds of sports when they were younger, and I'd always enjoyed football, but as soon as they got on that court, it was clear they'd found where they belonged. We've been a basketball mad house ever since. Even Grace loves watching it, and she hasn't got a sporting bone in her body."

"It's cool that you're so supportive. I know it means a lot to them. Walker speaks very highly of you and the way you and Sandra raised them."

That comment seems to make him happy.

He's got a game on the TV now, and he's looking more at that than he is at me, but it's not in a rude way, I get the feeling he's somewhat uncomfortable with making too much eye contact, so the screen provides a nice buffer.

He seems happy enough to chat away to me though, and it's nice. I know Walker was a little nervous about this meeting.

He asks me about my family, my dad, my mum. I tell him everything he wants to know, and he listens intently, like he's filing it all away for future reference.

He's the first person that I've talked to who hasn't said they were sorry for my mum dying. Not that the statement has ever made much sense to me. Some random person has nothing to be sorry for, but it's the expected reply, I guess – and there's nothing wrong with it. But Paul doesn't say sorry, instead he tells me that my mum would be so proud to have a daughter like me.

That's it. He makes no apology for her death. He doesn't give me *that look*.

I don't know why, but it gets tears pooling in my eyes. There's no shame in dying, and while I appreciate the sentiment of support from anyone who cares enough to give it to me, this makes for a welcome change.

I don't know if he notices my reaction or not, but he pushes on, going as far as to ask me about childhood pets and if I remember living back in Australia.

The guy could talk the back legs off a donkey once you get him going.

I don't know how long we've been talking, but when I do look up towards the kitchen, I find Walker standing in the doorway, his big body leaning against the frame as he watches us.

He gives me a look that threatens to melt my entire heart.

This man.

There's just something about him. The way he looks at me.

"I'm a baller." I point at the game on the TV.

"Okay, Chingy, I see you." He smirks.

His dad starts chewing his ear off about game

scores and player stats, and all kinds of chat that mostly goes right over my head, but Walker comes and sits next to me with his arm slung over my shoulders, and I'm perfectly content here, with my boyfriend and his parents.

It's nice.

I'm already looking forward to the next time.

"I'm telling you, they loved you."

"You don't know that. They're polite people."

"They're more honest than they are polite, if I'm being real with you."

I have to laugh. "I did notice your mum didn't hold back when she was talking about the outfit Radford's wife wore to that charity event."

"Ma rarely holds back, and I honestly think that maybe Dad is on the spectrum or something, because he doesn't have much in the way of a filter. He pretty much just says what he thinks."

Maybe that's where Tom and Walker get it from.

"You really think they liked me?"

"I know they did. Ma was picturing the wedding and grandkids already," he teases.

"No pressure, Mrs. Daniels."

"Surprised she didn't start trying to measure you up for a wedding dress."

I poke out my tongue at him.

"It's all fun and games now, but you just wait. You should have seen how passionate she got when my sister got married. Poor Gracie had to recruit me and Tom to keep Ma in check. I think Tommy had to physically pick her up and carry her out of the venue at one point because she was so concerned that every single centre piece wasn't one hundred percent perfect. The woman legit lost her mind. But Grace had a perfect day. Every last detail was immaculate, and while Ma ran herself into the ground over it and had to sleep for a week afterwards, I know she'd do it all again in a heartbeat for any one of us."

Morgan better hire one hell of a wedding planner if her and Tom ever tie the knot, because they're going to have live up to the Sandra Daniels' standard.

"She's a proud mama."

"She's definitely that."

"I'm just glad they approve of me."

"A first for me."

That causes me to pause. "What? Really? They never approved of any of your old girlfriends?"

He shakes his head. "Nope. I don't think she had any problem with some of them, but she's a smart woman, she knew none of them were end game for me. She told me as much after a year of dating Rachel Gavin when I was in my mid-twenties."

"What did she say?"

"She sat me down and asked me if I loved Rachel. I couldn't say yes. She said that she was a very nice girl and that she thought I could easily spend years with her, but that she deserved to be with a man who was crazy about her. She gently suggested that I not waste any more of her time. Rachel wanted marriage and babies, and I was never going to give that to her. She has both now – met her husband a few months after we broke up. We ended on good terms and I still see her around sometimes. She's got no idea that my mother had to tell me I needed to break up with her."

"Oh my god, that's pretty classic."

"That's Sandra. There were a couple she didn't even pretend to tolerate. She just straight up said no."

I lose it at that. Sandra is a sweetheart, but I can't imagine she's about the bullshit. She wouldn't tip toe around her opinion.

Her and I have that in common.

"But she really likes you. I can tell. She's still a little iffy on Morgan I think – multi-million-dollar recording artist with a crazy life and all that – but she sees how happy Tom is, and that's all that matters."

"Well I like her and your dad too. They're good people."

"Two of the best. I hope Dad didn't say anything too outrageous to you."

I smile as I think back on our conversation. Quite the opposite, actually.

He slips behind me and wraps his arms around my middle, hugging my back to his front.

"Nah he was perfectly fine. We had a good chat, actually. I like talking to him." I turn in his arms so I can look up at him.

"And he kept his pants on the whole time, so that was a plus."

I look at him in confusion. What an odd thing to say.

He laughs loudly at the look on my face.

"The man doesn't like wearing 'em in the house. Don't know what it is, but if he can take them off, he will. He was under strict instructions today to keep them firmly in place."

"Wow, that's ah… that would have been interesting."

"Yeah, I'm not sure you'd be emotionally prepared for the sight of my dad in his tight whites."

"Probably best to leave some mystery in the relationship."

"You could have expressed that sentiment before you let Ma show you all those nude photos of me as a child."

Gosh, he was an adorable kid. He sure liked to get his bits out a lot though by the looks. It was fun looking back on all their memories. Every now and then one of them would see a specific photo and it'd launch them into a huge story about what was happening when the picture was taken.

I loved it. It was a privilege to be included in the trip down memory lane.

"I especially liked the photos of you and Tom in those matching tutus. I can't believe you guys let her take those."

He chuckles. "I'll admit, mistakes were made."

One of the things I like most about him is how he owns his shit. He's not embarrassed easily. He's not the kind of guy that's going to be peer pressured into anything or shamed into acting in a way that's not him. He just does what he thinks is the best call. He is who he is.

"They love you very much, you know?"

He nods and smiles a little to himself. "I do. I'm blessed when it comes to family."

"I think they're pretty lucky to have you too."

"Goes without saying," he boasts.

I roll my eyes at his antics. He's always playing, this man.

"You know, while you were sitting there in the living room, all I could think about was the things I wanted to do to you when I got you home."

His smirk turns devious.

"Is that so?"

He nods, and I can see that look in his eye already.

I have a feeling that we're going to be up for hours yet.

CHAPTER
EIGHTEEN

WALKER

Fuck man, whoever is blowing up my phone needs a bullet.

It's Sunday morning and I was trying to sleep in for once. Elly and I were up half the night on Friday, and I need my beauty sleep.

I ignore two more back-to-back calls before finally sitting up and turning on the lamp. Whoever it is, is clearly not going away any time soon, I'm going to have to see what they want.

I grab my phone off the nightstand and see I've had a dozen missed calls from Tom, all within the past hour.

Something must be going on if he's calling me like this before eight on a Sunday. I hit call and it only rings once before I hear him on the other end answering.

"This better be a fuckin' life or death emergency," I growl.

"Not quite, but close." He sounds pissed. "Where have you been?"

"Sleeping," I mutter. "What's the problem?"

"It's another ex, threatening a tell-all interview."

Fuck, hardly worth calling me a million times, but nothing like flying into a blind panic, I guess.

"Then *chill*. We'll dig out the NDA and solve it the same way we did last time." I don't know why he gets so worried about this shit, but he's extra precious about his business being aired since his private affairs all included Morgan.

He's quiet for a second, and I know then that this is something else. Something not so easily solved.

"That's the problem, bro, there is no NDA. This time it's *your* ex, not mine."

Oh shit.

Well, this is an entirely different beast. Maybe his worry *was* justified for once.

An ex of mine…

I just knew one of those bitches was going to come back and bite me one day.

In the past, it never occurred to me to have a woman *I* was dating sign a non-disclosure. I'm not a big deal – I'm not a pro athlete anymore, so I didn't think it mattered. It seems I was wrong.

This is the problem with crazy exes, if you don't have that sheet of paper signed, they can say whatever they want, and it's a lot of work to do something about it. It doesn't matter if they're telling the truth. The tabloids don't care, not really. They just want to make money, and they're prepared to do that at anybody's expense.

"Who is it?"

"Nadia." He sounds disgusted, and with good reason.

Shit.

She's the craziest of all of the crazy girls. She's a freaky bitch too. We got up to some stuff, she for sure has some stories. Not ones I thought she'd be willing to tell about herself, but some stories nonetheless.

"What's she saying? I don't really care if she brings up old shit about me."

"She's not saying it's *old shit,* bro. She's saying you've already got a kid together and that she's pregnant with another one."

"What the *fuck*? That's bullshit."

"That's what she's saying."

"She is balls-to-the-wall insane. What the actual fuck is wrong with that bitch? A *kid*? Since when?"

"That's not all."

Ah shit.

He's saving the worst news for last, I can tell, and that's beyond worrying. I don't know how it could get worse from here.

I'm scared of what he's going to say next.

"She's saying she's got a copy of the contract between me and Morgan. That she's going to air our relationship as a PR stunt."

What the fuck.

How could she know that?

The implications of this start to hit me, one by one, and they don't stop. It's a long list of crises.

What an absolute clusterfuck.

"What do we do?" I ask, my voice hoarse.

"I think *I'm* meant to be the one asking *you* that question."

My head is spinning.

I have no idea how Nadia could possibly have found out that information but given she shouldn't know a thing about it in the first place, this is a problem, and it's a *big* one.

Tommy and Morgan might be all legit and real now, but the reality is that it didn't start out like that, and we don't need the sponsorship and endorsement deals turning to shit if that comes to light.

I don't think the fans would be too happy to know they'd been duped, either. People don't like being lied to, and while it's all too common in Hollywood, we don't need the drama that would undoubtably come with Morgan and Tom's followings feeling like they've been deceived. They'll lose faith in the whole thing.

"There's no way. I can't see how she possibly could have got her hands on that. She can't have."

She shouldn't even know of that contract's existence. Nobody does.

"Well fuck, Walk, she's saying otherwise, and what she's saying about it checks out. She knows things she shouldn't."

"I keep the documents at home. I didn't even want to risk anyone in the office getting wind of it. It's in my cabinet, in my office, at my house, how could she have seen it?"

"I think we need to worry a little less about how

and focus on what the fuck we do now. Morgan is freaking out."

Fuck. Morgan. *Elly.*

"Does Elly know?"

"Of course Elly knows. Morgan called her at seven, and unlike you, she picked up first try."

Fuck, fuck, fuck. Logically, I know the real problem lies with this contract, but I can't stop thinking about the bullshit Nadia has spouted about being with me, about having a kid with me and another on the way. This is going to crush Elly. She doesn't deserve to look stupid because of me, even if none of it is true.

I need to hear these claims she's making.

This is so chaotic it's giving me whiplash.

"I really don't think now is the time to be giving me shit about sleeping in. Bigger fish to fry, my friend. I need to see what we're dealing with."

"I'll send you the links for the articles."

I chuck the call on speaker and wait for him to message them through to me.

I open the first one and skim it. She's claiming that we have a one-year-old kid together and that when I found out she was pregnant with that baby, I told her to either get a termination or leave. She's saying she chose to leave but decided a few months ago that she wanted her daughter to have a relationship with her father, so she came to my house to tell me about her. She's saying we slept together that night and she got pregnant again. Now she's crying and playing the victim, because I've been swanning around with Elly, and refusing to take Nadia's calls, or responsibility for my children.

I've never heard so much bullshit in my life.

"Jesus. What the fuck?" I breathe.

"Tell me you're not playing with that sociopath again?"

"Fuck no," I growl. "I wouldn't touch her with someone else's dick. I'm not playing *anything* with *anyone*. I'm with Elly."

"That better be the truth."

It's a little hurtful that he thought I'd be that stupid, but I guess my track record would lead him to that conclusion. I haven't exactly been smart.

"You didn't sleep with her again?" he confirms.

"No. *Fuck no.* I learnt my lesson there. No sex is worth that amount of crazy. And if I have to repeat myself again about the fact that I'm committed to Elly, it's not going to go well for either of us."

He ignores my threat.

"When did you last see her?"

"I haven't actually spoken to her since we broke up, but I did see her about a week ago, I was meeting with Rusty in a café downtown to iron out the contract for that electrolyte drink he's releasing, remember I told you about that? The one I'm really pumped about?"

"I remember."

"Yeah, so we were in the café, and she turned up there. I didn't think much of it at the time. She came in and looked around like she was waiting on someone, but I never actually saw her meet up with anyone the whole time she was there. She didn't look surprised to see me there though, now that I think about it."

"Did you talk to her?"

"Nah. She just glared at me across the room while she sipped her iced coffee bullshit that she loves so much. Didn't say a word to me."

"She didn't overhear you say anything she shouldn't have?"

"*No*. I didn't say anything I wasn't meant to, and even if I had, she was on the other side of the room. She wouldn't have heard a word I said about anything. I don't know what to tell you, Tommy. I don't know how she got that contract; I don't know how she got into my house."

"Yeah, well, neither do I, but you better find out and you'd better do it fast."

This isn't the kind of conversation you have over the phone, but I don't have a choice. She's out of town and we can't just ignore it until she gets back.

Each ring of the phone seems like I'm inching closer and closer to a death sentence.

I haven't done anything wrong, but it's still all my fault.

She's going to be hurt. She's probably going to be mad. And she should be.

"Hello?" Her sweet voice answers.

"Hey, kitten."

She sighs heavily.

"Are you okay?" I ask her.

"Did you really call me to ask me if I'm okay, slick? I don't mean to sound like a bitch, but I don't need questions from you right now, I need answers."

I guess that's fair enough.

"She's my ex, she's crazy, and I don't know what she's playing at," I offer.

"Is she crazy? Or is she just speaking out?"

I know what she's getting at, but I'm not one of those men who bag their exes after having treated them so badly that they act insane. I didn't make her crazy.

Nadia was insane when I met her, she was insane while we dated, and she was just as insane when we broke up. The only thing I did wrong was make a questionable choice about the type of woman I let into my life.

"Both by the sounds."

"Was she in your house, Walker?"

"I don't know. But I know I didn't let her in."

"She couldn't have got a copy of that contract from anywhere else."

"I know that. It doesn't make any sense, Elly. I don't know how she could possibly have got into my house without me knowing."

"You know how lame that sounds, right? She was *in* your house. She's saying the two of you were together. She's saying you hooked up... that she's pregnant with your baby... that you have a child together." Her voice cracks at the end.

Fuck, I feel terrible. This is hurting her deeply.

"She's lost her mind, Elly. I'm not *with* her. I haven't slept with her for over two years. If her and I were together, why would she be running to the media to tell them all this, it makes no sense."

"Maybe it's because she found out about me? There are photos of us out there now. She's saying you dropped her for me. She wants to hurt you."

"It's all bullshit," I promise her.

"*Am I* the other woman? Is that what I am?" I think she's crying now.

"There is no *other* woman, Elly. There's just you. From the moment we met. I promise you; I haven't touched her. I wouldn't. I couldn't do that to you."

She doesn't respond right away, I can't be sure, but I think she's trying to compose herself again. When she does reply, her voice is small.

"Why was she in your house then, Walker? Make that make sense."

I wish I could, but I can't – because it *doesn't* make sense. None of it makes sense.

"I don't know what to say. She's *insane*. Maybe she broke in. I don't even know if she *was* really here. I don't know how she got copies of those documents. I don't know how she knows anything at all. But I swear to God, Elly, I'm not with her."

"Okay, maybe I can believe that I'm not the side chick in your relationship with her –"

"I don't *have* a relationship with her," I interrupt her.

"Maybe she's pregnant, maybe she's not, *whatever* – that's not my problem," she carries on, as though I didn't even speak. "My problem is that she's got her hands on highly classified information that you should have kept locked down tighter than that."

It's a colossal fuck up, I'm prepared to admit that. If Nadia releases that contract to the media – to the public – shit is going to hit the fan.

"I know."

"And now you're telling me that you think she broke into your house, stole the contracts between Tom and Morgan, and then leaked them to the press along with a classic story time of how you two are lovers and have a secret love child, totally out of nowhere?"

"She's a money-hungry whore, maybe she's broke and wants money, saw the photos of us all in the media and thought she'd try and make a buck."

"So, by that logic, if you did have a kid, wouldn't she have come after you for child support a long time ago then?"

"I wouldn't be surprised if she doesn't even have a kid. She's a compulsive liar and she's got one hell of an imagination."

"She said you were trying to get her to have a second abortion."

I'm not even sure Elly is listening to me. She's just firing off questions and statements. I think she might be in shock.

"I'm not trying to get her to have *anything*. If she's knocked up, it's nothing to do with me."

"Have you ever gotten her pregnant?"

I pause for long enough that I don't need to answer the question. It's obvious.

"It was a long time ago."

"Oh my god, it's true, you really do have a kid with her, don't you?"

"No," I answer quickly. "She can't have. We got pregnant, yes, but…"

"She terminated the pregnancy?" she guesses.

"Yes."

"Her call or yours?"

"I don't see why it matters, but it was *her* call. I supported her decision. I might have encouraged her, but I'm not sorry, I never planned to have a child with that crazy bitch."

"But what if you *do*, Walker? What if she never went through with the abortion? Are you one hundred percent certain that she did?"

"I made the appointment for her… offered to drive her… she was sick afterwards and wouldn't let me see her. I thought she was emotional and mad."

Fuck.

I don't even want to consider that Elly could be right about this, that maybe I *do* have a kid. That maybe Nadia never got the termination in the first place.

We broke up a month after, and I didn't see her again until over a year later.

It's possible, but unlikely. I wasn't kidding when I said she was a money-hungry whore. I just can't imagine her having a baby and not demanding that I pay my way with it. It'd be so out of character for her.

"You must see how bad this looks, Walker."

"I can appreciate it doesn't look good."

"I'm not sure what you expect me to do here."

I don't know what she should do. Hell, I don't even know what *I* should do.

"I honestly don't know what to tell you, Elly."

"And I don't know what to believe."

She sounds so broken, it's killing me. This feels like the end, and I'm on the verge of going into complete ruins.

"Are you breaking up with me?" I manage to get the words out.

I didn't fuck around, I shouldn't have to find out, but that's life – Elly doesn't owe me blind trust. No one owes anybody that. Just because someone is in your life, doesn't give them automatic immunity to any accusation. Especially not one like this. It's rough, but I can't take her response personally – she's just protecting herself.

"No," she replies swiftly. "But I do need some space, okay? I'm not going to say or decide anything now, but I need a break. A timeout. Whatever you want to call it. I need time to think this through and figure it out in my head."

Alright, *Rachel.*

"Okay. I hear you."

"And you really need to figure out if there's a kid running around who shares your DNA, okay? Because I don't even know what to say about that."

That makes two of us.

CHAPTER
NINETEEN

ELLY

"Come on, Els, you've been in this business long enough to know that you can't believe ninety percent of what you read in the media. Remember that time they were convinced I was entirely bald and was wearing wigs all the time?"

She's still baffled by that one. I think we all are, but when you get people together in masses, crazy shit is always going to come out of nowhere.

"I'm not saying I believe *all* of it, but she was *in* his house. She had to be. There's no way she could have got copies of those documents if she wasn't."

"Why don't you try giving him the benefit of the doubt? Maybe listen to him tell his side? Take your time and think it all over. It doesn't have to be today, but think about it? Sleep on it a couple of nights and then maybe you might feel ready to hear him out."

Bold of her to assume I'm sleeping at night.

She's right though. Walker said he didn't know how she could have possibly been in his house, and at the time it all sounded like a big, poorly covered lie, but he's never done anything to give me any reason to doubt him, and he deserves the benefit of the doubt. I just have to be brave enough to give it to him.

The thing that bothers me most is that she *had* to have been there. That's where it all comes unravelled in my mind and I freak out, because *why* was she inside his home if they're not seeing each other... If it really has been a couple of years since they were officially together, and the same amount of time since they've fucked, then why was she there within the past couple of months...

I wish I could call my mum and ask her what I should do. These are the moments where I miss her most. She always knew what to do. She was the best at getting me to chill out and see things logically when all sense was being overruled by emotion.

"I'll try," I tell her. That's the best I can do at the moment.

She nods in understanding, but her expression looks sad. I think she feels sorry for me.

"What does Tom think of this chick?" I ask her.

"That she's *awful*. He said she was the worst of any of the girls Walker dated. Actually, he said she was the most mental female he's ever met. And that's including the chick his teammate Zayn dated, and he had to take his used condoms home with him because he was so worried the girl was going to dig them out of the trash and get herself pregnant."

"Oh my god." I shouldn't laugh, none of this is funny, but fuck that's next level. Girls like that give us all a bad rap.

"I know."

"This Nadia must be all kinds of bad news if she's *worse* than the condom girl."

"Right? I'm almost scared to hear it all." Morgan grimaces.

"Well, she's saying that the full interview is *coming soon*, so we might not have to wait long."

"Can't we just pay her off?"

I sigh. "We could, but she isn't asking for ransom, not yet anyway. Seems like she wants her five seconds of fame and she's getting it."

"She looks like a dirty tramp. He's really upgraded with you."

"I'm not sure he's with me anymore."

She rolls her eyes. "Oh, come on, Elly, stop being so stubborn and admit that you miss him like crazy. You're miserable. You've been miserable for days. Just accept that you want him."

"I'll accept that I want Walker when you accept that you love Tom."

"Too easy," she replies quickly. "I *do* love Tom."

Well shit. I've clearly overplayed my hand.

"Wait, what? You *love* Tom?"

"Of course I love Tom." She's smiling and blushing and it's so adorable. "He can handle my shine," she says with a shrug.

That's the only explanation she needs to give.

My god, she's *glowing*. It's so nice to finally see her in a relationship where the real her is not only embraced but celebrated. He's not threatened, not self-conscious, he's *thrilled* that he's with her, and her feminine energy is thriving because of it.

Tom is the definition of healthy masculinity. I hope the next generation of males stand up and take notice, and then follow his lead. Gone are the days of being embarrassed to be in love and adoring the woman you're with. It's the era of the simp.

"Since when?!" I demand.

"We said it for the first time a few days ago, but I think it's been hiding under the surface for a while now."

"Oh my god, I'm so excited for you."

It's not like I didn't see this coming, but I'm still shocked. I'm so happy for her.

I think poor Tom has been holding it in for half of his life, so I'm beyond happy that he's got the girl. I've never seen a man hustle so hard. He deserves it.

It's ironic that their feelings are finally real at the same time they're being accused of being fake.

This contract drama isn't great news for them, her and Tom are getting called out pretty hard online. The 'I told you so' brigade has turned up in full force. We haven't acknowledged Nadia publicly, haven't addressed the rumours, and haven't changed any of our plans, and that's exactly the strategy I plan to push forward with. We remain unfazed, and eventually people will move on and stop talking about it. It's not like they're going anywhere. People can speculate all they like.

Like Tom said, maybe in five years they'll stop questioning if the relationship is real.

Despite this drama, Morgan is still selling out stadiums and making record-breaking profits. Her fans are loyal. It's the haters who like to doubt.

We'll straighten this out, eventually. Stopping that contract from being released is priority number one.

Without any evidence, she's just a crazy lady with a theory. Her producing something concrete would change our approach drastically.

I just have to hope that we can stop her before she does it. I'm not in the mood for crisis mode.

"Are you stressed about this situation?"

She thinks for a moment. "No. Not really. I'd much prefer that she doesn't air all our private shit to the media, but if she does, and we can't do anything to stop her, then we'll deal with that."

"Very sensible."

"Tom and me, we talked about it. We're just going to focus on us and what happens, happens."

"Good. It's not your job to worry, that's what you pay me for," I insist.

"That's right, but you need to remember it's not your job to be miserable over a man who adores you."

That statement makes me feel like crying.

"Are we going to address the elephant in the room?" she asks cautiously.

"By elephant, do you mean possible child?" I sigh.

"Yeah... that's kind of a big deal. But maybe it's all a load of crap too."

"Maybe. Maybe not. They did get pregnant, you know? Back when they dated."

"Tom told me about it. They agreed not to keep the baby and she got a termination."

"That's what she said, but I'm sure she wouldn't be the first woman to lie about keeping a baby."

"Would it be a deal breaker if he did have a daughter out there?"

"If she's lying about everything else then him having a daughter would be nothing to me – I love kids and if he comes with a little girl then that's more than okay with me, it's not the fact that he might have a child… it's everything else."

I don't want to believe that Walker would hurt me, but when it matters most, I seem to be a terrible judge of men. Always have been. I thought maybe things had changed – that maybe I'd learnt to run away from red flags instead of towards them, but recent evidence would suggest that I'm still out here acting like an enraged bull.

"I knew that's what you'd say."

"Yeah. I mean, if he'd known he had a daughter when I started dating him, it wouldn't have made me any less interested. If anything, it'd probably have increased his chances. Single dads are hot."

She laughs. "I can appreciate that a good-looking man doting on a little kid is enough to get the ovaries fluttering."

Just for a moment I let go of the mind fuck that is my life and allow myself to just imagine that every-thing will work out okay.

"We joked about having kids once. Holy cow, he'd look so sexy holding a baby. I wouldn't be able to let him out of the house unsupervised. The vultures would be all over him."

I can picture it all in my head. It's not a fantasy,

because in all honesty, I can see it happening. Walker and I, a little older, a little wiser, doing the best we can with a couple of kids.

"Holy shit, you're in love with him," Morgan cries, interrupting my daydream.

She's right, I realise in that moment.

I'm in love with him.

I fell in love with him and I've never fallen back out.

"I think I might be." I huff out a breath.

She gapes at me, at a loss for what to say.

It's fair enough, I don't think either of us were expecting today to have all these declarations of love.

"You might be?"

"Who am I kidding? I'm *completely* in love with him," I confess – to her and to me.

I love that man.

I love him more than anything or anyone else.

Now I have to decide what to do about it.

WALKER

Endless research and numerous tails on Nadia, and no one has seen any evidence of a child with her.

The report says she goes out, drinks iced lattes, gets her hair, nails, lashes, tan, and whatever the hell else needs doing, and then disappears again. Maybe she might shop a bit, she might meet up with some friends, but there's never any children, and she's never with a man.

Whoever knocked that psycho up, doesn't seem to want to be seen in public with her. Can't say I blame him.

I've seen the pictures of her strolling around the city, coffee in hand, but as far as a kid goes, I still don't know if it exists.

I've had my team dig around birth announcements and they did what they could with hospital records and birth registries, but they're not exactly willing to hand out that kind of information to just anyone. We've come up as good as empty.

Nadia's friends won't talk, and she doesn't have much in the way of family. She burned all her bridges a long time ago with her partying and her bullshit.

I'm at a loss.

I don't know what to do. I don't know where I go from here. Her story is mostly all a load of shit, but the one element that could have some truth to it, is the existence of a toddler.

I just can't find any confirmation of that.

She doesn't drop a kid at daycare, she's not spending all her time at home, and I'm certain she couldn't afford a full-time nanny while she's out living the life every day.

I think I'm going to have to come to the conclusion that she was lying. There is no kid.

There's just something niggling away in the back of my brain though, something that just doesn't sit right with me. I can't put my finger on it.

I should have insisted on going with her for the termination. Then at least I'd know for sure, one way or the other.

I'm not saying that if we do have a child, that I wish she'd terminated it, but at least I would know for sure if she'd let me come with her that day.

I'd never have pressured her to go through with something she didn't want to do, but I sure as hell wouldn't have been okay with being cut out of my child's life either.

I didn't see her afterwards – she said she wanted to

be alone – and then not long after that we were over. She could have hidden it from me.

It's entirely possible that she never even went to the clinic. That she kept the baby, laid low until it was born and then just never told me a thing about it.

Fuck, maybe she gave it up for adoption.

The idea makes my blood run cold.

I wasn't prepared for the idea of being a father before she came out with all this talk, but the thought that she might have given birth and then walked away – just like my mother did to me – makes blood whoosh in my ears. I don't know what I'd do if my child was out there, living their life with another family.

The thought makes me feel sick.

I don't know how I'd cope if I found out I had a daughter, but I was never going to be able to see her.

I wish I could say that Nadia wouldn't do something like that to me, but the fact is, Nadia would screw over *anyone* if it meant she got a leg up in life. She doesn't care about what's right and what's wrong, she only considers if it's good for her. She's a money- and fame-hungry whore.

I don't doubt that she'd bat an eyelid about being a terrible person.

I quickly type up an email to one of the best guys on my team, asking him to see if he might have any luck with checking local adoption agencies.

I don't think it'll turn up anything. Not without Nadia's contact info. All these agencies and hospitals are doing their jobs a little too well for my liking.

I just need one person to slip.

Which person, and where, is the real problem. It's

like searching for a needle in a haystack. There are so many possible scenarios, so many outcomes, locations, possibilities… it's ridiculous.

She could have never been pregnant in the first place.

She could have terminated the pregnancy.

She could have lost the baby.

She could have given birth.

She could have given the baby up.

She could have kept the baby.

She could have had the baby taken from her.

It just keeps going, around and around and around inside my brain until my skull feels like it's going to blow apart into little pieces from the stress.

I need to talk to Nadia. She's the only one who can tell me for sure what's real and what's not.

The problem is, I don't know where to find her. Other than her daily Starbucks visit. My guys don't seem to be able to tail her home. She gets on trains, cable cars, in taxis and Ubers. She'll jump on the metro underground and they can't track where she ends up without going full stalker.

I've told them not to worry about it. I'd prefer they kept their distance. I don't need to know where she lives yet.

She'll have to surface again soon – she's talked a big game to the media, and she's meant to have a contract to deliver.

The whole world is waiting for it.

I still doubt that she has it.

I don't know how she possibly could.

But that's not even my main concern at the

moment. Right now, I care more about whether or not my reckless decision-making has led me to having a mini version of myself running around somewhere or not.

I'm so restless, I'm probably not far off wearing a track through my carpet with the way I'm pacing back and forth.

I've called every reporter I've got a working rela-tionship with, asking them if they can put me in touch with her, but no one can. They're all waiting on her too. Waiting for her to show up with the evidence.

I've messaged her on all her social media, and I've tried her old email and phone number. Everything is either cancelled, bounces back to me or I'm blocked.

I toss my phone onto the couch and run my hands through my hair as I keep pacing.

I stride back to the couch and grab it again. Maybe Tom will know what to say.

Walker: I can't find anything. It's driving me crazy.

Tom Spanks: Maybe there's nothing to find.

Walker: I've got a feeling.

Tom Spanks: I've got lots of feelings man, doesn't mean I've got kids running around the city.

Walker: You know what I mean. I feel like I'm losing my mind.

Tom Spanks: Hang in there, Walk, we'll figure it out.

Walker: I'm starting to think I'll never know for sure.

**Tom Spanks: What are you doing right now?
Want to get a beer?**

God, I wish I could talk to Elly.

She'd know what to do. She's so much smarter than I am. She's the smartest person I know. She'd help me, and if she couldn't help me, she'd support me anyway.

Except she isn't here, because somehow, my fuck ups are having a hell of a time catching back up to me.

The dildo of consequence rarely arrives lubed.

I don't blame Elly for needing some time and space. All evidence points towards me being a total scumbag, she's an intelligent woman, and she needs to take a step back so she can get some perspective and figure this all out.

It's completely understandable. If it were me, I'd probably have been stupid and stubborn and thrown in the towel on the spot. I could learn a lot from Elly. I hope I get the chance to.

I miss her like crazy.

It's been the longest week of my life without her.

I never thought I'd ever feel this way about someone to the point where not having her near me, not knowing if I'm ever going to touch her again, is causing me physical pain.

She's left a permanent mark.

My gaze falls to the lanyard hanging on the back of my door. The little photo of Morgan on the front gives me an idea.

I might not be able to get close enough to Elly to actually talk to her, but I can keep my word.

I told her I was going to be at the show – she gave me the pass – I think it's time I used it.

Walker: I don't want a beer, but I can think of something else we can do.

TWENTY-ONE

ELLY

"Get me Elly!" I hear Morgan yell. "Quick!"

"Elly!"

"Elly!"

"Elly, we need you."

I can hear about fifteen people calling my name.

Fuck me, where's the fire?

I run towards where I know Morgan will be getting changed from her 'Timeless' outfit into her 'New Me' one.

"What? What is it?" I demand.

Her eyes are wide like she's just seen a ghost while the wardrobe team push and pull on her limbs, getting her changed.

I *hate* being backstage, it's exciting, but the chaos is too much for me. It's all controlled chaos, every single person knows precisely what their job is and does it to perfection, but it's so hectic I can barely stand to watch it.

The look on her face makes me think I don't want to know whatever it is she's got to say.

"He's here," she tells me.

I already know who the 'he' she's talking about is, but I have to ask anyway. It's either confirm my fears or run away.

My heart slams into my ribcage. "*Who* is here?"

Time stands still as she answers me. "Walker. He's here. Right up front. Tom too. They didn't tell me, I swear."

"Thirty seconds," I hear someone say, and everything speeds back up again.

"Shit," I hiss.

"Second row, black t-shirt," she tells me before she's whisked away towards the stage.

She shoots me a sympathetic look over her shoulder.

I take a deep breath. It does less than nothing to get my heart rate to chill the fuck out.

I don't want to go and look, but I already know I will. I'm a complete sucker for this man. I can't help myself. I've been punishing myself all week by looking at every picture of him I can find online, whilst ignoring every one of his calls and messages.

He's been photographed more in the past five days than he has been in the past year, and it's not doing me any favours. I can't help but think he's doing it on purpose.

I know I need to talk to him. I can't keep hiding out like a chicken shit.

All this has hurt me, but maybe I need to be the bigger person, hear him out, give him a chance to apologise – if that's what he wants to do – and then try and move on with my life if what he says breaks me.

I don't have the luxury of being able to avoid him.

Morgan and Tom are the real deal. That's not going to change. Anyone with eyes and half a brain can see that this is permanent. They're endgame.

She's finally found the man for her.

It's either quit my job, or hand over the day-to-day of Morgan's management to someone on my staff, or learn how to deal with a man I'm still insanely in love with.

None of those options sound good to me, but I'm a grown woman. I can put on my big-girl panties and deal with this.

Clearly, he's not going to just disappear quietly like a guy with manners might. He's *here*, for fuck's sake, at her concert.

He's used the damn unicorn pass.

I regret giving him that thing. He wouldn't have been able to get in here without it; this show has been sold out for months.

Morgan is back out on stage, singing one of my favourite songs, but I can barely even acknowledge what she's doing or that she's doing it in front of all these people, there's only one person on my mind, and I have to go and see if he really is here.

I slip around the side and down into the area the crew uses. I sneak around to where I can get a good look at the front few rows and brace myself.

I know how my body is going to react. It's not

going to listen to my brain. This body wants him, no matter what.

I peer around and it's as though I know exactly where to find him without having to search.

He's in the second row, and he's every bit as gorgeous as the day I fell in love with him.

He's towering above the group of early twenties girls that are in the row in front of him. I actually feel bad for the people behind him, they've paid for premium tickets, and they'll be getting a heavily obstructed view.

He's got on a black t-shirt, just like Morgan said, but what she failed to mention is the pink glittery writing across the front that says 'Elly-May's man'.

He's singing along with Morgan, and for a man who claims this kind of music 'isn't his jam', he sure seems to know a lot of the lyrics.

His big body is moving to the beat. It's not until he leans over and speaks to the person next to him that I even notice Tom next to him.

His brother has unfiltered access to VIP tents, they both do – so their choice of seating is *very* intentional. He's here for me. He said he was going to come, and he did.

He's trying to keep his word.

Walker says something in Tom's ear and he turns to look at something. There's two teenage girls down the row from them who are clearly beyond excited to be sat so close to Morgan's new man. Tom wiggles his fingers at them in the most ridiculous wave.

They look at each other and scream.

I glance around and it seems like there's as many

people with their phones pointed at Tom as there are at Morgan. It's lucky he's not camera shy.

Walker chuckles and shakes his head. I'm trying to lip read, but I can't make out anything the two men are saying to each other. Tom is watching Morgan on stage again, he clearly can't keep his focus off her for long, even though he's seen this show a few times now already.

Walker yells up at Morgan through cupped hands, something that sounds suspiciously like "yassss, queen, slay."

I hate that it makes me smile.

He glances around, and I hold my breath as he turns in my direction. He looks around and skims over the place I'm hiding like a coward.

I exhale heavily, relieved that he didn't spot me, but I realise I've celebrated far too soon as his eyes dart back to me as recognition dawns.

Oh no.

His expression softens and the confident, cocky mask he wears slips, revealing the broken man beneath.

I've never seen someone so strong, look so helpless.

The pain in his eyes is so evident it makes me hurt with him.

I want to turn and flee, but I can't, I'm stuck on the spot, frozen by my emotions.

We look at each other like that for what feels like forever, but in reality is probably only a few seconds.

He looks away first as he reaches down onto the

ground to pick something up. I watch as he holds up a sign, pointing it in my direction.

'I'M SO SORRY. PLEASE TALK TO ME.'

He shrugs. The look on his face... he's barely holding on by a thread. Just seeing me is breaking him. Seeing him is breaking me.

How can two people feel like this about each other and still it's not easy or simple? It's not fair.

I feel like I'm going to cry.

I don't know what to do, I don't know what to think... so I stick with the coping method I've employed lately and turn and run away.

I'm hiding in a dressing room, bawling like a baby when I'm found.

I didn't expect anyone to come looking, let alone find me here, but when I look up and see Tom giving me a sad smile, I'm not all that surprised.

I'm sure Walker sent him.

His unicorn pass is good, but it won't get him back here without Morgan's say so. The boyfriend of the musician pass works wonders though. Tom could probably get anywhere he liked in this venue.

"Oh, Elly." He sighs when he sees the state of my face.

He sits down next to me and offers me a packet of tissues.

This is a man who has come fully prepared for what he knew he'd be walking into. He really is a sweetheart.

"Thank you." I sniffle as I take them from him.

I'm being silly. Sitting here crying isn't going to help anything, but I can't seem to stop myself. I've held it in for so long but seeing him again tonight broke me.

I want to talk to him so badly, but I don't know how. I don't know what to say.

I love him – I'm in love with him, and while I'd love to sit down and let him tell me that everything is okay, that none of it is true, that he didn't betray me, there's every chance that he wouldn't be able to tell me that, and then what? Maybe he did betray me. Maybe there is some truth to even one small element of it.

That'll crush me.

I need to hear it, but I'm not ready. I'm not strong enough to handle all the possibilities.

Another heavy sob wracks through me, catching me off guard. That's a trauma response. This situation is bringing up all kinds of old shit for me.

"Oh, honey." He puts his arm around me and pulls me into his side.

Tom is a good man.

I'll forever be grateful for him shooting his shot with Morgan and winding up here at her side. He's the kind of man she deserves.

"Are you okay?" he asks when I finally settle down.

I don't know how much time has passed since he's

been stuck in here with me, but I've made a huge wet patch on his shirt as he's hugged me.

"Sorry," I say as I pat at it with a tissue.

He laughs, and it sounds just like Walker's. "Don't worry about it. It'll dry."

"You don't have to sit here with me. I'm sure you'd rather be watching the show."

He shakes his head. "I'll catch the next one."

I sigh heavily. This is so embarrassing. I bet I look like a train wreck; my eyes will be all puffy and red, and my makeup will be long gone. My nose is snivelly and my hair is bound to be a mess.

It's lucky Walker can't see this. I'd have no pride left.

"I'm sorry about all this." I gesture to my face.

"Don't sweat it, you look good with panda eyes."

"This is embarrassing. I don't even know why I'm crying." I laugh.

"Because you're hurt," he says simply.

"And scared," I admit.

He squeezes my arm. "Fair enough. I don't think anyone would blame you for being hurt and scared, or embarrassed, or nervous."

"I just don't want to be one of those girls, you know? The ones that get presented with a bunch of evidence, but they're too stupid to believe it so they stay... and keep getting broken over and over until there's nothing but pieces left."

"No one wants to see you in pieces, Elly. Especially not Walker."

"Am I being stupid?"

He sighs heavily. "Look, my brother can be an

idiot, and I'm not going to sit here and tell you that he has a squeaky-clean record and hasn't ever put a foot wrong, because you're too smart to believe something so stupid, but I can promise you, Elly, he didn't cheat on you. He didn't get some girl pregnant. He's not been seeing you on the side of his real relationship with her. When it comes to the way he sees you, you're it. You're the whole picture. There is no one else."

"Do you really believe that?"

It's a stupid question; he wouldn't have said it out loud if he didn't believe it was true. He's not a bull-shitting kind of guy.

"Every word," he promises me.

That makes me feel at least a little bit better.

"I never thought I'd say this – in fact, I'm pretty sure I made a hundred dollar bet a couple of years ago that this would never happen – but Walker's found his person."

I look at him with glassy, unblinking eyes.

"I mean *you*, just in case that wasn't clear."

A laugh bubbles out of me. "I figured that but thank you for making sure."

"Can't be too careful with an emotional female," he teases.

"But what about Nadia?"

"Fuck Nadia."

"What if they have a kid?"

"Then he'll cross that bridge when he comes to it, and maybe he'll have you there to hold his hand while he does. And if they don't, then there's nothing to consider."

He makes it sound so simple.

I didn't account for a child when this whole thing started, but I have to admit, that if he had a child when we started dating, it wouldn't have changed a thing for me. I'd still have been as taken with him as I am.

"She's saying horrible things about you," I tell him.

"Me and Morgan are going to sue if she keeps this up," he reassures me. It's ridiculous that he's the one reassuring *me* when it's him being dragged through the mud. I'm the least affected party in this whole mess, yet I'm the one crying like a baby.

"I don't understand what she's doing."

"That makes two of us."

"If she has the contract, why hasn't she leaked it? Why is she still holding on… is she waiting for a better pay day?"

"Doubt it," he scoffs. "If she had it, it'd be released by now. I don't think she's got shit. She wanted money, thought she could make a quick buck and didn't think it through."

I'm inclined to think he's right. I've been somewhat behind that theory after two days went by and she didn't release it. I don't think she ever had it at all, but that doesn't explain how she knew it existed in the first place.

"It still makes no sense; if she doesn't have it, did she just happen to guess exactly right? That doesn't really track. She knew specific details."

"I don't know. Walker doesn't know either. But he's determined to get to the bottom of it."

"That's the part that keeps tripping me up. I want to trust him. I do. But I need facts. She didn't guess. So how did she know?"

"I think that's fair enough. But just don't lose sight of the man you know him to be. That's who he really is. The rest of it is just… noise."

"There's a lot of noise. Everyone is talking about this all being a PR stunt online, you know that, right?"

He shrugs. "At this point, I don't really care. People can speculate all they like, they'll get bored after five years, or ten. Maybe it won't take that long. Surely they'll believe it when I marry her one day."

It gives me the warm fuzzies to hear him talk about her like that. He really does love her.

She deserves a real love – like the one he's going to give her.

I deserve that too.

Maybe I might still have that. Tom seems to think I do.

I need to talk to Walker, and not just to see if there's anything to salvage between the two of us, but to do my job.

If nothing else, I *will* be good at my job.

It's been the one constant in my life for years, and as much as I was hoping that I'd have a new constant with Walker, I can live through work being my life again if I *have* to.

WALKER

"Just call me *Quasimodo*."

"*Why* would I call you *that*?" Tom asks.

"Because I had a hunch."

"Hunchback joke. You're a strange man, you know that?"

"I like to keep things diverse."

"Are you going to tell me what you're banging on about? Or are we just going to shoot the shit all night?"

"Sorry, got caught up thinking about animated films."

"Walk, man, spit it out."

"Right, got it. So, I went back to that café I met Russ in, ya know, the one where I last saw Nadia, and asked them if they had any footage I could look at.

Lucky I went when I did, it was only a few days away from being deleted."

"And then?" He's waiting not so patiently.

"I couldn't shake the feeling that I was missing something there. She doesn't live in that area, and she's a terrible actress, so it seemed like she was there for me, somehow."

"Checks out. Sounds like something a crazy bitch would do."

"Yup. So, I found the time we were there, watched us arrive, and then Nadia about fifteen minutes later. She sits. Russ and I talk. We've both got laptops open on the table. After about another forty-five minutes, my phone rings and I get up from the table and go outside."

"Did you leave anything on the table?"

"Yeah. I'd forgotten about that. I left my laptop and a stack of papers and went outside. You can see Russ sitting there for a few minutes, his gaze flickering from the door I disappeared out of, to over to Nadia's table, which is weird, right? He doesn't even know Nadia."

Tom looks like he's trying to solve a puzzle in his head.

A few minutes pass and she gets up and makes a beeline for Russ. They talk like two people who know each other – actually it looks like they even argue before she sits down in my seat and starts clicking around on my laptop. He gets up and walks away to the other side of the café. Looks to me like he's keeping an eye out for me – so she can do whatever the hell it is she's doing in my business, but he doesn't look happy about it."

"*What*? She's just brazenly going through your shit in full daylight?"

"Sure as hell looks that way."

"Call the police."

"Already did. I'm taking the footage down in an hour."

"What a slimy bitch! And Rusty? What the hell is his deal?"

My thoughts exactly.

"That I *don't* get. I'm going to that asshole's place after the police station, and I'll be getting answers one way or another."

"Want me to round up some of the boys? Really get him shaking?"

"No need, bro, I could take on ten of him at once and still come out on top with the rage I'm feeling right now. I think the look in my eye will be enough."

"Try not to get arrested."

"That would be inconvenient. He'll be lucky if it ends without a black eye though."

"Can't say he wouldn't deserve it. But back to the story... she's going through your laptop?"

"Right. You can see me spend another ten minutes on the phone outside and eventually Rusty gives her a signal that I'm coming back, she gets off my laptop and scarpers like a cat on a hot tin roof. Rusty sits back down, and I come in, none the wiser to the fact that my shit has just been combed through."

"So I'm guessing you have a copy of the contract on there and she's emailed it to herself or something?"

"No. No electronic copy of it exists."

That's had me confused too.

"Maybe I've taken one too many basketballs to the head, but I don't know where this is going. The suspense is killing me though, you should tell stories more often, you've got a real knack for it."

"I'll have you over for story night sometime, we can roast marshmallows."

"Sounds good, cupcake. First tell me how she got the contract if it's not on there?"

"The actual contract itself isn't on there, but I think she might have gone through the emails between me and Elly. There's a thumbnail of the cover page of the contract in one of them, and our email chain pretty much paints the rest of the picture if you know what you're looking for."

"So how'd she get it then?"

"I'm not convinced she did."

"You think she's bluffing about having copies of the actual documents?"

"Bingo. She's full of shit. That bitch has *not* been inside my house. She doesn't have them – there's no way she can. All she's got is a bad attitude and probably some kind of STD."

"Is she waiting for us to offer her a payout?"

"I dunno. I'd guess so. She's probably waiting for me to reach out and beg. She's not taking any of the payouts she's been offered from the media though, which pretty much confirms she hasn't got it."

"Sounds like our strategy of completely ignoring any and everything to do with this saga, may have been the best idea after all?"

"I do love it when a plan pays off."

We haven't acknowledged this at all publicly. I've

seen how things like this go, and anything you say will get twisted and thrown back at you. Sometimes it's better to just shut up and say nothing at all.

"So her entire story is all crap?"

"Well I sure as hell haven't got her pregnant recently."

"What about her saying you've got a kid with her?"

"I don't even know what to do about that. If I've got a daughter out there, then fuck, I'll take on my responsibilities, but I've got some serious fucking questions, that's for sure."

"Is it wrong that I kind of feel excited that I might be an uncle?"

"That's all kinds of fucked up, bro."

I know what he means though. I don't know how I feel. I really don't want a child with Nadia – she's certifiably insane, but I've always wanted a daughter. I've always wanted to be a dad one day.

"What now then?"

"Police. Russ. Hopefully get some answers. Then beg Elly for another chance. Maybe throw some eggs at Nadia if I can track her down. I don't even know where to start looking for her, though."

"Why do you think she did all this?"

I run my hand through my hair in frustration. That's the bit that has me really stumped. I have no idea what would have possessed her to do this now, or how she's manipulated Russ into co-operating. I don't know the guy well, but we've worked with him on a few endorsements over the years and he's never shown himself to be a slimy little weasel until now.

"Your guess is as good as mine. Other than the classic *bitches be crazy*, I have no idea. She didn't take our breakup well, but it was years ago."

"Yeah, that's sociopath shit."

"I'll let you know when I've talked to Russ. See what that good for nothing dickhead has to say for himself."

"If you need reinforcements, call me."

"Yeah, I bet Coach would just *love* me if I called out half a dozen of his players for a brawl during the business end of his Championship season."

"Coach is an OG. He knows how it is."

"Coach *is* an OG. But I've got this."

If it weren't for the fact that this related to two very successful, and wealthy people, I think the cops would have just thrown it out.

The video is pretty clear cut, but without audio, without being able to actually see what she's doing on my laptop, without being able to prove it's mine and she didn't have permission to touch it, they can question Nadia, but I doubt they'll be able to press charges. Not unless she actually comes out and produces something to implicate herself. Right now, she's just running her mouth.

I've already filed a defamation case for Tom, and Elly has done one on Morgan's behalf, but nothing moves quickly in the legal world, so it'll likely be weeks before I hear anything about that. I didn't bother doing one for myself about all this crap she's spewing, it's not worth the hassle to me.

The cops took a copy of the footage; I filed a full report, and they sent me on my way. I'll have lawyers handle everything with them from this point on.

I'd rather the cops weren't involved with the next part of my plan.

I have Rusty's home address from the last contract we signed. He told me he's restructuring his business and working from his house. I'm pretty happy with that outcome – I'm less likely to have an audience at his home than I would in some office building.

I scope the place out as I pull up outside. Pretty standard-looking stuff. No indication that a backstab-bing douche bag lives inside.

I get out of my car, go through the front gate and down the path to his door.

I knock three times, cross my arms across my chest and lean my shoulder against the house to wait for him to answer.

I hope he shits himself when he sees me standing here waiting for him.

The door swings open and it's me who shits myself at the sight on the other side of the door.

"*Nadia?* What are you doing here?"

She scowls at me, but it does nothing to cover her obvious shock. "*I* live here. What are *you* doing here?"

I look back at the street. I'm sure I'm in the right place.

What the fuck is going on.

"I'm looking for Rusty."

She looks panicked. She also looks pregnant – I hadn't noticed on the camera footage. Maybe one part of her ridiculous story wasn't complete bullshit after all.

"Who is it, babe?" I hear a voice call out. Not just any voice; Rusty's voice.

Babe.

Everything clicks into place.

She's *with* Rusty. This is *his* baby.

He walks into the hallway behind her, and I watch as the colour drains from his face.

"Walker – *what* – ah how did – what are you doing here?" he stutters his way through his question and does his best to school his features into something barely resembling composure.

The dude can't even get that right.

"I came to talk to you about why you let *her* go through my shit in the café the other day, but it's all becoming clear to me now."

I glance back and forth between the two of them.

Nadia tries to shut the door on me, but I push my arm out to stop it.

"Yeah, I don't think this conversation is over just yet."

She takes a couple of steps backwards, but I don't follow her in. she looks scared, and while I'd never lay a finger on her, she *should* be scared.

She's just saved me the job of tracking her down, and filled in a lot of the blanks I had about the details of this saga.

She takes another step back.

Fucking Rusty has made no move to get in between us, to protect his woman. He's such a pussy.

If some guy turned up to my house, as wild as I am right now, there's no way in fuck I'd let him anywhere near Elly. Sure as fuck wouldn't let him anywhere near a pregnant Elly.

Just proves what I suspected about him – that he's got no backbone.

"You can't be here," Nadia says, suddenly finding that sass she's been splashing around the media.

"And you can't be telling people that I'm fathering your children, but here we are," I drawl.

She's getting redder and redder by the second, and Rusty, he just looks like a beaten spouse. It's pathetically clear that this is all her scheme and he's just doing what he's told. He's so weak it's almost funny.

"I can tell people whatever I want, Walker, that's the beauty of free speech."

"You're playing with fire, Nadia, and I promise you, you'll get burnt if you carry on."

"What are *you* going to do?"

"Sue you, most likely," I reply.

She looks a little worried, but not as much as I'd like her to be.

"Do we have a daughter?" I demand.

She looks like she's weighing up whether or not to tell me the truth. "No. I got a termination, *remember*?" she replies sourly.

"There is no kid?"

"No," she snaps. "No kid." She doesn't even bat an eyelid.

I feel disappointed, but relieved. It's a weird sensation to experience both simultaneously.

"You are seriously the worst kind of human on the planet. Who lies about having a child, Nadia?"

I glance at Rusty, and he looks fifty shades of guilty.

"You can't prove I lied."

"I can prove I'm not that baby's father." I point at her belly.

"Pfft." She rolls her eyes. "Your name will be mud by the time you prove that. Your pretty little doll of a girlfriend will have left you and I'll have made bank selling my story."

If she could 'make bank', she would have done it already. They're offering money for evidence, and she has none.

"Is that what this is about?" I smirk. "You're *jealous* of Elly? I didn't want to be with you, but I want to be with her…"

"This isn't about *her*," she snaps.

"Isn't it though? Seems to me like you saw the pictures of her and I in the media, and you lost your fucking mind."

That would explain why she was deep diving in the emails between Elly and me. She was likely trying to find a way to break us, but like the opportunist devil she is, she got wind of the contract and decided to run with it. Added the rest of her lies in for a bit of razzle dazzle.

She looks like she wants to scream at me. "I'm *not* jealous. Don't flatter yourself."

"And then you realised that I was doing work with

your pathetic excuse of a man here, and you thought you'd use that to try and gather intel, am I about right so far?"

"Pretty much," I hear Rusty mutter.

Nadia turns and glares at him.

"You saw a chance, you took it, committed a serious crime, and still found nothing."

"I didn't find *nothing*, and you know it."

"Where's your proof, Nadia? If you had anything to show, you'd have shown it by now. You haven't got shit and we both know it."

"You can't even prove I touched your computer. You're as full of shit as I am."

That actually does make me laugh. She's going to wish I had nothing.

"You're obviously not aware the café has CCTV footage. The police already have a copy of you caught in the act. They're taking it pretty seriously – high profile case and all." It's my turn to bluff now.

Her mouth opens and closes like a fish. She doesn't know what to say.

"Jesus Christ, Nadia, I told you this was a bad idea," Rusty says, but it's quiet and with absolutely no power, like the pathetic human he is.

"What's the move, Nadia? We know you don't have any kind of contract to release, it's obvious that that baby isn't mine and that you're in a relationship with this dipshit. It's all lies. You're sunk. No one is going to buy this bullshit story from you anyway because we've threatened every channel with a lawsuit if they put out something that isn't true. No one wants to play these games with *Morgan Rhodes*, the woman is too influential."

More bluffing, but she doesn't need to know that.

"Fuck Morgan. *You're* the one I wanted to hurt."

And there it is. Finally, a truthful word comes out of her mouth.

"You don't have the power to hurt me."

"She left you, didn't she? Now you know how it feels." She looks smug as fuck.

"Don't pretend to know anything about the woman I love."

Her eyes widen and it gives me great satisfaction to know how much that statement hurts her. She was a stage-five clinger when we dated and took it up to a stage seven when I told her it was over. I had no idea she held a grudge all this time though. That's next level.

"She's not going to believe you, not until it's too late. I'm going to sell my interview about you trying to force me to get an abortion, and how you tricked me into sleeping with you again."

"It's no worries, if she's got any questions, I'll just have her listen to the recording of this conversation."

Nadia looks confused, but as I slide my phone out of my pocket, recognition dawns. I've been recording every single word she's said.

"That won't hold up in court," she hisses.

"I won't need to take you to court, Nadia, because you're going to retract your statements, and disappear back into the hole you crawled out of."

"And if I don't?"

"If you don't, then Morgan and Tom will take you

to court. I don't give a fuck what you've said about me, but they're important people and you're dragging their names through the mud."

"This is bullshit, you know it's true. They're not even a real couple. I saw it. Tell him, Rus."

I look at the spineless little snake.

"I didn't see anything. I just know what you told me," Rusty admits.

The look she gives him is so feral, I'm surprised he doesn't burst into flames.

She focuses her disgusted stare back on me. "You *know* it's true."

"I don't know what you're talking about. I've never seen two people as smitten with each other as those two."

She shrieks, out of pure frustration if I had to guess. She knows she's not going to win here.

"If you want me to stop telling my truth, then you need to pay me for my silence."

She's really pulling out all the big guns now. If she thinks I'm going to pay her, she's really got another think coming.

"It's time you got a life, Nadia, and stopped trying to mess with mine. You're having a baby for fuck's sake. Grow up."

She looks like she wants to say more, but she doesn't. She storms off down the hallway, pushing past Rusty without so much as a glance.

I almost feel sorry for him. Almost, but not quite. He's made his bed.

I turn around to leave, but look back, one last thing needs to be said.

"Tear up the paperwork for that deal we were talking about signing. Tom won't be associated with you ever again."

He looks like he wants to beg, but I'm not going to stand here and watch that. I've seen enough humiliating behaviour from him to last me a lifetime.

"And seriously, bro, have some dignity for the love of God. You're an embarrassment to men everywhere."

He doesn't even try to argue with me.

ELLY

I'm going to kill Morgan for this.

I *know* it was her doing. She's a meddley little meddler, with sticky little mitts.

I should have known she was up to something. She never calls me like that and insists that I be somewhere so quickly.

Half the time she asks me to do something for her, she acts like she's sorry for asking, and that I could hit her with my car to make up for the inconvenience. But today she was all demands.

Walker is sitting at the table in the middle of the empty café, a bunch of flowers on the table in front of him.

The owners of this place are the best, and it's not unusual for Morgan to eat here with friends or family when they're closed for the day to the public. They offer her privacy, and she offers them a more than fair financial incentive to keep it that way.

So the location it was demanded I go, wasn't out of the ordinary.

Only today, Morgan isn't here. Walker is.

It's just the two of us.

I don't know what to do. I don't know if I'm ready to have this conversation. I haven't made my mind up. I haven't figured anything out.

I can't make sense of any of it, but I'd like to.

I want to give my mind a break from the constant back and forth. I know I need to talk to him; I've been hovering over his name in my contact list ever since I saw him at the show, but something has stopped me from hitting the green call button.

I'm scared of what he's going to say.

He's got the power to crush my poor, fragile little feelings and I'm terrified that's exactly what's going to happen when he opens his mouth.

We're here now though. The power has been taken out of my hands. There's no time to overthink. It's classic for Walker and me. Maybe this is exactly how it needed to happen.

I walk slowly towards the table, and he gets to his feet, picking up the flowers as he stands.

God, he looks good. He's seriously gorgeous. Like, I can't even believe how appealing this man is to me.

He smiles at me, a crooked, lopsided smile and my heartrate speeds up.

"Elly-May," he breathes. He holds the flowers out

to me, but I don't reach for them, instead slipping into his arms, and wrapping mine around his middle. Something comes over me and I just need a hug like it's as essential as my next breath.

I don't care that he might have hurt me, I don't care that we need to talk about everything. Right now, I just need a hug from the man I'm in love with.

He freezes up for a second, I've caught him off guard, but then he melts into me, pulling me tight against his body.

I think he needs this as much as I do.

I can't remember the last time someone gave me a real hug. Not a polite hug, but an all-encompassing bear hug.

"I missed you," I tell him. "I know that's probably not what I'm meant to say."

"You can say anything you want. And I missed you more, kitten."

We stand there for a long time, just holding each other before I finally pull away.

He smells *so* good, he's so big and warm. I'm never going to be able to have an objective conversation with him if I don't get some space.

I take a step back and he hands me the flowers, a shy smile on his face. It's adorable really. He's such a big teddy bear.

"Thank you, they're beautiful."

He pulls a chair out for me, and I take a seat, laying the flowers on the table in front of me.

"You have no idea how good it is to see your face."

He looks like a man who's been starved for days,

and someone just sat a huge plate of food in front of him.

I think I might be able to relate to the way he feels, but I need to protect myself and not say too much. I'm afraid if I open my mouth, I might tell him I love him and that I don't care about any of this nonsense – I just want him.

But the problem is, I *do* care. I don't think I believe what that woman's been saying, but I need answers.

I need to look into his eyes while he tells me his side of the story. It's the only way I'm going to know if he's telling me the truth or not.

"I'm sorry about the other night."

He's shaking his head before I even finish speaking. "You have nothing to be sorry for. You were upset. I told you I'd give you space and then I turned up to the show. It was a bonehead move."

"You are kind of a bonehead."

"I'm also a *Rhode Runner* now. The girl puts on a good show. I've had her songs stuck in my head since."

"I did try to tell you."

His gaze is roaming over my face, like he can't get enough.

"I guess we should talk," I say with a shrug.

I hope I look more relaxed than I feel. My pulse is racing.

"I actually brought you something else too."

I hope it's not another gift. I've never been great at accepting gifts, especially not expensive ones.

He pulls out a folder from somewhere under the table and slides it across to me.

My brows pinch together as I look at it. I flick it open and it's a bunch of pictures and documents.

I flick through the photos of Walker sitting at a café table with some guy, until I get to one where he's halfway across the room and the guy is still at the table, and then another where a woman is sitting in the same spot he once was.

It's that woman – Nadia – and she's touching Walker's stuff.

"What is this?"

"Nadia snooping. She went through my laptop while I was on a call. It was during that endorsement meeting I was telling you about."

"Why didn't that guy stop her?"

His expression darkens. "That sack of shit is her boyfriend it turns out. That crotch goblin she's growing is *his*. I caught them out yesterday."

I frown, I don't understand what's going on.

He can see I'm confused.

"Listen to this," he offers as he pulls his cell phone out of his pocket. "I went around to confront Rusty."

I don't know what I'm about to hear, but I'm so focused, I don't want to miss a single word.

The recording starts playing and I listen intently as he confronts this Nadia chick, and the guy called Rusty – who I assume is the guy from the café – the one Walker was signing up a deal with.

My eyes get wider and wider as I listen to every-thing they're saying. It's only Walker and Nadia really, the other guy sounds like a complete pussy.

Walker was telling the truth. And not just part truths, but the *whole* truth.

She's not carrying his baby, not that I ever really believed she was, but it's beyond reassuring to know that she wasn't really in his house.

I'm also thrilled that she doesn't have that contract. All she's got is a suspicion, and she can have that. I don't give two shits what she knows, or who she tries to tell, as long as she hasn't got the proof to back it up. People make crazy allegations about celebrities all the time – this will just be another one of those.

My god, I could cry, I'm so relieved.

I don't know what else to do, so I just let it all out.

Tears pour out of my eyes and land in heavy drops on the table in front of me.

I feel so silly and so reassured simultaneously. I can love him – if he'll still have me after I bailed on him these past few days.

He reaches across the table and takes my hand in his.

"Those papers in there are copies of cease and desist letters. I've sent them out to every news station, talk show, radio station and tabloid that I can think of. Anyone airing that bullshit she's been spouting will be getting a call from Tom's lawyer. This is as good as over."

He's been doing a better job than I have been. Not that it's hard – I've been a waste of space.

"She doesn't have the contract. She hasn't been in my house, certainly not in my bed. She's just a crazy, jealous bitch who can't handle the fact that I've moved on with someone who is better than she could ever be."

"Walker, I... I'm sorry."

"You don't need to apologize. I don't expect you to just blindly believe anything I tell you. We haven't been together long enough for me to have earned that right."

He's so calm, so understanding and reasonable. It makes me feel like even more of an asshole.

"It's not that I *didn't* believe you, but when you're being told something and there's no other logical explanation... I just didn't want to be some dumb woman who winds up looking stupid and getting hurt. I needed some space to think straight."

"I would have done the same thing."

I don't know if he's just saying that to make me feel better or if he really feels that way, but either way, it eases some of the guilt I'm feeling.

It's like he can sense it's still eating away at me. "Elly-May, I don't ever want you to feel bad for needing some time to clear your head and process. You're allowed to feel hurt. Just because I didn't do anything to cause you pain, doesn't stop you from feeling it."

Jesus. That is one emotionally mature man.

I don't know how I got so lucky. Maybe that cocky swagger he carries like a badge of honour really is justified.

"She lied about you having a daughter."

"Yeah." He shrugs. "She lied about everything else, so I guess it tracks. Can't say I was surprised."

I can see a hint of disappointment behind his casual façade. He may not have wanted a kid with her, but I can tell he's a little hurt that he thought he had something and then had it taken away.

"Are you okay?"

He nods.

"Really?"

"I'm alright. I have to admit, the idea of having a daughter, even amongst all this mess... it made me feel good. But it wasn't real, and I shouldn't have believed it ever could be."

"Don't be so hard on yourself. She managed to sell a pretty good story – about the contracts too – she's sneaky."

He nods his head in agreement, but I can tell his thoughts are far away.

He zones back in, in a flash and his gaze caresses my face again.

"You've got no idea how much I've missed you," I whisper.

"I guarantee you that I know *exactly* how much. I don't plan on letting you out of my sight for a very long time."

"Bold of you to assume this thing is back on," I tease him.

He pins me with an intense stare. "It was never *off*, kitten, you never stopped being mine."

I want to say something smart, but the quip gets lost on my lips.

The way he's looking at me has rendered me silent. I kind of want to cry, part of me wants to jump up and down in excitement. I'm just so exhausted from life.

"Don't take this the wrong way, but you look tired." He reaches out to softly cup the side of my face and runs his thumb over my cheek.

Wonderful, I obviously look exactly the way I feel. Like shit.

"I can't sleep. And not in a good way."

His expression softens into sympathy. "I promise I'll make sure you sleep well tonight."

I believe him. I've learnt my lesson about doubting him. It won't happen again.

WALKER

"I'm looking forward to the makeup sex."

I laugh as she throws a grape at me.

"As full of confidence as ever, I see," she says with a roll of her eyes.

"Some things never change."

"Are you sure you're okay? With the whole… you've got a kid, oh no, just tricking… thing."

She's an observant woman – or maybe it's just me she can read well. She's right – I am a little gutted about it. It's silly – you can't miss something you didn't have.

I'll be over it soon – the only person I'm actively looking to have children with is the one sitting next to me.

"I'm good, kitten, I promise."

"You know you can tell me if you're not. Not just now, but any time. Anything."

Well while we're on the topic of coming clean and confessing feelings, I think it's about time Elly knows exactly how I feel about her. I've been holding this in too long. I'm one long look in her eyes away from spilling my guts anyway.

"I've got everything I need right here," I reassure her. "Good food, a cold beer, the woman I love, the –"

"*The what?*" she interrupts me, those pretty green eyes almost bugging out of her head.

I grin at her. "You heard me."

"Say it again."

"How are you going to make me?" I smirk.

"By asking nicely," she whispers, her eyes still as wide as saucers. "Please?"

There's no way I could deny her something, even if she didn't ask me nicely. I'm putty in her tiny hands.

I lean in closer, and lightly grip her chin between my finger and thumb. "I love you, Elly-May."

It's crazy the way I can see her whole body almost absorb the words right into the centre of her. Like she's waited her whole life and now she's finally whole.

"And I love *you*," she breathes.

Thank fuck for that.

"I love you more."

"Always have to win, huh." She shakes her head at me.

Pretty much.

"I can't believe you just told me you love me."

"I've been holding it in for so long," I admit.

"Me too. I told Morgan already and everything."

He chuckles. "So, you're telling me I'm not even the first person who knows that you love me?"

"Girl talk, slick, you'll get used to it."

"I don't know whether I'm insulted or not."

"I think if you have questions about it, then you aren't."

"That's a fair point."

"Girls tell each other everything. Maybe I'll tell her about what you're packing in those shorts," she taunts, playing with me.

"Don't even think about it," I warn her playfully.

"Oops." She smirks and shrugs her dainty shoulders. "Might be too late."

"Don't make me punish you, Elly."

Her eyes are burning. I think she'd like nothing more than for me to do exactly that.

She shrieks as I grab her by her waist, lowering my hands to grip her ass and lift her so she's sitting on my dick that is now undeniably hard inside my shorts.

She lets out a soft moan when she feels it.

I grab a hold of her silky hair and force her face up to mine while she's straddling me, her knees on either side of my hips.

She lifts her ass so her cleavage is right in my face, but I don't look down, instead training my gaze on her bright green eyes. It's no small feat – she's got one hell of a body.

"You have the most beautiful eyes I've ever seen."

She blushes and sits back down so I can feel her again.

This is the life, leaning back on a couch while a gorgeous woman gently rotates her hips over my crotch. She leans forward, her breath heavy on my face, and I kiss her, tasting her sweet lips.

She tugs on the hem of my shirt, wanting it gone, and I scoot forward so she can pull it over my head.

I return the favour – lifting her dress from the hem and dragging it up over her head, revealing that she's got nothing on underneath.

Just when I thought there was nothing hotter than those skimpy little sets.

"You're so fucking sexy."

"*Show me* how sexy," she whispers.

I growl as my lips get to work. I don't need to be told twice. I kiss her pouty mouth, her neck, her breasts. I'm so rock hard for her, it's out of control.

It's been too long since I've had her – I'm going to embarrass myself if I'm not careful.

I don't know how the fuck I'm meant to be careful when I'm so desperate to taste her.

I lift her off me and throw her onto the couch. She gasps as she lands. I know from experience that my girl likes being thrown around.

It's so sexy how effortlessly I can do it.

She's on her back, legs open, looking like a snack I'm about to devour.

I move between her thighs, kissing up the inside of her legs, getting close to where she wants me before pulling back.

She bucks her hips as I do the same on the other side, moaning in frustration as she does.

I chuckle. My little kitten, so eager.

I give her what she wants, my tongue running

through her centre. She lets out a satisfied sigh at me finally making contact.

Her hands find my hair as I settle into a rhythm. I can tell she's close as her grip tightens on my hair, pulling it painfully.

So fucking hot.

Her moans get louder and louder as I put my mouth back on her sensitive clit, bringing her to the brink.

She's so close, but I'm in one of those moods. I don't want to make it too easy… I want her to beg for it.

I change my tempo, stopping her from falling off the edge.

"Walker," she moans.

"What's the matter, kitten?" I smirk.

"*Walker*," she repeats. She sounds half delirious.

I run my finger over her clit and slip it inside her. I watch as her lids flutter and her eyes almost roll back in her head.

She's fighting for her life right now.

"Please." She begs, "I want to feel you."

There she is. That's my girl.

I sit up on my knees, tugging my shorts roughly out of the way and palming my dick.

"I'm so fucking hard for you."

"Do something about it then," she half challenges, half demands.

I plan to do exactly that.

I tease her, rubbing my dick between her legs, but not letting it slip in. She's gripping my shoulders so hard, she's desperate for a release.

I know this isn't going to last long once it starts, I'm way too wound up, so I need her so close to the edge that she's pretty much coming undone as I slide into her.

"*Please*," she whimpers. "I need you inside me."

That's all the restraint I've got left in me.

I line up and push into her wet heat with one fluid stroke.

Fuck, she feels amazing. I'm a total goner.

She lifts her hips and I push deep, sliding out a little before pushing in again.

It only takes another couple of thrusts before she's crying out in pleasure. I know exactly how my baby likes it.

"Oh my god," she breathes.

Oh my god is right.

I hold on as long as I can, moving in and out of her, dragging out her release. But all too soon I'm following after her, coming so hard my ears are ringing.

It's been a long time, and I haven't even been touching myself, so there's probably going to be a major clean up in aisle three.

"That was intense," she says, her breathing laboured.

It was fucking explosive.

I'm still inside her, I don't have the energy to move.

"That wasn't exactly what I had in mind when I said I was going to come over to hang out," she admits sheepishly.

"Really? It was *exactly* what I had in mind." I smirk, a shit-eating grin stretching across my face.

"I bet it was." She raises an eyebrow knowingly. "I'm certainly not mad about it though."

"You and me both, kitten."

Fuck, an after-sex nap really slaps different.

I'm all kinds of satisfied. Morgan is tucked into my side, and the midday sun streaming through the window is warm enough that we don't need a blanket.

This is my kind of perfect.

I stretch a bit, being careful not to jostle her.

She looks so peaceful. I wasn't sure if I was ever going to get to see this sight again in real life, or if my memories were as good as it was going to get.

I reach my arm out and grab my phone off my nightstand, so I can snap a photo of her. I don't ever want to forget this.

I get a photo and then nearly drop my phone on her head when it abruptly rings in my hand.

"*Shit.*"

Her eyes open and she looks at me in confusion.

"Sorry, kitten, I didn't mean to wake you."

She yawns and looks at the still-ringing phone in my hand. "Are you going to answer that?"

I finally look at who's calling and nearly drop it again when I see it's Rusty.

"What the fuck, why is Rusty calling me?"

"Maybe answer it and you'll find out," she suggests sleepily.

Very clever.

I don't really want to talk to that cunt, but I'm intrigued. Curiosity killed the cat and all that.

"I thought I told you to lose my number," I answer.

"I know, man, I know. But I need to tell you something."

"I can't imagine there's anything you can say that's going to be of any importance to me."

I'm about to hang up, but the way he speaks has me pausing. He sounds broken.

"I wish that were true, Walker, I really do." Me and Elly exchange a look. "You have to hear me out."

I don't know what the fuck he thinks he's trying to do here, but I'm not a patient man.

"Spit it out, Rusty, but I'm telling you now, Tommy isn't signing up for anything you're involved in. That working relationship is done."

"No. This isn't about Tom. It's about Nadia."

Elly scowls. She doesn't like that name any more than I do.

"And why the fuck would I care about Nadia?"

"Just listen to me, Walker, it's important. She lied to you the other day."

Hardly surprising, all that bitch does is lie.

"About what this time?"

He sighs. "About you two having a kid."

I swear to God, my heart stops beating.

Elly's eyes are wide as saucers as she hears everything I'm hearing.

"She's got a daughter. She's one and a half, and I

don't know for sure, Walker, but fuck man… she's got your eyes. Nadia told me when we met that she didn't know who the dad was, and I believed her, but now she's been running her mouth, and I think she was telling the truth about you being the dad – for a minute at least. Ever since Tom started dating Morgan and you've been in the media a lot, it's like she's totally off her head."

"She's got a daughter?" I say the words slowly, testing them out.

I'd put this issue to bed. Made peace with it. Accepted it was over.

I feel like I'm stuck inside a yo-yo, going up and down, back and forth.

"Are you fucking with me?" I demand. "I swear, if you're fucking with me I'll –"

"I'm not fucking with you," he cuts me off. "Her name is Stevie."

I don't know what to say, I don't know what to do. I'm full blown panicking. I should never have taken Nadia's word for it. I should have dug deeper.

"I don't understand."

He exhales heavily. "That makes two of us. She hides the pregnancy and kid from you, then goes to the media for a pay day, then lies to you again. I think she wants money, but she's seriously unhinged at the moment. I don't know what her game is… I don't even know if she does. I don't even recognise the woman I fell in love with."

Stevie.

"You really think this little girl is mine?"

"I can't say for sure, but the other day when we

met up was the first time I've seen you since she started saying shit, and I swear her eyes are a carbon copy of yours. She looks just like you."

"Where is she?" I demand, sitting up straight.

I don't even know for sure that this kid one hundred percent exists, let alone that she's mine, but I feel fiercely protective either way.

If there is a little girl, and she's spent her entire life with Nadia as her only parent, she's going to need saving if she's got any chance of growing up without a million issues.

"Is she at your place?"

Mentally, I'm already in the car with the keys in the ignition.

I don't know when I got to my feet, but I'm standing, and Elly is standing in front of me, looking as ready for action as I am. Despite the fact we're both naked.

"No. Take a breath, Walker. It's complicated."

"It's only complicated if I commit murder over this," I growl. "Where. Is. The. Girl?"

If this fucker doesn't hurry up and tell me, I'll end him. I've got no patience when it comes to this.

"She lives with Nadia's mum at the moment."

What the fuck. "What? Why?"

"It sounds like Nadia wasn't exactly… *on the rails* after Stevie was born – well actually, no pun intended. Ironically, from what I hear, she loved a good rail… but anyway, she was a mess and Jessie took Stevie on. When I got together with Nadia, she was off the drugs, and she still is, but it was like she'd completely disassociated from Stevie. We had her with us for a bit, to see if the bond could be built back up, but Nadia wasn't interested. She sent her back to her mum's."

"She's keeping my child from me, and she doesn't even look after her?"

I didn't know Nadia's mum Jessie well, but from what I do remember, she was an older woman, and in poor health. I can't imagine she's been handling a one-year-old with ease.

"It's fucked up. I don't think she even considers herself that little girl's mother. She got pregnant again, which honestly now that I've taken off the rose-tinted glasses, feels very intentional, and she's talked about this baby being her 'fresh start', and her 'miracle baby'. I'm sure I heard her call herself a first-time mum. It's like Stevie isn't alive and well and here waiting to be loved."

Jesus Christ. Nadia is so much more unstable than I ever could have imagined.

If Rusty has any sense, which I'm not at all convinced he does, he'll file for full custody of that baby the minute it's born and get as far away from nut case Nadia as possible.

"I'm going to need you to email me everything you have; I need contact details for Jessie, and I want a copy of the birth certificate if you can get it."

I'm not really asking him if he might be able to get it – I'm telling him he has to.

"She's going to lose her mind if she finds out I told you anything."

"Do you think I give a shit?"

"No." He pauses. "But she's carrying my kid, man. I'm stuck between a rock and a hard place."

More like between a psycho and a hard place.

I do feel for the guy, I know how charming Nadia can be, she's all sexy and sweet… until she's not.

Unlucky for him, he hasn't figured that out until too late – we might have that in common by the sounds.

"I won't tell her that you had anything to do with it, but I have more questions than you could possibly have answers – I need to talk to someone who can give them to me."

"Thank you. I get it. I'll do my best."

I do appreciate him doing this for me. He didn't have to call me today, but he chose to do the right thing. Maybe he's not a total prick after all.

He agrees to dig around and find whatever he can this afternoon while Nadia is going to be out getting a facial and a massage, and we finish up the call on better terms than I ever could have imagined.

My hands are shaking as I pull the phone away from my ear.

"You heard all that?" I ask.

She throws herself at me, wrapping her arms tightly around my middle. "Every word," she whispers.

I don't know what to do now. My body is tense and ready for action, like I need to do *something*, I just don't know what. I feel like I'm going to cry, my eyes are pricking with tears.

I might be a *dad*.

I can't even begin to process that. I don't know what that would mean for my life, but if she is mine, I'll do whatever I have to, to get her.

I need to remember to chill, though. I don't want to get ahead of myself. My ex having a kid with grey eyes doesn't make her mine.

God, I hope this isn't too much for Elly. I only just found her, I wouldn't blame her if it was, and she wanted to bail on me and my crazy situation.

"I'm sorry," I murmur.

"For what?"

"For all this bullshit. You didn't sign on for crazy exes and potential illegitimate children."

"*Walker*. It's not your fault."

"No, but it is my problem. It doesn't have to be yours. I'll understand if you want to walk away."

She looks up at me with a look so disgusted, it's like she's just watched me drop kick a puppy.

"You're so *stupid* sometimes."

I chuckle. "Why are you insulting my intelligence?"

"Because you and your big dumb mouth are insulting *me*."

"How did *I* insult *you*?"

I'm having a hard time stopping myself from laughing at how serious – and pissed off she looks.

"Did you not hear me say that I love you, you idiot?"

"I heard you."

"Yeah, well I don't only love you if life is perfect and easy."

She's still scowling up at me. It's so adorable. My feisty little kitten.

"Okay?"

"So, if you do have a daughter, then I'll *still* love

you, and we'll figure that out together. I'm not going to stop loving you because some crazy bitch kept your baby from you – I will question your past taste in women, because *my god*, Walker, are you insane? *But* I'm not going to bail on you, so get that out of your head and don't you dare mention it again."

God, I love this woman. I'm head over heels, crazy about her.

"Yes, ma'am." I nod.

As entertaining as I find her little outburst, and I certainly do find it entertaining, I can feel my heart swell at the way she's responded.

I might not have a say in this whole kid thing, but it'd break my heart to lose Elly over it. We're just starting out, and I wouldn't blame her, but I'd be devastated.

"Walk away..." she mutters, feigning disgust. "You're an asshole."

"But you love me anyway."

She meets my eyes again, and her furious expression softens. "I do love you."

"And I love you."

CHAPTER
TWENTY-FIVE

ELLY

"Thank you for being here," he whispers, squeezing my hand.

"No where else I'd rather be."

Today is the day we finally get to meet Stevie.

It took a while to get through to Jessie – Stevie's grandmother – and to organise a paternity test, but she eventually agreed. She also agreed to keep Nadia out of it, at least until the results were back.

They arrived a few days ago.

She's his. I think I knew she would be.

Walker made the choice not to even see her until he got the results back, and I supported that decision. No use in getting attached to a kid that isn't his. That would just make life harder for us, and for Stevie.

He spent the time getting all his ducks in a row, operating under the assumption that she was his daughter. He's got a lawyer fully informed and on standby to deal with whatever is going to come next.

Now that I'm seeing her in real life, I can see the DNA test was a waste of time and money. She's got her daddy's eyes alright. She looks exactly like him – in a tiny little girl way.

It's mind-blowing how genetics work. She's the prettiest little girl I've ever seen, yet she so closely resembles her absolute mountain of a man, blokey father.

The main way they differ is their hair. She's got a mane of brown hair so dark it's nearly black.

Jessie informed us that Nadia's blonde locks aren't natural, and that Stevie gets her dark hair from her mother.

I hope that's all she inherits from the piece of shit who gave birth to her.

I don't know how anyone could look at this beautiful little angel and not want her. It breaks my heart.

She's going around the room picking up random items and holding them up for us while loudly saying 'this' or 'that'. She's not shy at all. She's been all over us since we arrived.

Apparently, she spends three days a week in a daycare centre so that Jessie has a chance to rest and get some jobs done. She seems very well socialised because of that.

Jessie was a little standoffish with us when we first got here, but she's opened up as time has ticked on.

She's confided in us that while she loves her granddaughter, she can't manage on her own very well. It's been hard for her.

She's begged Nadia to reconsider the arrangement, but like Rusty said, she's not interested. I can't fathom how she doesn't see herself as this baby's mumma. Poor Jessie is doing the best she can, but she can't keep this up. We've only been here a couple of hours and even I'm a little worn out.

Such a tiny little person, but so much energy. I need some of whatever she's on.

Jessie is putting Stevie down for her nap in a minute and then we'll be able to discuss with her where we go from here.

I'm nervous. I can't imagine how Walker feels. This is his daughter – his baby girl – and the fate of her future is in someone else's hands.

Nadia didn't put his name on the birth certificate – which Rusty managed to produce for us – so right now, he has no rights.

As soon as we got the positive paternity test results back, Walker submitted the paperwork to have his name added. I'm sure it won't be a quick process, but at least it's under way.

I'm not sure what Walker is hoping for out of this – I don't even know if he knows – but I can't imagine that Nadia is going to be accommodating about it.

That bitch is difficult through to her core.

"Alright, missy, bedtime," Jessie tells Stevie.

"No, no, no, no." She waggles a finger at her, all sass and attitude.

"Yes, yes, yes, yes."

Stevie tries to run away, hiding behind Walker where he sits on the floor.

She's giggling as he pretends to shelter her.

My god, my heart. Watching how sweet and gentle he is with her is making me fall even deeper in love with him. The man takes everything in his stride.

I think he loves her already; I can see it in his eyes.

Jessie manages to wrangle Stevie off with the help of Walker, and she waves at us as she's carried off for her nap.

Jessie is back only a few minutes later, and I can hear the sounds of Stevie babbling to herself through the baby monitor.

"That kid sure can talk. She usually jabbers away in there for about ten minutes and then she'll be out like a light."

"She's a sweetheart," I tell her.

Walker hops up off the ground and comes to sit next to me where I'm sitting at the table.

Jessie seems to sense the meeting is in order, and she joins us too.

She looks between the two of us, and I sense that she feels worry, but maybe some hope too.

It's obvious she loves her granddaughter, but it's also clear she can't go on this way.

"I guess we should address the elephant in the room," she says. "What are we going to do about Nadia? I know she's not around, but I'm going to have to tell her."

Walker nods his head. "I agree. She needs to know."

"And then what's your plan?"

She's very calm, like this is a business transaction. I wonder what she used to do for a job.

"That's what we need to discuss," Walker says softly.

I reach under the table and take his hand in mine.

"I don't want to come in here and start making demands, or to take her away from you. You love her and you've done a great job raising her so far – Stevie is a real credit to you, Jessie."

She looks like she's got tears pooling in her eyes.

"Thank you. Sometimes I worry I'm not up for it… I went wrong somewhere with her mother after all…"

"Stevie is a happy little girl. She's loved and cared for. You're doing great," I reassure her.

"Like I said, I'm not looking to come in and call the shots, but I want my daughter in my life," Walker continues. "It doesn't seem like Nadia is coming back for her any time soon, if ever. Do you have any kind of formal custody of her?"

"The courts gave me temporary guardianship, so I could get some benefits to cover some of the costs, but that's all at this stage."

I hadn't even thought about the financial burden this must have been on her. Her home is small, but clean, tidy and cosy, everything is very basic in here. It looks like she gets by but doesn't have a lot to spare.

Walker brought a huge box of nappies with us today, some outfits and a big bag of toys, but I know he'll be leaving this woman with money too. If I feel bad for her, he'll feel at least ten times worse. His compassion is unmatched.

"Does Nadia contribute anything?"

She shakes her head. "Never. She hasn't even been by for months."

"I'm just going to put it all on the table, Jessie. I've been talking with a lawyer, and once my name is on the birth certificate, there's nothing stopping me from getting at least fifty-fifty custody of Stevie, and ultimately, I want that, at the very minimum. I'd do right by her, we can take things slow, and you can have time with her too if that's what you want, but she's my daughter. I've already missed a year and a half of her life. I don't want to miss any more."

The silence stretches between us, and it's not until I run out of air, that I realise I'm holding my breath.

It's no small thing, to come into someone's home and basically tell them you want to take away a child, at least part time.

"I think that would be the best thing for that little girl," she finally says.

Walker's shoulders visibly relax. "You really think so?"

"I'm seventy-five, I can't keep up with a toddler full time. You both seem like nice people. Obviously I'll want to get to know you a little better, and we're going to have to deal with Nadia, but if you can make that happen, I think Stevie would be better off with her father than with me."

"I really do appreciate you saying that." Walker smiles at her, his relief evident. "And you let me deal with Nadia."

"She's going to start World War three over this."

"But she doesn't even want Stevie," I say quietly.

Jessie sighs. "I know, but there's no logic to the way she operates. I know I shouldn't talk about my daughter like this, but she's not right in the head.

There is something wrong with that woman, and I believe she needs help, and medication most likely, but even then, I'm truly not convinced that she's a good person underneath it all."

That's so sad.

Every mother's worst fear, I'm sure. I'm sure Jessie did her best, and her daughter still turned out insane. It must be a difficult pill to swallow.

"Would you support me, in court, if it comes to that?" Walker asks her.

"I don't know what kind of mother it makes me, willing to go up against my own daughter, but yes, I would. If you really are everything you say you are, and you're the man you seem to be, then yes. For Stevie. She would be lucky to have you."

"I really appreciate that, Jessie."

"I'm still so mad with her. For abandoning Stevie, but also for lying about you. She told me she didn't know who the father was, but all this time she did. She could have given her to you when she was a baby. I know she's got her issues, and honestly, I'm glad Stevie isn't with her when she so very clearly doesn't care about her, but to deprive that poor little princess of both of her parents is unforgivable."

She's tearing up now. This poor woman is spent. I can't imagine being her age and being handed a baby, but she's stepped up.

Now it's our turn.

"As much as I love that little girl, it'd be a relief to not stress about how I'm going to pay for food, and daycare, and everything else. Let alone all the running around and all the things she'd miss out on with me."

"I'll handle the expenses from now on, and I'll help you out with anything you need. I'd like to see her, every day if possible, and when she's comfortable I could take her out, give you a break."

You can almost see the weight being lifted off her shoulders. She's not silly, and she's not going to be willing to hand Stevie over to just anyone, but she has hope now. Hope that she probably didn't think she'd ever have. It's a reprieve, if nothing else.

"I can't ask you to do that."

"You didn't. I insisted. I owe you months of child support, consider it back payment."

She wipes at a tear in the corner of her eye.

"If you're sure."

He's sure. I know he is.

"I'd love to be able to just be her grandma one day. Have her for a night sometimes, pick her up after school. Just enjoy the fun times and not be responsible for the rest of it. That probably makes me sound horrible."

I reach over and take her hand in mine. "There's nothing horrible about that."

"That's your right as her grandmother," Walker reassures her. "You shouldn't have been forced to be a parent to a child that isn't yours.

"You promise you'll keep letting me see her?"

I think Jessie has already accepted that Walker is going to do whatever it takes to get his daughter back, and that when he does, she'll eventually go to him full time. I think we've all accepted that this is going to happen.

He's a determined man with a lot of resources, and

more than that, he's a good man. A real one. He's not going to stop until she's where she should be.

"I would never keep her from someone who loves her," he promises her. "You'll always have a place in her life."

"And what about Nadia?" she asks cautiously. "I know it probably makes me sound naïve, but I still have hope that one day she'll sort her life out. That maybe one day she might try to fix things with Stevie."

Walker looks her right in the eye. "I can promise you, that no matter what, I'm always going to do what's right for Stevie. I'll do whatever I have to do to get her with me, and I'll keep her safe. If Nadia proves one day that she's worthy of being in Stevie's life, I won't stop her."

"Thank you. I know she doesn't deserve any of that, but thank you."

"I'll do right by her, Jessie."

"I'm worried something is going to go wrong. Nadia is… crafty. She has a unique ability to manipulate people and situations. I just hope you're prepared."

"She can be as crafty as she wants. It's not going to stop me from being with my daughter."

He's a dad already. Not just a biological father, but a *dad*. He's already putting her above everything and everyone else, and he's only met her once. I know he's going to be the best dad when he's got the chance to embrace it completely.

TWENTY-SIX

WALKER

"What the hell is this? An ambush?" Nadia demands as she swings the door open.

"Something like that," I reply.

"Fuck off, Walker." She tries to shut the door on me, but I know exactly how to stop her.

"I got a DNA test, Nadia. I know about Stevie, I know you didn't go through with the abortion, and I know she's my daughter."

The half-shut door slowly opens up again. She looks like a deer in the headlights. I think that was about the last thing she expected me to say.

"Have you been talking with my mother?" she demands.

At least she's smart enough to recognise that there's no point in trying to deny it. Unlike her with that contract saga, I'm not bluffing, I brought receipts.

"Who I've been talking to is irrelevant. What matters is I have a daughter, and you kept her from me, and that's over now."

"You don't get to come in here and start making demands. You're not legally her father."

"Actually I am."

She smirks. "No, you're not. I didn't put your name on her birth certificate, so good luck with that."

"It's nothing a paternity test and a few forms can't fix, Nadia."

Her eyes narrow. She thinks I'm lying. "It's already done." I shove the copy of Stevie's new birth certificate at her.

She looks it over and I see her eyes widen when she reads my name printed there alongside hers.

"You can't just DNA test my child without my permission."

"You're not even her current guardian. I don't have to ask your permission."

She looks like she's about to blow a gasket. She tears the sheet of paper in half in a fit of rage.

"You can keep that, it's your copy," I tell her with a smirk.

"What do you want, Walker? You're not getting *anything* from me."

"I just want my daughter."

She scoffs. "Well then you may as well hit the road because it's not going to happen."

"Or maybe you could lay off being such an insufferable bitch for five minutes and listen to my offer."

I don't know if it's my tone, or my expression, or

the word 'offer' that catches her attention, but she doesn't argue further – not yet anyway.

"We have a proposition for you."

She looks between me and the man standing next to me.

"Who's *he*?" She points at Jeff.

"My lawyer."

"You brought a *lawyer*?" she demands.

"You're lucky I didn't bring a police escort."

"You make out like I'm some kind of crazy bitch," she hisses, outraged as hell.

Fuck me.

She's got to be fucking kidding me. She's totally bananas. She's the definition of a crazy bitch and she thinks *I'm* the one who's being unreasonable.

My flabber is definitely ghasted.

I'm not even going to engage in that comment. That's half the reason I brought Jeff with me – to ensure I keep my cool. That, and to witness the level of mental I'm dealing with firsthand. I'm also hoping it'll speed this whole thing up. We've come prepared, with a contract drawn up, all ready for her to sign. In fact, I have three different contracts at the ready, depending on how this conversation goes.

I warned him what we were going to be dealing with, and I'm sure he's seen worse, but this isn't going to be fun for him. He'll probably charge me a fortune for this afterward.

"I'm going to be in my daughter's life one way or another. Let's make life easy. What's it going to take to get you to play ball with this?"

She laughs. "What? You think you're going to get

me to play nice and sign over my rights just to keep you happy? You're dreaming."

She's so fucked in the head she can't even see this isn't about her, or me. It's about our daughter.

"I came here for Stevie, Nadia, and if we can't come to some kind of arrangement today, then I'll be seeing you in court."

"Maybe I'd rather take my chances in court."

"If you think anyone is going to side with a mother who hasn't seen her own child in months, who contributes nothing financially and who hid that child's existence from her father, then you're out of your mind."

"I don't need them to side with me, as long as they don't side with you."

She's actually demented. She doesn't even want Stevie – she just wants to make sure that I don't get her either.

"Are you really so fucked up that you'd disadvantage an innocent child – your own flesh and blood, just to try and hurt me? I can give her a good life, I can love her and take care of her and give her everything she needs. I know that you don't care about her, and I know you hate me, but there has to be some good, somewhere inside of you, there has to be something in there telling you to do the right thing. I'm not going to quit. I'll win, one way or another, Nadia, you may as well get something out of it."

She doesn't say anything for a few minutes. I'm about to start talking again when she finally replies.

"I want money."

"You want money?" I repeat.

This isn't a surprise to me. I don't know what debt she's got going on, but I'd be willing to bet it's out of control.

She nods. "You pay me, and I'll sign over my rights. She's all yours."

"How much?"

"Half a mil."

I can't believe that she's willing to give up her child for something as stupid as money. I've only spent a month with Stevie, and there isn't a dollar figure in the world that could get me to give her up. Nothing. Certainly not five hundred thousand dollars. It's a lot of money to a lot of people. Hell, it's a lot of money to me, but I'd give that and more if it came to it.

"Done."

Her eyes widen. "Just like that, you're going to hand over half a mil?" she asks, barely hiding her excitement.

"Sign the documents we've got here; legally forfeit your rights as her mother and you'll get your money."

Nothing about this really sits right with me... paying off a mother for her child feels so wrong, but I don't care. Nadia isn't doing anything a mother does. She was nothing more than a surrogate to Stevie anyway. I'm willing to do what I have to do, for my girl.

This past month has been the best of my life. I've been seeing Stevie every day; Elly comes with me most of the time too. After the first couple of weeks of visiting at Jessie's place, Stevie was more than comfortable with me, and Jessie felt like she knew me well enough to have me and Elly take Stevie out to do stuff. Yesterday we spent half the day at the zoo, and I was loving it as much as she was. She's started calling me 'dada' and it melts me.

"Hand them over," she says, totally emotionlessly.

She's a heartless bitch and I couldn't be happier for that fact right now.

I mentally prepared myself for this to go to shit. I was convinced I was going to have to go to court and fight over hot coals for this to get resolved.

I didn't let myself hope that she'd disappear entirely.

I know there's nothing stopping her coming back in the future, she's still her biological mother and she'd likely have some rights, even with the paperwork in place, but I'll cross that bridge if and when I come to it.

For now, for *today*, this is a big win.

I gesture for Jeff to take over. He's got the documents prepared, and he'll file everything as soon as we get done here. Once I have official confirmation, I'll settle the money with Nadia.

He steps forward and asks if they can go inside to look over the documents – all business.

She doesn't look happy about it, but she allows him inside and I follow after.

He pulls out the papers and reads through them to Nadia – I can tell she's not even listening. All she wants to hear is that cash hitting her bank account. He fills in the amount – five hundred thousand dollars – and instructs her of where to sign.

She scrawls her signature on the document, and I do the same when Jeff directs me.

He's telling her about the process and she's sitting there like a bored, sullen teenager.

She may as well be chewing gum. It's fucking ridiculous how little fucks she gives about something so serious.

"That's everything. I'll have a copy emailed to you within the hour," Jeff tells her.

"*Cool.*"

I've seen enough. Being here, being around her is just making me angry. I turn around and walk away for what I hope is the last time. I can hear Jeff following after me.

"Pleasure doing business with you," she drawls.

"Go fuck yourself," I growl.

She doesn't reply.

"Oh, and Nadia," I call, without bothering to turn around, "I would have paid *way* more than that."

"Well joke's on you, because I would have accepted less," she snarls.

The fact that she thinks that makes her a winner, is the saddest thing I've ever heard.

I feel for the child she's carrying, I really do, but I can't worry about that. I've got enough of my own shit going on. Rusty can handle that one – good luck to him – he's going to need it.

I walk out the door and don't look back.

I'm leaving poorer, but so much richer in the ways that really matter.

People tell you that time flies when you have a child, but I never imagined it would go this fast. It's already been three months since Nadia signed over her parental rights and the legal process was completed, and one whole week since Stevie officially moved in with me and Elly full-time.

I didn't anticipate having one woman live with me so soon, let alone two, but things happen when they happen, and sometimes, everything just aligns to fall into place perfectly.

That's the best way I can describe my life. Perfect.

It's challenging, hard and tiring. There's temper tantrums, dirty nappies and sleepless nights, but there's also so much love, laughter and growth, and the good stuff far outweighs the bad.

Every single day, I wake up so excited that I get to live *my* life.

The best part of it all is that I get to do it with Elly by my side.

She's the light of our lives. She's always there with a smile, a hug, some solid advice, and she's always about five steps ahead of me, effortlessly making my life easier as she goes.

I *could* live without her, but I never, ever want to.

"How are my girls?" I ask as I walk into Stevie's room and find her and Elly lining up all of Stevie's soft toys.

There's a hell of a lot of them.

Apparently, Tom and Morgan have got absolutely no grip on the real world whatsoever, at least not when it comes to what is and isn't an appropriate number of gifts to give a toddler. My parents aren't much better.

Every single time they turn up here, which is at least once a week, they bring her some over-the-top present. Last time was a pink stuffed dinosaur that's the size of Elly. It's beyond a joke.

I've tried to have a word to Tommy about it – at this rate I'm going to have to buy a bigger house just to accommodate all this shit – but he won't hear it. Only the best for his little princess.

He's obsessed with that kid.

I can't really blame him. I think we all are.

She can scream like a banshee, but she's the sweetest little thing.

Elly smiles up at me.

"We're good. We're just trying to decide if Patrick bear wants to sit next to Stretch the giraffe, or that weird little duck thing that freaks me out too much to name."

She gives the weird little duck the side eye.

I chuckle at her. She's hated that thing since it arrived, and so of course, it's one of Stevie's favourites and gets lugged around from room to room.

I'll have to start hiding that ugly little thing around the house to freak Elly out.

"Dada, sit," Stevie instructs, pointing to the spot on the floor next to Elly.

I haven't sat on the floor this much since I was in kindergarten. I'm not exactly built for it either, so half the time I'm folding myself like an origami crane, trying to squeeze into the space it's been insisted I sit.

Elly had a good old laugh the other day when Stevie *demanded* I sit with her at her little table and chairs for a pretend cup of tea. I got stuck and ended up having to stand up with the whole table stuck over my quads.

Stevie thought it was hilarious too. Jokes all round apparently. They're already teaming up against me.

I drop to the floor and attempt to cross my legs underneath me. My knees don't really bend the way they used to.

"Dada, raffe," Stevie cries, plonking herself and her toy giraffe in my lap.

"Yeah, baby, that's your giraffe, mama says his name is Stretch."

"*Retch*," she repeats. "Mama, retch."

"Good job." I kiss the top of her head.

I glance over at Elly and she's giving me that look again. I've never seen her look at me like that, so often. It's like I can see her physically melting at the sight of me and my little girl.

I swear her ovaries are about to explode.

I can't wait to put a baby in her one day.

She's an incredible mother already and she'll be no different with any other children we have. She's going to give Sandra a real run for her money.

Ma will probably let her take the title; she's chasing after Grandma of the century these days.

She's probably not far off it already.

Stevie's got the whole lot of us wrapped around her little finger.

The thing I love most about Stevie getting to know my family, is how much she loves my dad. I think Pop-pop might be her favourite person in the whole world.

They share something special – did from the moment they laid eyes on each other. It's pretty special. Dad is chuffed about it all. Never seen him look so proud. Telling them they had a beautiful little granddaughter was one of the best days of my life.

Ma and Jessie have become close friends too, they've really bonded over Stevie, which I couldn't be happier about. It's just one big happy family over here – Nadia thankfully excluded.

I haven't heard a word from her since she got her money, but I've been told she's rolling around in a brand-new Range Rover and still making Rusty's life hell.

I hope he has the backbone to get that baby out of there when it's born. It might not be my kid, but it is Stevie's biological half-sibling. No child deserves to have a mother like Nadia.

"I'll take her to the doctor this afternoon to get that rash checked out," Elly tells me. "Can you let the daycare know that she'll go on the trip they have planned and that one of us will make sure we can come along?"

"Already did it." I smile at her.

She raises a brow at me. "Well, look at you go, slick."

"You don't call me daddy for nothing." I wink at her.

"Ew." She grimaces. "That's icky."

I chuckle, her expression is hilarious.

"No daddy kink for you, huh?"

"Zero out of ten rating on that one."

She gets up off the floor, kisses Stevie and then me. "I'll go do the laundry, you make lunch?"

"Deal, kitten."

She strolls out the door and Stevie starts handing me random objects and jabbering away about each of them.

This is it. This is our life now. It's not glitzy or glamourous, it's not high profile or splashed across the tabloids, it's just real, down to earth and filled with love.

A man couldn't ask for anything more.

EPILOGUE

ELLY

One year later

I know this isn't technically part of my job description, but as one of Morgan's closest friends, I feel responsible for making sure that Tom gets every little detail right of this proposal.

I've been running around behind the scenes acting like a crazy person to try and make sure the flowers were delivered on time, that the lighting people got let in – that the champagne has been put on ice…. There are so many little things that go into a proposal. I'm glad this isn't what I do for a job.

This year's NBA finals couldn't be more different from last years.

Last year, Morgan was courtside watching the performance of a lifetime while Tom's team went all the way and earned themselves another championship title.

This year, Morgan is watching the game courtside with Tom next to her. The Bears finished in fourth in this year's playoffs, and while it wasn't the result they were hoping for, they played a solid season, and Tom personally grew to a new height in his game.

The next season is going to be crazy.

I think we can all tell Tom is on the verge of becoming one of those players that's not only the best while they're in their prime, but a player that is idolised for generations to come. He's one of the best the game has ever seen, and he's not done yet. He's got so much more in him professionally and personally.

He's about to have his ring on the finger of one of the most successful singers of our generation.

What a power couple.

Walker: Can you come to the suite for a minute please?

I thought he'd never ask.

I've been dying to see what it all looks like put together. He insisted that I stay out so that I could get the full experience of all my decision-making and hard work, as it was intended.

Tom is going to be bringing Morgan up here after the game, in only a few short minutes, and then he'll be getting down on one knee and asking her to be his wife.

I'm literally sweating, I'm so excited.

I hope I've done everything right. I want it to be perfect for her.

I skip down the hall, heading for the suite that would normally be filled with people watching the finals. I'd hate to know what Tom had to pay to get this room left empty.

He'd been hoping that his team would have made the finals again, and he'd get to propose on home ground, but it wasn't meant to be. I know Morgan won't care what stadium it happens in. She's got everything she needs when she's with him. She's home wherever he is.

I pause outside the door; I can hear some music playing softly from inside. I take a deep breath, hope like hell that we've got it perfect, and open the door.

I gasp as I see the dimly lit room.

It's absolutely filled with lit candles – total fire hazard – but the most beautiful thing I've ever seen.

It smells like heaven in here – the hundreds of flowers that are placed around the room have the most divine scent. I step into the room and let the door shut behind me, and that's when it hits me.

It's *perfect*, but none of it is *right*.

The flowers are carnations, not roses.

The candles are pink, not black.

The song playing is *my* favourite, not Morgan's.

All of the framed photos are of Walker and I, not Morgan and Tom.

All of the air is stolen out of my lungs as he steps out of the corner of the room and into the candlelight.

He looks so unbelievably handsome.

"Walker? What's going on?"

My heart is smashing against my rib cage. I'm freaking out. My body and brain are in overdrive. I know exactly what's happening, and also cannot possibly comprehend it, all at once. I'm so nervous my hands are shaking as he walks towards me, with such casual confidence.

He's got that sexy smirk I love so much on his face, and I don't know if I can take it right now. I feel weak in the knees.

He hasn't said a word to me.

I forget how to speak as he stops in front of me and drops to one knee.

I'm losing my mind internally, but my body has frozen. I'm pretty sure my jaw has fallen lax as I stare at him in disbelief.

He takes my hand in his and looks deep into my bewildered eyes.

"Elly-May, I don't even know where to start. Nothing I could say is ever going to be enough for you to understand exactly how I feel about you. I've known for a long, long time that I was going to get down on one knee and ask for permission to put my ring on your finger, but now that it's really happening, I don't know what to say. I had a whole speech prepared."

I just stare at him. I can't believe this is really happening. I don't speak, so he carries on.

"Elly, I love you. You make everything better and I can't imagine a happy life that doesn't include you in every part of it. You've made me a better man, you're helping me be the father I always wanted to become, and you're undoubtably the best thing that ever happened to me. You're the best bet I ever made. I want to spend forever trying to be all that and more for you. Will you marry me?"

Oh. My. God.

I can't believe this.

I just planned my own proposal.

"But… but it's only been like a year. Are you sure?" I whisper.

He looks amused. "Kitten, I knew last season that I was going to marry you."

"*What?*"

He nods. "But I couldn't ask you then. That was Tom's moment."

"You knew *last year*?"

He nods. "Of course I did. But I had to wait. This is *our* moment now, Elly-May, will you let me spend the rest of my life loving you? Will you marry me?"

I finally notice the ring, and when I do, I start crying. It's the beautiful, ridiculously expensive ring I loved in the boutique jeweller I went to with Tom. It's not the ring I suggested he buy for Morgan – it's far more my taste than hers, but it's the one I couldn't take my eye off. It's the most stunning piece of jewellery I've ever seen.

"You tricked me." I sob.

I can see now exactly what he's done. He and Tom,

they've led me to believe that I was choosing all the details for Morgan. I couldn't help but give my opinion along the way, and now that I realise how blind I've been, it's so obvious. Every time I said something like 'I think Morgan would love this', Walker or Tom would ask me what I liked, and because proposals and romance and planning excite me, I rambled on and on about the things I thought were sweet and beautiful.

They took notes.

He's done every one of them.

Walker gives Tom a hard time about being a hopeless romantic, but I think he's even more of a romantic. This is so dreamy; I can't even believe it's real.

"I wanted you to have everything you ever dreamed of. I added in a few things, but this is *your* dream proposal, Elly, all you have to do now is say yes?" He looks a bit nervous that I'm going to say no.

"Oh my god, yes!" I throw myself at him, tears still streaming down my face. "Yes, a million times, yes."

In my total and complete shock, I forgot to answer him.

Of course it's *yes*. As if I was ever going to say no to this man.

His lips find mine and we kiss each other like the world is about to end. It's messy and passionate and I never want it to stop.

I'm going to marry this man.

This cocky, frustrating, sweet, infuriating, kind, loving man of mine.

I wouldn't change a thing.

He pulls back, and he's got tears in his eyes too.

He slides the stunning ring into place on my finger, where it'll stay for the rest of my life.

It fits perfectly, of course. Tom's sneaky doing, no doubt. He had me trying on all sorts of rings and different sizes.

I can't believe how well they pulled the wool over my eyes. I *never* saw this coming.

"Oh my god, I can't believe this is really happening." I wipe at my eyes and then stare at my ring again. It's so beautiful.

"I'm just glad you said yes." He chuckles. "You were making me sweat a bit there."

"I'm sorry." I laugh. "I thought maybe I'd passed out and I was hallucinating."

He tips his head back and laughs. "No hallucination here, kitten, just me and you forever."

Sounds like something out of my wildest dreams.

"This ring is so beautiful."

I bring my hand up to rest on his shoulder so I can admire it again.

"Can I ask you something about that ring?" he asks me. He's got this cute little look on his face like maybe he's feeling a bit shy about whatever he's about to ask.

"Of course..."

He's got me intrigued.

"Is it *really* the one you liked when you were with Tom? You didn't pick out a different one?"

"He didn't tell you?"

"He was... *vague*. We walked in and he told me to look at all the rings and pick out the one I thought you'd have chosen."

Of course, these two made it into a game.

"Okay, so what did you pick?"

"You're wearing it." He shrugs.

I don't know why that makes a fresh wave of tears pool in the corners of my eyes. He chose my ring. We chose the same ring.

That makes it even better.

"I looked at every single one, and I can't really explain it, but that one just felt like you. I showed him my choice and he just said *my work here is done* and walked out of the store. Didn't answer my texts or calls. So, I eventually bought it."

"Oh my god." I laugh.

"I know. That guy working in there thought I'd lost my mind. I stood there holding it for over an hour, and then I imagined giving it to you, and I could see you saying yes, and I figured that was enough for me. I paid for it and left."

It's adorable that he thinks the ring he chose would have made a difference to whether I said yes or no.

He could have picked out the ugliest piece of jewellery I'd ever seen, and I'd still have accepted.

Although, I doubt anyone in their right mind could say no to *this* ring.

"That's the ring I loved, slick. You did good."

"Really?"

"*Really.*"

We both just smile at each other in silence for a moment, soaking in our happiness.

"Fuck Tommy is a dickhead. I've been stressing about that for *weeks.*"

I can't help but laugh. Classic brother behaviour.

"He had me get it sized right and everything, but

the prick still wouldn't tell me which ring you picked out in there."

"Aw that's so mean. I love it."

"I'm starting to think you might be a sadist." He eyes me with fake suspicion. "The both of you, actually."

"I'm sure he would have told you if you'd picked any other ring."

"I don't know… I think he would have just used it as prime entertainment."

I laugh and the sight of his ring on my finger steals my attention again.

"I wish your mum were here to see you now," he murmurs.

Oh, my heart.

"Me too. But I like to think she's watching us from somewhere."

"I bet she is. She wouldn't miss this." He smiles at me so sweetly, it warms my heart. "I went and told her, you know. That I was going to marry her baby."

"What?"

"I went out to New York to visit your dad and get his blessing, and I called in to see where your mum is laid to rest. We had a long chat about you. She's a really good listener."

I'm crying again now. And not just a little tear in the corner of my eye, I'm full-on bawling.

This man has spent the past year not only making me fall deeper in love with him, but he's also fallen so deeply in love with me that he knows exactly what I need before I even do.

He visited my mum.

My god, my heart.

He's too perfect.

And he got my dad's blessing and everything. I know it's probably outdated and old fashioned, but I know that would have meant a lot to my dad. It means a lot to me too.

I know it'll mean a lot to Walker one day when Stevie is older, and someone wants to put a ring on her finger.

I can't believe I'm getting married. Everything for the rest of my life is going to include him and that makes me feel like I'm on top of the world.

"Do you still want to have two boys one day?" I tease him. "I want to know what I'm getting myself in for in this marriage."

"Better make it three. Our girl is gorgeous, she's going to need some brothers to watch her back."

I love how he considers Stevie to be as much mine as she is his.

She's nearly three years old now, and she's called me 'mama' ever since we got her. I've taken a leaf out of Sandra's book and treated her like I gave birth to her myself. It hasn't been hard to be her mama. She's an angel. She throws horrendous tantrums sometimes and recently went a whole week without sleeping more than two hours at a time, but I love her.

I love being her mama.

We're a happy little family and this ring only makes it more official.

"Three boys you think?"

He chuckles. It's a running joke with us now. We both know we'd be happy and fortunate to have another child one day, and neither of us could care less if we were blessed with a boy or a girl. A future NBA star would just be a bonus to keep Uncle Tom on his toes.

He might have one of his own by then anyway. It's still a secret, but Morgan is ten weeks along with a baby they didn't plan but are eternally grateful for.

I've never seen two people so happy to be new parents. They're so sweet and in love – it's beautiful to watch.

There are still people who think it's all a PR stunt, and once upon a time, they were right. Those days are long gone.

"Wait, so Tom *isn't* proposing?" I ask.

I know he will one day, and as excited as I am for myself, I'm kind of sad they're not engaged now too.

"Don't worry, kitten, he really was taking notes. He's a man with a plan. He's going to do it just like you told him. He's been wanting to propose for a while now, but he didn't want to steal my thunder."

I laugh. "What? does he think the whole world is going to go crazy about it or something?"

Walker chuckles. "Self-indulgent much, right?"

"Bless his heart."

"They're throwing us a party. We should really go."

"*What?*"

"Yeah." He shrugs like it's no big deal. "All our friends and family are waiting to celebrate with us. They've all been out in the crowd watching the game."

"You're lucky I said yes."

His grin is blinding. "You always say yes to me, kitten."

That I do.

I've got a real weakness when it comes to this man, and I'm more than okay with that, it's a weakness I can live with.

"It's so pretty in here though, I don't want it to go to waste."

I look around the picture-perfect room. He really did so well. I'm very impressed.

"It's all getting packed up and taken back home with us."

He really thought of everything.

He kisses me again. "Fuck I love you."

"And I love you."

I still pinch myself daily that my life has turned out this way. That a guy who was nothing but a thorn in my side has turned out to be the most important person in my life. It's crazy how things work out.

"Hey, guess what?" I ask him, smiling.

"What?"

"You've got a fiancée." I wiggle my ring finger.

He chuckles. "And guess what?"

"What?" I grin.

"So do you."

If I never have anything more in my life than I do in this moment, I'll have lived a happy and full life.

THANK YOU!

Thank you for reading 'Public Relations'. I hope you enjoyed it.

If you did enjoy it, please consider leaving a review; they give authors valuable feedback, help other readers find new books, and I'd really, really appreciate it!

If you are interested in getting sneak peeks into my work, freebies and giveaways, you can sign up for my newsletter.

Thanks again!

ALSO BY

<u>Love like Yours Series</u>

Rushed – Book 1

Pierced – Book 2

Hunted – Book 3

Chased – Book 4

Love like Yours Box Set – Books 1-4

<u>All Access Pass Series</u>

Paper, Scissors, Rock – Book 1

Hide and Seek – Book 2

One for the Money – Book 3

<u>My Heart Duet</u>

My Heart Needs

My Heart Wants

Every Last Beat – The Heart Duet Box Set – Books 1 & 2

<u>Calendar Boys</u>

Mr. January

Mr. February

Mr. March

Mr. April

Mr. May

Mr. June

Mr. July

Mr. August

Mr. September

Mr. October

Mr. November

Mr. December

Calendar Boys Box Set – Books 1-4

Calendar Boys Box Set – Books 5-8

Calendar Boys Box Set – Books 9-12

Master Manipulator

The First Rule

<u>Royals of Westlake</u>

The King of Black Diamonds

The Ace of Westlake High

PLAYLIST

I Can See You (Taylor's Version) – Taylor Swift
Easy – Camila Cabello
Power Over Me – Dermot Kennedy
Halo – Beyonce
Style – Taylor Swift
Boys Like You – Anna Clendening
Fireball – Pitbull and John Ryan
Love Story (Taylor's Version) – Taylor Swift
Apologize – OneRepublic
Royals – Lorde
Dress – Taylor Swift
exile – Taylor Swift and Bon Iver
Supercut – Lorde
I Think He Knows – Taylor Swift
Start of Something New – Troy, Gabriella Montez,
Disney
Red – Taylor Swift
Breaking Me – Topic and A7S
King Of My Heart – Taylor Swift

You Make It Read – James Morrison
End Game – Taylor Swift
Future Looks Good – OneRepublic
I Knew You Were Trouble (Taylor's Version) – Taylor Swift
Wicked Game – Parra for Cuva and Anna Naklab
All Of The Girls You Loved Before – Taylor Swift
I'm Ready – Sam Smith and Demi Lovato
Getaway Car – Taylor Swift
Can't Help Falling In Love – Kina Grannis
Stay Stay Stay (Taylor's Version) – Taylor Swift
Secrets – OneRepublic
Back To You – Selena Gomez
Mine (Taylor's Version) – Taylor Swift
Delicate – Taylor Swift
How You Get The Girl – Taylor Swift
Flowers – Acoustic Version – Jonah Baker
Mastermind – Taylor Swift
Don't Blame Me – Taylor Swift
Wildest Dreams (Taylor's Version) – Taylor Swift
Little Bit More – Suriel Hess
I Will Follow You into the Dark – Death Cab for Cutie
Call It What You Want – Taylor Swift
…Ready For It? – Taylor Swift

ABOUT THE AUTHOR

NICOLE S. GOODIN is a romance author and mother of two from Taranaki in the North Island of New Zealand.

In mid-2015, she started to write about a group of characters who wouldn't get out of her head. Her first book, *Rushed*, was published in mid-2016.

Nicole enjoys long walks on the beach, pillow fights, and braiding her friends' hair. She dislikes clichés, talking about herself in the third person, and people who don't understand her sense of humour.

Please feel free to contact her either via email, Instagram, Twitter or on her Facebook page, she would love to hear your feedback. If you're feeling really game, you can even sign up for her newsletter HERE.

UPCOMING TITLES BY NICOLE S. GOODIN

Royals of Westlake

The Queen of His Heart